SOMETIMES THERE ARE HEROES

Lightning flared overhead; the puddles reflected it until the ground seemed to be on fire. Thunder followed, a roar at first, then fading through a rumble and a growl into silence. The silence lasted only moments before another thunderclap broke it, without lightning. The thunder seemed to be going on, too, with little pops and cracks—

"Down!" screamed Kennedy. Grant stared in confusion as a black ovoid the size of a hen's egg hit the tent roof and rolled down into a puddle.

"Get down, damn it!" shouted Kennedy, his voice a little more under control. "That's a grenade!" Grant dove for the ground as Kennedy lunged for the grenade. She buried her face in her arms, not wanting to see an act she'd heard described several times—a man throwing himself on a grenade to muffle the explosion with his own body.

A PEACE COMPANY NOVEL

THESE GREEN FOREIGN HILLS

ROLAND J. GREEN

ACE BOOKS, NEW YORK

This book is an Ace original
edition, and has
never been previously published.

THESE GREEN FOREIGN HILLS

An Ace Book / published by arrangement with
the author

PRINTING HISTORY
Ace edition / December 1987

ISBN: 0-441-65741-9

Ace Books are published by The Berkley Publishing Group,
200 Madison Avenue, New York, New York 10016.
The name "ACE" and the "A" logo
are trademarks belonging to Charter Communications, Inc.

PRINTED IN THE UNITED STATES OF AMERICA

10 9 8 7 6 5 4 3 2 1

ACKNOWLEDGMENTS

Special thanks to Scots folk singer Andy Stewart, for his moving rendition of "A Scottish Soldier."

I. DRAMATIS PERSONAE

A. The Peace Force

CORPORAL JOHN BREZEK—Supply Company, Group 14.

CAPTAIN DANIEL COOPER—Captain, Peace Cruiser *Ark Royal*.

CAPTAIN SONDRA DALLIN—C.O., Transportation Company, Group 14.

CORPORAL JOSEPH DIETSCH—Headquarters, Group 14.

COMMANDER MARIE DUBIGNON—Executive Officer, Peace Cruiser *Ark Royal*.

MAJOR-GENERAL JEANPIERRE DUCHAMP—C.O., Greenhouse Expeditionary Force, replacing Haskins.

FIRST LIEUTENANT KATHERINE FORBES-BRANDON—Naval Liaison Officer, Group 14.

ARTHUR GOFF—Mediator, Group 14.

SERGEANT MICHAEL GUSLENKO—Mechanic, Transportation Company, Group 14.

BRIGADIER-GENERAL FRANCIS HASKINS—First C.O., Greenhouse Expeditionary Force.

LANCE-CORPORAL PAUL HAGOOD—Rifleman, Third Company, Group 14.

CAPTAIN CARL HANSEN—C.O., First Company, Group 14.

MAJOR STEPHEN HUGHES—X.O., 31 Squadron.

PRIVATE JAMES KENNEDY—Rifleman, First Company, Group 14.

MAJOR GEORGE KUZIK—C.O., Support Squadron, Group 14.

CAPTAIN MARIAN LAUGHTON—Medical Officer, Group 14.

SERGEANT MAJOR MARIA CAMILLA Di LEONE ("Dozer")—Support Squadron First, Group 14.

COLONEL KIRSTEN LINDHOLM—Chief of Staff to General Duchamp.

LIEUTENANT-COLONEL DAVID MacLEAN—C.O., Group 14.

WARRANT OFFICER YUKIO OHARA ("Geisha")— Chief of Maintenance, 31 Squadron.

SERGEANT MAJOR JOHN B. PARKES ("Fruit Merchant")—Group First, Group 14.

FIRST LIEUTENANT BERTHA SIMMEL—C.O., Third Company, Group 14.

CORPORAL THOMAS SYKES—Launcher squad leader, Third Company, Group 14.

FIRST LIEUTENANT WILLIAM TEGEN—Computer intelligence officer, attached to HQ, Group 14.

ELIZABETH ("Betsy") TYNDALL—Younger sister of Sergeant Patricia Tyndall, K.I.A. on Bayard in *Peace Company*.

MAJOR JESUS DESIDERIO VELA—C.O., Field Squadron, Group 14.

SERGEANT MAJOR CHARLES VOORHIS—Field Squadron First, Group 14.

B. The planet Greenhouse

ARMAS DOZO Y CERRAR—Mountaineer weapons firm.

BARRON, ALLISON, & McNEIL—Builders of the Mountains of Steel railroad.

ROGER CAREY—Metallurgist on the University of Scotia archeological expedition.

MAJOR ENRIQUE DOZO—Assistant to Colonel Limón.

PROFESSOR JEAN GRANT—Head of the University of Scotia archeological expedition.

MAJOR SIMON KABUELE—C.O., Kabuele Company (Black Star mercenaries).

COLONEL BERTRAN LIMÓN—Chief of Intelligence, Mountaineer army.

COLONEL MARTIN MACOMBER—Officer, Utopian militia.

FIRST LIEUTENANT KYRIL NGOMBA—Kabuele Company.

OLYMPUS MACHINERY LIMITED—Forbes-Brandon family firm, with subcontracts from BAM.

CAPTAIN HUGO OPPERMAN—X.O., Kabuele Company.

CORPORAL OKAN TSOBO—Headquarters, Kabuele Company.

ALEXIS WERBEL—Daugher of Julius Werbel.

JULIUS WERBEL—Terran author.

TENG XIA—Union Ambassador to Utopia.

C. Hrothmi

Hrothmi names have the following form:
(Personal name) m'no (a male)/m'ni (a female) (bond name)

CHABON M'NI LUURN—Training Officer, the Hrothmi Company.

GILA M'NI MERSSA—Company clerk.

KILAA M'NI IFARN—Leader of Hrothmi working for the University expedition.

KOYBAN M'NO SHREEN—Officer in the Hrothmi Company.

KUFSA M'NI TERSA—Member of University work team.

PEIRA and NILA M'NI SIMAS—Twin sisters; recruits in the Hrothmi Company.

RIBON M'NO BERUS—Hrothmi homesteader.

SHIPO M'NO HERU—C.O. of the Hrothmi Company in the service of the Republica de las Montañas.

TSIGO M'NO CHURAF—Bond and second-in-command to Kilaa in the University work team.

II. GLOSSARY

A. Military Abbreviations

C.I.D.	—Central Intelligence Division.
C.P.	—Command Post.
E.E.	—Electronic Emissions.
E.R.	—Efficiency Report.
I.C. 52	—Incendiary Compound 52, a bomb filling.
I.F.F.	—Identification, Friend or Foe.
J.A.G.	—Judge Advocate General.
L.Z.	—Landing Zone.
M.D.S.	—Missile Defense System.
N.L.	—Naval Liaison.
R.H.I.R.	—Rank Hath Its Responsibilities.
S.P.	—Self-propelled.
S.U.F.U.	—Situation Unbelievably Fouled Up.
S.W.A.G.	—Scientific Wild-Ass Guess.
V.T.O./ S.T.O.	—Vertical/Short Take-off.
X.O.	—Executive Officer.

B. Hrothmi words

The human pronunciation of all Hrothmi words is strictly phonetic. Due to differences in mouth structures, human efforts to match native pronunciations are hopeless.

alkli—Respectful diminutive of *alklo* ("chief"), best translated as "boss."

cheeness—Hrothmi fighting knife, literally "debt-payer."

cuirna—Term of endearment, roughly "sweetheart."

demashirhi—One thousand *shirhi*.

feyos—Domesticated herbivorous pet, about the size of a large squirrel.

hinia—Matchmaker or go-between.

Hygar—Freedom fighter.

iskupi—Communal digging insects native to Hrothma.

jag-hirmi—Cannon fodder.

jag-rufai—Untrained or inexperienced soldiers, less pejorative than *jag-hirmi*.

jagrun—The most common Hrothmi term for a soldier.

jag-tsari—Berserker; literally "death-vowed."

kanai—Traitor.

kasir—Flower whose dried petals are smoked by the Hrothmi in pipes.

kukmar—Bondless individual (derogatory).

kukos—Individual guilty of sexual misconduct within the bond. An obscenity in most Hrothmi cultures and a mortal insult in those that still practice duels and the blood-feud.

rygu—Domesticated slothlike food animal.

ryon—Unit of distance, about .75 kilometer.

shedni—(Female) scholar.

shirhi—Unit of measurement, about 1.68 meters.

steki—Domesticated fowl, about the size of a turkey but even more stupid.

te—Honorific suffix, as in *"Shedni-te"*—"Respected Scholar (female)."

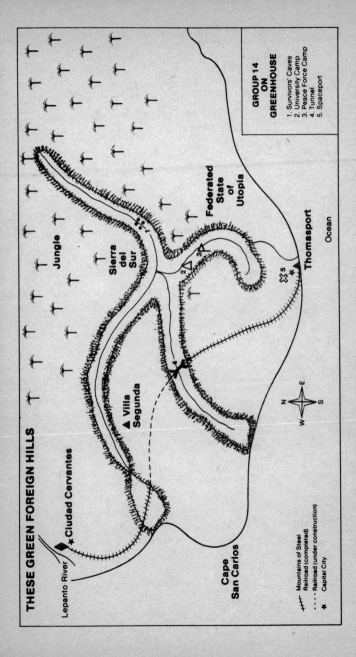

THESE GREEN FOREIGN HILLS

Lepanto River
★ Ciudad Cervantes

Jungle

Sierra del Sur

▲ Villa Segunda

Cape San Carlos

Federated State of Utopia

Thomasport

Ocean

N
W — E
S

GROUP 14
ON
GREENHOUSE

1. Survivors' Caves
2. University Camp
3. Peace Force Camp
4. Tunnel
5. Spaceport

━┿━ Mountains of Steel
┿┿┿ Railroad (completed)
- - - Railroad (under construction)
★ Capital City

Prologue

PROFESSOR JEAN GRANT woke up and rolled over on her sweat-soaked cot. She was too tired to do anything more, after a long day spent preparing for the move to the caves and barely two hours' sleep. Maybe she wouldn't have to do anything more. Maybe she'd only dreamed that she'd heard an explosion close to the camp.

Whooomp! Whooomp! Whooomp!

Three more explosions. Now that she was awake, none of them could be dreams. It sounded as if they weren't up here on the hilltop, with the living quarters and the main dig.

Another explosion. Whatever was happening, it was happening down the hill, by the storage sheds and boat landing on the riverbank.

At least none of the University team or the work gang were down there in the line of fire. Maybe nobody would be hurt unless the intruders came uphill, and if they did—

Grant sat up. Too fast; her cot teetered ominously. She reached for a handhold to steady it and knocked the ultrasonic pest repeller off the trunk at the head of the cot. It sparked, hissed, and died. She started to swear in both Anglic and Gaelic. Even here in the foothills of the Mountains of Steel, the Greenhouse night brought out fifty different kinds of vermin. Some crawled, some flew, all bit or stung. Without a pest repeller, sleep was hard to come by. If you did sleep, you woke up with what looked like tribal tattoos—at least until the infections, fevers, and hatching eggs hit.

An automatic weapon hammered from downhill. A couple of pistol shots replied. Grant stood up and snatched trousers, shirt, and shotgun off the top of the trunk. Even after a Standard Year on Greenhouse, it took her a moment to adjust to the heavier

1

gravity—four percent greater than Terran Standard, six percent greater than her native Scotia.

She nearly dropped the shotgun, fortunately before chambering a shell. Then she found herself putting her right leg into the left arm of her shirt. She took a deep breath and forced herself to finish dressing slowly and carefully. By the time she picked up the shotgun again, her hands weren't even shaking very much. She chambered a shell as she trotted out of her tent.

From downhill the automatic weapon was still firing, short bursts but lots of them close together. Grant couldn't hear if the pistol shooter was still in action. She knew who it had to be—Julius Werbel or his daughter Alexis. Werbel was a Terran novelist who'd joined the University's Greenhouse expedition to research his next novel in the Startreaders family saga. They'd camped by the river—the farther from the main camp, the better for the research, or so Werbel told her—and both had pistols. Grant hoped both knew how to use them, because now they had to be right in the middle of the shooting match downhill.

They also had to be within twenty meters of the team's store of blasting explosive. The work gang had hauled it down for loading on the boats, more than half a ton of it. It wasn't supposed to go off from a solid slug, but if the attackers had explosive or incendiary rounds, let alone grenades . . .

Bad news. And once the attackers had finished along the riverbank, they could come uphill. Kilaa M'ni Ifarn said the path should be easy to defend, but with only shotguns and pistols against automatic weapons . . . ?

Grant was more scared than she'd ever been in her life, except for the time she and her surfboard parted company off Stornoway Beach and the wild board nearly knocked her out. No, this time was worse, because she had to be afraid for others as well as herself. The ten archeologists from the University team were all going to depend on her translating that fear into sensible orders.

Two of the Hrothmi were already standing at the head of the path, shotguns aimed downhill. Another was climbing a tree to the left of the path. Before Grant saw anybody else, she heard two pistol shots, then a woman's scream.

Grant found herself struggling in the muscular grip of one of the Hrothmi.

"No, no, *Shedni-te*. Not go down. They wait for you at bottom, like we wait for them at top."

"I've got to go down! Let me go, you—" She punched the Hrothmi's thick arm and hairy shoulder. The second Hrothmi stepped closer, to help his friend. Grant kicked him in the shins and he started, losing his balance and stumbling against his friend. That broke the first one's grip on Grant. She plunged down the path, with just enough sense left to hold the shotgun at high port so she wouldn't shoot herself if she tripped and fell.

She'd just passed the purple weeper halfway down the path, when the blasting charges went off. Even filtered through the trees, the flame lit up the whole hillside. The blast stripped leaves and branches from trees all around Grant and caught her in mid-stride. Her foot came down on glass-slick mud and went out from under her. She sat down on the mud and tobogganed completely off the path, to turn a half somersault and land facedown and rump in the air in a stand of blade-eater.

She had just time to thank God that it was an old stand with most of the thorns on the underside, when she heard a deep Hrothmi laugh close to her left ear. She knew what kind of a spectacle she must have made of herself—and without giving any orders, sensible or otherwise. She still started to swear again.

"*Alkli*, are you all right?"

"Kilaa?" Nobody else was that informal or spoke Anglic with so little accent.

"Of course. Tsigo and I thought we'd best take a place down here, where we could greet our visitors if they came up the path before you were ready to receive them."

Grant felt herself gripped by four hands larger, hairier, and stronger than most humans could have claimed. She gasped as thorns raked her skin, then felt herself lifted completely off the ground and set on her feet. She wouldn't have minded lying down, but she'd be damned if she'd make herself look weak as well as stupid. Not in front of Kilaa and her camp-bond, Tsigo M'no Churaf. Both were ex-*jagruni,* and she'd seen them digging all day with cracked ribs only bound up.

As her hearing returned, Grant realized that the gunfire downhill had also stopped. She controlled a wild hope that the attackers had blown themselves to bits, and turned to Kilaa. She and Tsigo were carrying shotguns, pouches of extra shells, and bush knives. Kilaa was carrying her old *cheeness* as well. Anyone coming up the path without their invitation would have had a much warmer welcome than they would have appreciated, in the short time they had to appreciate anything.

Now figures were coming slowly down the path, both Hrothmi and human, all armed.

"Professor Grant?" Roger Carey, the team's metallurgist and

jack-of-all-trades, was leading the column, probably by virtue of his one term in the New Inverness Fusiliers.

"Here I am, alive and well—I think," she added, flexing her limbs to make sure they were all attached in their usual places and worked in the usual fashion. "Down here, with Kilaa and Tsigo. They were laying an ambush."

"I think we should all stop talking before our friends downhill lay one for us," Kilaa said briskly.

"Now, look here—" began Carey.

"She's right," said Grant. "Let's be quiet and wait a few minutes, then go downhill."

Carey turned away, muttering something that sounded like "Furballer," but not loud enough to be worth noticing. Grant wanted to swear again. Carey didn't like Hrothmi, and they returned the compliment. She was going to have to complain about him to the University when they got home. He wasn't fit for duty with mixed-race teams. If that meant he would be denied tenure and forced to leave the University, that was his problem, not hers or the Hrothmi's.

The reinforcements distributed themselves under cover on either side of the path, and everyone settled down to wait. It seemed that the blast had stunned or frightened away the usual population of insects, reptiles, and unidentifiable small nuisances. In ten minutes Grant was stung painfully only once, and felt an uncontrollable urge to scratch only twice.

At the end of the ten minutes the silence from downhill was unbroken, except for the murmur of the river. Grant thought she heard a faint whimper once or twice, but knew it could also have been some native life form whose call she didn't know. Greenhouse's jungles could surprise even people who'd lived all their lives on their edges.

At last Kilaa and Tsigo rose as silently as cats and started down the path. Grant was starting off after them when she heard not-quite-stifled laughter from behind her. She realized that her clothes hadn't survived her plunge off the path any too well. She hitched up the remains of her trousers and tucked the remains of her shirt into them, achieving at least minimal decency, if not respectability.

As Grant reached the foot of the path, she heard an agonized wail from close to the riverbank.

"Dad! Dad! Oh, Dad! Why you?"

The voice was Alexis Werbel's. Then came Kilaa's, trying to

soothe her in Anglic while Tsigo said the Prayers for the Dead Bond-Kin in Hrothmi.

When Grant reached them, Kilaa was holding Alexis against her chest while the girl sobbed on her shoulder. Alexis wore only the remnants of a nightgown and both the gown and her skin were liberally smeared with mud and blood. One whole side of her face was black. Grant's stomach twitched at the thought of such a burn, then she saw it was only a plastering of mud. Alexis seemed to be in good hands, so Grant turned to her father.

Julius Werbel was lying where the explosion had hurled him, jammed between the roots of a huge slingtree. The explosion had only hurled a corpse, though. One solid slug had pierced his chest and another had nearly ripped off his left arm. At least he couldn't have felt much or for long.

"Tsigo, get the medical kit for Alexis. Also some clean clothes, and boil water over the Werbels' stove." If they had a stove, which she couldn't remember for sure now. If she couldn't remember something like that, what kind of a war leader was she?

No worse than most other professors of archeology at the University of Scotia, came the voice of common sense. *Certainly the best the team has. Unless you want to turn the job over to Carey?*

Grant's stomach twitched again at the thought, and she almost lost her dinner. Tsigo handed her a canteen, and when she'd finished drinking, she found she could give more orders. Find stretchers for both Werbels, post sentries, count damage and casualties . . .

The casualty count was mercifully short—the two Werbels and one Hrothmi. Grant refused to let herself be counted, in spite of Kilaa's urging and the stinging of her thorn scratches and bug bites as sweat poured over them. The Hrothmi was the one who'd been climbing a tree to take a sniper's perch; the blast knocked him out of the tree, and he sprained a wrist landing. He seemed more ashamed of his clumsiness than concerned about the injury.

Damage was another matter. Everything in the three tents closest to the explosion was ruined, as well as four of the five boats and all their motors. Far from being ready to start for the caves at dawn tomorrow, the team had no way of reaching the caves and precious little gear to do anything once they got there.

Grant wanted to cry—for the death of Julius Werbel, for the wreckage of the expedition's plans, and for what her own stupidity had done to cause both. She knew she would never have accepted Major Kabuele's proposal to withdraw the whole expedition into the secure area along the railroad until the terrorists were tracked down. But if she'd accepted his proposal to station half a platoon of his mercenaries at the camp, at least it might have been the terrorists who got the nasty surprise, not two innocent Terrans.

Now, of course, she *would* have to pull the expedition back into the secure zone. They'd lost too much equipment to be able to do anything here that was worth facing another attack. Not to mention that another attack might be aimed at people, not equipment. Major Kabuele and Captain Opperman would dig the information about the expedition's situation out of someone, whether she ordered everyone to keep their mouths shut or not. When they'd done that, there would be no arguing with either of them.

As Jean Grant stared into the sodden darkness, thunder rumbled overhead. A moment later she heard the thin rustle of wind in the high leaves, and a moment after that the spattering of the first drops of rain. She gripped a climbing vine on the trunk of the slingtree and bowed her head. The rain would doubtless wash out all the footprints and other traces the terrorists might have left behind, but it had one advantage. Now she could cry without anyone being the wiser.

1

"O God, whose mercies cannot be numbered: Accept our prayers on behalf of your servant Patricia, and grant her an entrance into the land of light and joy, in the fellowship of your saints; through Jesus Christ our Lord, who lives and reigns with you and the Holy Spirit, one God, now and forever. Amen."

SERGEANT MAJOR JOHN B. PARKES tried to give Master Sergeant Patricia Tyndall's funeral the attention it would have deserved even if Pat hadn't been an almost-friend who'd been killed at his side on Bayard. It wasn't easy, not when he'd seen at least fifty funerals of twenty different sects, cults, and religions.

That didn't count all the dead comrades, either, who hadn't even enjoyed the dignity of a funeral, let alone having their ashes shipped home for burial in their family's plot. All the dead of Peace Cruiser *Suffren*, endlessly orbiting Bifrost. The shuttle that went into the jungles of Greenhouse with thirty Peace Forcers aboard, gone as thoroughly as if they'd dived into a star. Even the two PFers of the Maritime Squadron, Parkes's own Group Fourteen organized on Bayard, whose bodies hadn't been recovered after their converted fishing boat *Ramilles* sank.

A minister, a well-kept plot in a well-kept cemetery, and family and friends all standing around as the urn was lowered into the grave—they were the trappings of a civilian death. To Parkes they almost seemed to rob Pat Tyndall's death of some of the dignity she'd earned in life as a good soldier.

"Heads up, Fruit Merchant," whispered a voice in Parkes's ear. The minister put his prayer book away, and Sergeant Major Maria di Leone stepped forward from her place behind Parkes to join the other three pallbearers. Parkes straightened to attention and saluted as the pallbearers lifted the urn and started downhill toward the grave.

He waited until about half the crowd had fallen into line behind the pallbearers before stepping off himself. It wasn't likely that anybody else had noticed his discontented wool-gathering. Dozer di Leone had the sharpest eyes Parkes had ever known for soldiers whose minds weren't on their jobs, whether they were new recruits or fellow sergeant majors. He didn't want to risk embarrassing the Tyndalls or disgracing his full-dress uniform.

He fell into route-march step as the procession wound down the hill. The familiar rhythm relaxed him. By the time the squad from the Militia Battalion of the New Athabaskan Regiment had fired the three volleys (not as raggedly as Parkes expected), he was even ready to face Dozer.

Theoretically it was ridiculous to be uneasy about facing Dozer. As Group First of Group Fourteen, Parkes outranked Dozer, the Support Squadron First. Theory didn't make much difference when you faced Dozer, and rank made hardly more. She was notorious for reducing all privates and N.C.O.'s and most officers short of general rank to the level of unruly children who'd talked back to their mother.

"What was getting to you, John? The funeral or the prospect of having to go home?"

"Will I get a straight answer if I ask whether you're telepathic?"

"Not unless you give me one first."

"And maybe not even then?"

"I'm reasonably honest."

"Unless it's a question of holding on to one of your best people in the face of a Priority One requisition."

"Guilty as charged. But that's not the question now."

Parkes made a millimetric adjustment in the angle of his beret. "No, I suppose I don't want to go home. I was lucky, having to report as Field First so soon that I had a good excuse. This time I've got most of a month's leave ahead of me. Of course, I'm Group First now, so I could cut my leave short—"

"John, one of these days you're going to have to stop letting your family put a bug in your brains. You said yourself that Voorhis isn't the kind who can cope with the Group First hanging over his shoulder. Particularly a Group First who knows the Field job better than he does. You want to muck up Voorhis just to make life easier for yourself? Then who's next, after Voorhis . . . ?

"Sorry. I'm coming down on you too hard. If I thought there

was anything you could do that wouldn't hurt the Group besides go home, I'd hand it to you on a silver platter with a ribbon around its neck. As it is . . ." She shrugged.

"As it is, it's the same old SUFU, and I'd better get it over with?"

Parkes wanted to snap at Dozer. That would be unfair, and even worse, a waste of breath. Good relations between the Group First and the Field First were *not* expendable, except in a much better cause than keeping the Group First from having to listen to his father's depressions and his stepmother's bitcheries.

"Couldn't have put it better myself. Tell you what—go down and do your duty by the Tyndalls, and I'll phone the Overlook Inn for a dinner reservation. With any luck you won't be home until everybody's gone to bed. Yeah, I know what your stepmother'll say about you sneaking in like a thief, but she'll say it after you've had a good dinner and a good night's sleep."

"The condemned man's hearty meal?"

"Have you got a better idea?"

Parkes had to confess that he was short of ideas, better or otherwise. He made another adjustment of his beret and turned uphill toward the open-air chapel, where the Tyndalls were forming their receiving line.

Parkes approached the Tyndalls with the firm resolution not to let his family troubles affect a single word he said to them. They'd given their daughter to the Peace Force with open eyes, and now had buried her without bitterness. He owed them a lot more than good manners, but he could at least give them that much.

His resolution wavered for a moment when he saw the sheer number of the Tyndalls. Pat had occasionally mentioned being one of five children and her mother being one of four. Parkes had never figured out what that meant in terms of aunts and uncles, cousins, in-laws, and nieces or nephews. The sheer mass of Tyndalls and their relations was daunting; even more was their obvious closeness. Right now they were sharing sorrow, but they looked just as accustomed to sharing joy. Parkes had to swallow a medium-sized lump in his throat as he contrasted the Tyndalls with his own family; the only closeness he'd known there for thirty years was with his sister Louise.

He kept aching envy of the Tyndalls out of his voice, but he didn't remember most of the people he shook hands with or most of what was said. He remembered one uncle mentioning a letter that Pat had written about applying for a commission, but not what he said in reply. Not surprising, when taking a commission was another place where Parkes's conscience was tender.

As he walked away from the line, he passed a girl who looked about sixteen, wearing a depressingly sober blue dress. She had sun-bleached hair, wide gray eyes, and looked as if she would have been more comfortable in slacks and a sweater.

Parkes booted his memory. "You must be the one Pat always called 'baby sister.' Sheryl—no, Elizabeth?"

"Call me Betsy." They shook hands, and she went on in a voice just above a whisper. "Can I talk to you later about joining the Peace Force?" She looked back along the line toward her parents. "In private, if you can manage it."

"I'll see what I can do."

From the sour look Betsy gave him, Parkes suspected he'd brushed her off like a girl instead of answering her like a woman. Parkes still didn't see what else he could have said. Of the five Tyndall children, four had already put on uniforms and three still wore them, one in the Navy and two in the Peace Force. The elder Tyndalls hadn't stood in their children's way, but that didn't change the fact that Pat was the first to die. They would have to be doing some serious thinking about having *all* their children hostages to the fortunes of war.

That in itself wouldn't have stopped Parkes from giving Betsy a few facts that weren't on any recruiting tape, if he thought they would do any good. As it was, Betsy looked remarkably like a young woman who'd made up her mind beyond being confused by facts. Everything Parkes said would likely end up pushing her further and faster than before toward a Peace Force recruiting office.

Parkes didn't want that on his conscience. Apart from what the Tyndalls might be thinking, he suspected that Peace Force duty was about to become more dangerous, and in some particularly nasty ways.

The alliance of the seven planets that had kept interstellar flight after the Collapse War on Earth was nearly two hundred years old. Its stated policy of promoting united planetary governments and economic development among the other sixty-eight human-settled planets was almost as venerable. So was the unstated policy of making sure that the seven worlds of the Planetary Union got richer in the process. The military arm of both policies, the Peace Force, had been organized for more than a century, although its clear superiority over most planetary armed forces was barely fifty years old.

In its career the Peace Force had unquestionably done more good than harm. It had improved the situation on more than thirty planets, until eleven of them had become Federated Allies of the Union. In the process it seldom had to either take or hand out really heavy casualties. As often as not, it expended more candy bars than ammunition and built more dams and roads than blockhouses.

Parkes believed that this happy time was drawing to an end. Before his promotion and assignment to Group Fourteen, he'd begun to suspect it on the basis of rumors, some confidential information, and veteran soldier's sixth sense for impending trouble. He'd been nearly certain ever since Group Fourteen went to Bayard with holes in its T.O. that you could fly a verti through, and a prime collection of odds and sods holding down key positions in that T.O.

The fact that Group Fourteen rose to the occasion and wiped Bayard clean of the agents of the Terran terrorist leader known as the Game Master, didn't change Parkes's opinion. In fact, he'd heard that two more Company Groups, Fifteen and Sixteen, were being organized with the same mixed bag. A few veterans held down key posts, with the rest of the T.O. filled with potentially talented but unproven newlies and a miscellany of others, down to pure barracks scrapings. Group Fourteen had proved that this offered a workable formula for an increase in Peace Force field strength that now seemed to be getting under way.

What was Peace Force Command expecting? One answer was obvious: the Union was running out of planets that it would be cheap and easy to pacify. Some of the remaining worlds were either too civilized to need pacifying or too barbarous to be worth more than an enforced quarantine. Others might need a Union-imposed solution, but would be ready and able to resist it. If the Union did choose to intervene, it would need more men and ships than in the past. The Bifrost Confederacy had faced the Peace Force with high-intensity air-ground combat for the first time. It wouldn't be the last.

The second answer was something that Parkes himself had shied away from at first. The Union had held together so far because over the mid- to long-term, everybody profited about equally. Sooner or later this would change. Union intervention would begin to look like a zero-sum game, with clear winners and losers among the seven planets.

Would the losers accept their status tamely? Not if they had thousands of starship crewmen and ground troops trained to Peace Force standards. The planetary governments could be financing the training of the cadres for possible civil war out of the Peace Force budget.

That thought didn't taste any better to Parkes the twentieth time than it had the first. The only difference was that now Parkes knew one thing to do: keep Betsy Tyndall out of uniform, or at least out of the Peace Force. Bifrost's two thousand Peace Force dead wouldn't be a record for long; he didn't want to see Betsy help set the new record.

He wanted even less to see her having to call in salvos on a company that a year before had been her comrades. Parkes had known too many veterans of civil wars and listened to them talking out their nightmares over far too many bottles and doses. If the Peace Force was going to end that way, Parkes wanted the dirty work left in the hands of old troopers like him and Dozer, who wouldn't have so long to live with the nightmares, even if they came out alive.

Looking for a tactful line of retreat, Parkes said, "Betsy, how old are you?"

"Seventeen."

"Then you can't enlist in one of the New Frontier combat arms without your parents' consent for another two years."

"I can enlist in one of the service units or a militia battalion."

"Yes, but you'll still have to transfer to a regular combat arm and do at least a year there before you can apply for the Peace Force."

Betsy's face told Parkes that he'd just put his foot in it up to the knee. "Pat said you were accepted for Peace Force duty after only six months in the Airborne Regiment."

"That was a one-in-a-million shot. I suspect that P.F. was hard up for recruits back then."

Betsy raised her eyebrows in a look uncannily like her dead sister's. Parkes wondered if, when Pat told her baby sister about his early entry, she'd also quoted her usual response to his efforts at modesty:

"With all due respect, Sergeant Major, I don't see any garden handy that needs so much fertilizer."

Before Betsy could follow up the raised eyebrows, Parkes saw a tall blond woman approaching. She wore a tailored green pantsuit that did justice to a more than admirable figure, a green cloak, and low-heeled brown boots. Lace showed at the cuffs and the elegant neck. Probably genuine lace too—Lieutenant Katherine Forbes-Brandon, Group Fourteen's Naval Liaison officer, came from a wealthy family, and had good taste to guide her in spending her allowance.

"Sergeant Major. They said I might find you here. Is Sergeant Major di Leone anywhere around?"

Parkes pointed toward the parking lot. "She's gone to make dinner reservations for us, Lieutenant."

"I'm afraid we'll be having dinner on the way back to Fort Crerar. The Group's on Alert Two."

A Grade Two Alert means off-planet within ten New Frontier days and all leaves cancelled. Parkes let Forbes-Brandon lead him out of hearing of any civilians before satisfying his curiousity.

"Where to this time?"

"Greenhouse. Apparently the situation between the Mountaineers and the Utopians is turning into a bit more than the PFers already there can handle. They're all air or engineer units, and apparently they need ground troops to defend the Mountains of Steel railroad. It's less than six months from completion, if the terrorists don't blow it up first."

Parkes mustered what he knew about the planet Greenhouse. Since he'd had a couple of friends aboard the shuttle that crashed into its jungles, that was a bit more than the average.

It had heavier gravity and higher temperatures than Earth, and a southern hemisphere that was largely ocean. Its tropics were too hot for human habitation. The one northern continent was divided between two nations, the Republica de las Montañas and the Federated State of Utopia. Between those two nations lay three thousand kilometers of the most nightmarish jungle on any human-settled planet.

Land communications through the jungle were impossible. Vicious storms, abundant reefs, and a shortage of natural harbors meant that communications by sea were difficult at best and impossible except with large ships. Unfortunately most of the iron-bearing ores needed for a shipbuilding industry lay in Utopia. Its agricultural communes lacked either the capital or the inclination for industrial development.

The Republic had a good industrial base of light metals and petrochemicals, and money to spare if not to burn. Obviously the best solution to the planet's geographically-imposed disunity was linking the two nations by an all-weather land route through the Mountains of Steel. Rising from the southern edge of the jungles, the mountains offered several routes of no more than seven hundred kilometers.

No economic idea is so good that politicians won't find objections to it. The politicians of both countries had spent nearly fifty years at that task. Three years ago they finally gave up and work began.

At first things went fairly smoothly. Each country provided security from its own armed forces. The main contractors—Barron, Allison, & McNeil—hired a company of Black Star mercenaries in addition. "Major Kabuele's company," added Forbes-Brandon.

"A good outfit," said Parkes. "Or so I've heard." Few Peace Forcers had much time for mercenaries. More often than not they were part of the problem rather than part of the solution. Black Star units tended to be better than the average, however, and Kabuele Company was one of Black Star's best.

"They're living up to their reputation," said Forbes-Brandon. Parkes looked a question at her, and she shook her head. "No, I haven't attended any briefings yet. My Uncle Henry is a director of BAM, and I borrowed him for a few minutes at our last garden party. He's never needed much prodding to talk about anything he thinks will impress people.

"Anyway, after about a year they started getting sabotage, minor at first, then major. After that came sniping on the new farms growing up along the railroad. A lot of them were settled by Hrothmi who'd served out their contracts in the Republic, moved to Utopia and homesteaded.

"Hrothmi in danger automatically moves the whole issue up to Union level. Nobody wants to give the Populists an excuse for making trouble. So they moved Air Command's 31 Squadron to Greenhouse, for airmobility and reconnaissance."

"What about cover against a Mountaineer attack?"

Forbes-Brandon ran a finger from the bridge of her prominent nose up to her hairline. "I didn't get the impression that things were expected to be that bad. Even if they were, I doubt that anybody would have been talking about it in my uncle's hearing. The Populists would just love an excuse to denounce Peace Force Command for planning to start a war."

Dozer had returned in time to hear that last exchange. Now she grunted. "Even though they've also been wanting to kick the Mountaineer's butts all the way to the Southern Ocean?"

"Did I say the Populists were logical or consistent?"

What would happen if the small but excellent Republican Air

Force did intervene against the project was too delicate a topic for discussion here, even if the lieutenant knew anything useful. Parkes looked a warning at Dozer, who nodded and lit a cigarette as Forbes-Brandon finished bringing them up to date.

The terrorist incidents had begun to look as if they were slacking off until thirty-seven days ago. Then a full-scale raid on the camp of an archeological expedition from the University of Scotia killed a visiting Terran author and wrecked the camp. Scotia was a Union planet, and what attacks on Hrothmi farmers began, this attack finished. Group Fourteen had been alerted to move to Greenhouse, improve security for the railroad, and if possible take the offensive against the terrorists.

Dozer was grinning by the time Forbes-Brandon finished. If she and the Group's Support Squadron didn't end up helping build the railroad, they would be tackling some of the most famous jungle humanity had ever tried to avoid. Either would be a first-class engineering challenge.

Parkes wasn't quite up to grinning. The jungles of Greenhouse were hot, humid, and loaded with insects, diseases, and dangerous animals. The extra gravity wasn't going to help matters either. He started making mental notes for a brutally realistic physical-training program. He'd never get away with all of it, but even half would help.

"The Alert reached me at home, and I knew you would be over here at North Crossing for Tyndall's funeral," Forbes-Brandon concluded. "So I borrowed a car and drove over. If you don't mind associating with officers, I can run you straight over to the airport."

"Thank you, Lieutenant," said Parkes. "Meet you at the parking lot?"

She nodded and strode off briskly down the hill. The green suit did as good a job setting off her long-limbed figure from the rear as it did from the front.

Parkes pulled his attention around from the departing lieutenant to Betsy Tyndall, who was trying not to look either forlorn or indignant.

"Betsy, what you've just seen is the kind of thing that always happens if you join the Peace Force. You can be dragged away from your personal business at a moment's notice. If you can't get used to it—"

"How do you know that I couldn't?"

"I don't. I also don't know that your parents wouldn't rather keep you at home for a few more years. I just think you ought to ask them before you assume they'll be happy seeing you in a Peace Force uniform."

"We've never been Populists!"

"I didn't say you were. Betsy, you've got a while before you have to decide what kind of a military career you want, or even if you want one. You can afford to give your parents some time to get over Pat's death. In your place I'd give it to them. They might need it."

"Is that all, Sergeant Major?" Very cool, trying to act grown-up and not entirely succeeding.

"No, it isn't, but I'm about to be carried off by superior rank. Tell you what. I'll write you some letters from Greenhouse."

"They'll be censored."

"Not for what you want to know."

Betsy's frown and outthrust jaw as she tried to make up her mind if Parkes could be trusted reminded him painfully of her dead sister. Finally she nodded.

"Word of honor, Sergeant Major?" Almost pleading now.

"Word of honor."

"All right."

Parkes felt almost as relieved to be away from Betsy Tyndall as he did about not having to go home, not to mention almost as guilty about feeling so relieved. *How many more time do I muck up this sort of thing?*

Since he hadn't had an answer to that question in fifteen years, Parkes wasn't surprised not to have one when he and Dozer reached the parking lot. Forbes-Brandon's car, a Rolls-Ferguson, sat purring at the gate. Parkes reached for the driver's door but the lieutenant shook her head.

"Climb in back, and if we shock the MP's, that's their problem. I'd rather explain to some rank-bound provost officer than listen to what our chauffeur will say if I let anyone else touch this lady."

Parkes quickly saw what she meant. The interior of the car was a symphony, or at least a concerto, in leather and fine wood, with a control panel that would have looked more at home on an all-weather attacker. Forbes-Brandon slapped a switch and one of the panels in the back of the front seats irised to reveal a small but well-stocked bar.

"Help yourself," she said, reaching down out of sight with one hand. A moment later one of her boots flew up on to the seat beside her.

"Sorry, but I like to drive barefoot."

Parkes had seen the lieutenant barefoot once, when he'd massaged the strain of a long hike out of her feet and ankles. That was about the first time she'd dropped the mask of being something superhuman, at least for him.

It wasn't the last time, though. Parkes remembered sitting on somebody's dirty front steps in Havre des Dames on Bayard, with a Katherine Forbes-Brandon who'd been drowning her nightmares in brandy nestled against him, heavy blond hair covering his shoulder and tickling his cheek. . . .

"What are you smiling about, John?" said Dozer.

"We're going back to work. Isn't that enough?"

"It's enough to justify a drink."

"So it is. Scotch, brandy, wine, or seven-juice?"

2

"YOU'RE QUITE SURE that no attempt was made to search for footprints or other traces of the terrorists?" said Captain Opperman.

Jean Grant stifled a sigh. "I didn't order that a search not be made, if that's what you're trying to find out—"

"It isn't."

Grant raised her eyebrows as far as she thought polite. "Only six of us were down there before the rain started. I'm sure you know better than I do what the chances of finding footprints would have been after more than five minutes of rain."

"Quite. Six of you. How many humans and how many Hrothmi?"

"Three of each. And if you're trying to imply—"

"I'm not trying to imply anything, Professor Grant. If I want to discuss something, I'll do you the courtesy of bringing it out into the open. Will you do me in return the courtesy of not flinging around wild accusations? I've had quite enough of that sort of thing from your Mr. Carey."

For the first time since they left Scotia, Grant felt grateful for Carey's loud mouth and tenacious prejudices. By getting Captain Opperman's back up, he'd done her a service.

She smiled. "Very well, Captain. The possibility of some of the terrorists being Hrothmi was one that didn't occur to any of us at the time, not even Carey. Also, we were much more concerned with getting Alexis Werbel to safety and posting armed sentries around the hilltop camp. We couldn't be sure the terrorists were gone for good."

"That pretty much confirms what I've picked up from the others. I wouldn't be raising any questions at all if it wasn't for Ms. Werbel's statement."

"Is there any witness to that statement besides Carey?"

"Do you think you're entitled . . ."

"I think I'm entitled to put your willingness to cooperate with a bigot before your commanding officer."

Opperman's face was tanned dark enough to make a startling contrast with his bleached hair and beard, but not dark enough to hide an angry flush. "I think that Major Kabuele will consider my service under his command carries more weight than your theories about what my ancestry might have done for my prejudices. I also think you might be interested to know that I have in fact turned up two other witnesses."

He named two Hrothmi, and now it was Grant's turn to flush. One was the camp cook and the other one of the carpenters; both were hill folk from Akkwa, and ex-*jagruni* as well. They were as likely to castrate themselves as to lie in such a serious matter.

"I won't claim that all the people of Nieutrek are that much of an improvement over our Terran ancestors. I'll merely suggest that you should look at some of your own prejudices, if you're so ready to suspect a Nieutrekker after he's done ten years with a Black Star mercenary company."

"That wouldn't guarantee you a clean bill of health, Captain. After all, you could be a cull that no other outfit would have"— she held up a hand as he flushed again—"except that I've looked up your combat record. I promise that I won't insult you or our Hrothmi witnesses by being uncooperative again."

"Good. Now, the fact is that Alexis Werbel's statement was made when she was in considerable pain, dosed with several drugs, and grief-stricken over her father's death. There's not even complete agreement on what she said.

"Also, my experience is that on a dark night it's not easy to tell a Hrothmi from a heavily-built human at a distance of more than twenty yards. Alexis hasn't said how far away the figures she saw were, and her father's wounds don't prove anything one way or the other. So I'm willing to label the question of Hrothmi among the terrorists 'Not proven' and pass on to other matters."

Opperman flipped up the screen on his portable computer and punched coordinates. The screen displayed a map; Grant recognized the area of the Survivors' Caves.

"You were about to head upcountry into the deep jungle to explore those caves. That's a long way from help if anything went wrong."

Ten minutes ago Grant might have flared up, suspecting that he was accusing her of having secret friends in the deep jungle, maybe even the terrorists themselves. Now she only nodded.

"We had arrangements for resupply airlifts with Barron, Allison, and McNeil. We were also going to pick a site on high ground where we could blast a landing pad, and use a balloon antenna until we'd found that site. You can check with BAM's Transportation Section if you want to."

"I already have. They confirm your plans. What I want to know is why you were going to the caves at all."

"Some of the ships that reached Greenhouse after the Collapse War were in pretty wretched shape. They had to land their people every which way. If they landed outside the few thousand square kilometers in each country that had been settled at the time, their chances weren't good. If they landed in the deep jungle, they didn't have much of a chance at all.

"About a dozen ships dropped their people in deep jungle. Most of them haven't left any traces except wreckage that shows up on metal detectors.

"The landing parties from *Deirdre* and *Wasserfall* were luckier. They came down on higher, drier ground, close to some caves that provided shelter and kept out the worst of the wildlife. Enough of the people survived to strike out for the nearest major river. Some of those got through to what passed for civilization in Utopia then."

"Did any stay behind in the caves?"

Grant nodded. "They wouldn't have survived until now, though. Between conditions in the deep jungle and inbreeding among a small population, they'd have died out within a couple of generations. They might have lasted long enough to leave some interesting traces, though. That's one of the things we'll be looking for.

"Another is the caves themselves. Most of the survivors who reached civilization were suffering from amnesiac fever, among other things. Also, most of them didn't go very far into the caves. A couple of people said they did, though. If half of what they said was really there, the Survivors' Caves dwarf Mammoth or Shamballah or Higgins's or any other cave formation that's ever been explored. That could be—oh, two or three thousand kilometers of passages, running down five or six kilometers."

"I *thought* your bio specs mentioned that you were faculty adviser to the University Cavers."

"Guilty. There's also more than just a lot of new caves to explore. The people who went deep both swore they'd seen passages that had been carved out artificially."

Opperman opened his mouth, then appeared to decide that a respectful silence was the best response to that possibility. It had been established since the mid-twenty-first century that life in the Universe was fairly abundant. Since the discovery of Hrothma in the mid-twenty-second century, even the inevitability of someday discovering (or being discovered by) a vastly superior sapient race was more or less taken for granted by most intelligent people.

What had everyone who thought about the matter for more than five minutes looking nervously over their shoulders was the question: *Where were they?* There was no more than a chance in a thousand that the Survivors' Caves held any answers to that question, but that was more than enough reason to convince Jean Grant that the caves were worth exploring.

"Of course, the survivors' accounts aren't much better evidence than Alexis Werbel's story. But you had to chase down every possibility, and so do I."

Opperman grinned. "I wasn't questioning your right to go. I was just wishing I could go with you. I've never gone caving, but I'm about a Grade Four rock climber, and I don't have claus—"

The door to the hut flew open and a gangling young man in green fatigues hurried in. The name *Tsobo* was stencilled over his breast pocket. Although his close-cropped black hair rose in tight curls, his skin was hardly darker than Opperman's.

"Captain! Word from the chief. The new firm's got the contract—oh, sorry," he added, as he noticed Opperman wasn't alone. Unabashed, he looked Jean Grant up and down and nodded approvingly.

Grant smiled. She wasn't ashamed that at thirty-eight she could still do justice to a shorts-and-halter outfit or draw admiring glances from young men. However, a "new firm" could mean a good many things—including serious trouble for her people if all the arrangements made with Barron, Allison, & McNeil would now have to be negotiated over again.

"What new firm?"

Opperman glared at Tsobo, looked up at the ceiling with a God-give-me-patience expression, then shrugged. "I think I can persuade Major Kabuele that you have a need to know. The 'new firm' is a Peace Force Company Group that's supposed to be on the way."

"Don't we already have enough Peace Forcers on Greenhouse?"

Grant was no Populist, although at the University it was wise

to be polite both to and about them. A good deal of practical
experience, however, suggested that soldiers and scholars didn't
always mix well.

"We have an Air Squadron. Their security platoon is needed
for base defense. Their ground crew can only fight in an emer-
gency, like an attack on the base.

"With a Company Group, we'll have a Field Squadron with
three rifle companies to chase terrorists, and a Support Squadron
to work on-site. The Support people can also down tools and pick
up guns any time they have to. That should free Kabuele Company to join the Field Squadron and track down the terrorists,
instead of sitting on our arses and leaving the initiative to them."

"I still think it would have helped site security to enroll the
Hrothmi homesteaders in a militia unit."

"Maybe, but that's not your decision or mine to make. If you
want to argue it, I don't have anywhere to go for a while, so if
you can produce some beer . . . ?"

"Hrothmi homebrew?"

"Fine."

Grant rose to get two mugs and put them in the refrigerator to
chill down before she opened the earthenware crock of beer. As
she opened the cabinet, she realized that perhaps this mug the
Peace Force was setting before her was half full rather than half
empty. She'd have to go through the whole investigation of the
terrorist attack again, of course, probably with people who didn't
know Hrothmi, and certainly with people who didn't know
Greenhouse. But if she made the right sort of impression on
them, maybe she could persuade them to let her reopen the Site
One camp, or even move out to the caves . . .

She smiled as she started wiping the rims of the mugs with a
clean, soft cloth. The people who said Jeanie Grant didn't care
about anything except being left alone to dig up her pots and
hairpins were quite right, up to a point. What they missed was
how far she'd go in order to *be* left alone.

Shipo M'no Heru held his glass of water up to the lamp bolted
to the slimy wall of the cave. Even the dim yellow glow showed
the cloudiness in the water. He tasted it cautiously. It wasn't bad
enough to be poisonous or even worth spitting out. The spring
had a few days, perhaps as many as twenty, before seepage
through cracks in the rock from the foul jungle outside made it
undrinkable.

If they could only draw their water from the deep borings

three *ryona* below ground level . . . ! But that was impossible without either a pumping system—which could hardly be brought to the caves, even if the Montañans were willing to supply it—or else moving the base so far down that it would be a major operation simply to carry offal to the surface for disposal!

There would also be the risk of being trapped like *steki* birds if some turn of war luck led Utopian or Union forces to the caves —not a dozen scholars and *kanai,* but companies of trained soldiers. Shipo's band had given its war luck another chance with the raid on the camp, but no more than a chance. They also had not brought out the man they'd come for. Shipo had his suspicions about how that had happened, but could do nothing practical about them without another raid, even deeper into the territory of a now alert enemy.

"Gila!"

"Yes, Captain?"

"Add to our next supply requistion water purification gear— filters, chemicals, or whatever the technicians think will do the best. I'm tired of being chased from one water supply to another by that bondless jungle."

Gila's fingers tapped the keyboard of the office computer. "Recorded, Captain. Colonel Limón called while you were drawing water. The message was scrambled and coded 'For your eyes only.'"

"Put it on my terminal."

Shipo pulled on the hushphones as Gila transferred the message. When the green light recorded a complete transfer, he pressed UNSCRAMBLE, then PLAY, then leaned back. Colonel Limón did the People the courtesy of being as many-worded with them as he was with his own kind.

"Greetings, Captain," the Anglic message began. "I have some news for you that cannot be called good. The Planetary Union has agreed to send an entire Peace Force Company Group to Greenhouse. They should arrive the middle of next month. No effort that would not reveal our cooperation was spared to prevent this. It grieves me that those efforts were not enough."

The grief was probably sincere. Shipo had never doubted Limón's commitment to helping the Alliance's operations here on Greenhouse. What he had doubted and would go on doubting was whether Limón had enough support among the Montañan military to let those operations continue in the face of serious opposition.

A colonel was high enough that it was an honor to the People that he was aiding them. He was also high enough that he might

be the leader of a whole ruling-bond—*faction* was the Anglic
word, Shipo recalled—of Montañans dedicated to helping the
People.

He would *not* be high enough to carry all the Montañans with
him if some of them doubted the wisdom of facing the Peace
Force. The Planetary Union had little love for the Montañans and
might be looking for an excuse to make war on them. Shipo knew
that this made the Montañans angry, but since they were not
jag-tsari, it also might make them cautious.

Shipo realized that Limón was now in the middle of a long
and detailed list of supplies and equipment. He ran the list back
to the beginning and listened to it with growing excitement.

Launchers and machine guns with proper sights. More rifles
and pistols. Body armor. Rockets, grenades, and small-arms ammunition, to give the cave band a hundred rounds for each heavy
weapon, two thousand for each rifle, two hundred for each pistol,
and twenty grenades for every fighter. Medical supplies, including water treatment chemicals and filters. Assault rations for the
field, and cooking equipment to let them live off the land—as
well as anybody could live off the jungle of Greenhouse—while
in the caves.

Best of all, fifty reinforcements—ten humans and forty
People. The humans would be weapons instructors and electronic
specialists, the People new recruits. They wouldn't be junglewise
yet, but for thirty days or so they would do enough by relieving
the trained jungle fighters on duty in the caves. Once they were
trained, Shipo would have more than two hundred of the People
ready to strike.

"It is almost certain that I can arrange enough airlift to bring in
even more supplies and reinforcements than this, right up to the
time the Peace Force enters orbit. It's even possible that I can
arrange enough tactical air support to make Peace Force operations extremely expensive. Then the Peace Force will have to
either reconsider fighting us or else consider fighting the regular
armed forces of the Republic. I doubt that the Populists will be
willing to strengthen the Peace Force enough to permit that, as
much as they dislike the Republic."

From what Shipo knew about the Populists, this seemed likely
enough. The breed of human who hated enemies but did not
prepare to fight them was one he would never understand, any
more than he would understand those humans who did not like to
see their females fighting. Who else had more at stake than the
life-bearers?

"I will be paying you a visit after the first load of supplies," Limón concluded. "If you see me again after that, it will mean that the tactical air support is coming. Then we can have the party of the century before we settle down to planning how to harvest the *cojones* of the Peace Forcers. Until we meet, farewell and good hunting, *Jagrun-Te*."

When Shipo pulled off the hushphones, Gila could have posed for a statue of curiosity. He grinned at her. "The Union is sending a Company Group of their Peace Force. The Montañans are sending us much of what we will need to fight the Peace Force. We can look forward to battles that will make our names forever."

Delight replaced the curiosity on Gila's face. Since she would surely spread the fact that the captain had received a scrambled message all over the caves, why not let her spread an encouraging version of the truth? Shipo hoped that no one would tempt the War Lord by celebrating victory too soon.

Indeed, he could do more than just hope. If Chabon M'ni Luurn reminded everybody that one dishonored a worthy foe by celebrating a victory over him before it was fairly won, they would listen. Chabon would have to know the whole truth about what was coming anyway, if only because of their twenty years of war-bond born as recruits and fire-tempered in the Akkwasi War. Then Chabon had been equally merciless to armed enemies, full bottles, and willing males, before the High Lord let her develop the weakness of trusting the humans to allow the Hrothmi into space.

If it was a weakness. Shipo would have preferred an easy answer to that question, or even better, not to have to ask it at all. He wasn't foolish enough to believe he could have either merely because they would make his life easier. Wisdom told him that those humans who wished the Hrothmi tied to their own world for centuries to come were the strongest faction, and would not weaken unless the Hrothmi were prepared to fight with weapons held in their own hands. Too many of the People's human friends would do everything for them except fight, and that made them a poor sort of friend.

"Gila, send a message to Captain Chabon that I would like to visit her once she's finished her meditations. Then sign yourself off-duty and draw us both a beer from that private stock you and the supply-section clerk keep for your nights together."

Gilda tried to look indignantly innocent, but spoiled the effect with a snort of laughter. "Yes, Captain."

3

THE SHUTTLE'S PASSENGER hatch slid open, showing the deployed landing stair and letting in a blast of hot air. By the time Katherine Forbes-Brandon reached the foot of the stair, she felt as if she'd stepped into a sauna. She tried to tug her uniform away from at least a few of the places it was sticking to her, then gave up the struggle for either comfort or dignity and concentrated on getting away from the shuttle. Away from the reentry heat its hull was radiating, things couldn't be as bad.

A minute later she stepped out of the shadow of the shuttle and discovered that she was wrong. Even filtered through yellow-gray clouds (vomit-colored, she christened them), Quixote's Star hammered down on the airfield until she could sense the glare even with her eyes shut. She couldn't stand still for long either; the heat of the plascrete underfoot was creeping through her shoe soles.

She slogged toward the Receiving Building, feeling as if there were weights tied to her ankles as well as hands pressing firmly on her shoulders. In spite of the extra gravity, she wished she'd worn field boots, with their heavier soles and ankle support.

She also wished for a moment that she'd worn a lighter uniform, then realized that was pointless. Anything more than a fig leaf would feel stifling on Greenhouse, while anything less than complete coverage outdoors could mean enough insect bites to put you in the hands of the medics.

Forbes-Brandon told herself that all these reactions were simply lack of acclimatization. In time she wouldn't find Greenhouse quite so appalling. The only problem would be surviving long enough to become acclimatized!

The Receiving Office was air-conditioned. Conscious of the rest of the shuttle load following her, Forbes-Brandon managed not to break into a run as she approached the climate-lock door.

She still got inside far enough ahead of the others to have a blessed thirty seconds alone to savor being cooled instead of boiled.

The Receiving Office was a standard Peace Force Grade-Two Field Building, but the furnishings were local, including the racked rifles by the rear door. So were the people at the main desk, except for one 31 Squadron corporal who looked as if he wanted to be somewhere else.

Looking at the Utopian militia, Forbes-Brandon decided that she agreed with the corporal. The Utopians had the indefinable scruffiness of soldiers who have either stopped caring about their appearance or else never started in the first place.

"Lieutenant Katherine Forbes-Brandon, Peace Cruiser *Ark Royal*, Naval Liaison Officer to Company Group Fourteen. I'm senior officer of this shuttle load. Here's my ID and the roster."

The senior receiving clerk, a master sergeant, took the two pieces of plastic with a limp hand and shoved them carelessly into the computer. Forbes-Brandon cringed, and wouldn't have blamed the computer for going down, as much trouble as that would have caused her and the shuttle load.

"All seems to be in order, Lieutenant," said the sergeant. "Now if you and your people will just wait while I call Security and arrange an escort to your Forward HQ—"

"Escort?"

"Base commander's orders, ma'am. I'm sorry for the delay, but ever since the attack on the Scotians, any unarmed party going outside the base perimeter gets a squad escort."

"Then we won't be an unarmed party. We'll just wait until our weapons are unloaded and—or is there something wrong with that too?"

"Base Commander's orders are that only duty sentries are armed except when a Red Alert sounds. Can't keep the weapons secure any other way."

All three clerks looked away from Forbes-Brandon's glare. She had her mouth open to damn them, the Base Commander, and all of his orders, when she realized two things. One, the Base Commander certainly outranked her, and possibly outranked Lieutenant-Colonel MacLean. This was a matter that would have to be put before the Expeditionary Force C.O. or even the Ambassador, if it was worth putting before anybody.

Second, the Base Commander might have a case somebody would listen to. It was a strict rule that in a combat zone everyone went armed at all times. The right to carry weapons elsewhere

was at the local commander's discretion—or in this case, indis-
cretion. Forbes-Brandon wondered if the Base Commander had
panicked on his own after the archeologists were hit. Or had
these Dystopian militiamen persuaded him to lock up the
weapons because they knew they could never face the terrorists if
the terrorists ever got their hands on some modern equipment?

These clerks in uniform weren't likely to know, or tell her if
they did. The sergeant's explanation had been more in the line of
trying to turn aside an officer's wrath than of giving information.
Meanwhile, what to do that would get her people out of reach of
these clowns fast without violating any standing orders?

It was a pity that Majors Vela and Kuzik had shuttled straight
down to the railhead airstrip, leaving her and Captain Dallin to
handle things in the Base Area. There was only so much that
MacLean could do from orbit, even if he had the rank, or at least
without breaking security. He wasn't scheduled to land until tomorrow morning.

Well, that schedule was going to have to be changed, and
maybe this would finally persuade the Peace Force Personnel
Division that Group Fourteen needed an executive officer and an
adjutant. All they'd received after Bayard were three lieutenants
and forty N.C.O. and enlisted replacements. This left MacLean
effectively sharing the adjutant's job with Sergeant-Major John
Parkes, the Group First, while Vela doubled as X.O. and Field
Squadron C.O. The available people with enough rank to do
some effective yelling and screaming were spread rather thin.

"Start processing our people, then," she told the sergeant.
"And give me a secured line to Communications. I want to talk to
Ark Royal."

About half the thirty people from the shuttle had been proc-
essed, and Forbes-Brandon was discussing scrambler codes with
Communications, when the rear door opened and Captain Sondra
Dallin walked in. She wore boots, fatigues, and an aircrew vest
with her bars tacked to the shoulders. Through the closing door
Forbes-Brandon glimpsed a six-wheeled truck with a machine
gun mounted on the cab.

"I'm here to escort Forbes-Brandon's party to our FHQ," said
Dallin. "We have authorized machine guns on all four vehicles."

Fear of a distant Base Commander lost out to fear of a captain
on hand and looking ready to pull rank. "Fine, Captain. They're
all yours," said the sergeant.

"All right, people. Let's mount up and move out. Lieutenant,
would you ride with me?" Navy lieutenants and Peace Force cap-

tains were equal in rank, but Dallin had two years more time in grade, which made her the senior officer present.

Also, Forbes-Brandon would have obeyed a pfc if that pfc had found a way of getting her people out of the Receiving Office and embarrassing those damned clerks into the bargain!

Dallin's command car, the light reconnaissance vehicle, and the two trucks were all clear of the base perimeter before Dallin stopped looking out the window as if she expected an attack at any moment. Finally she leaned back, wiped her face with her sleeve, and lit a cigarette.

"*Are* there any terrorists around here?" asked Forbes-Brandon.

"Your guess is as good as mine," Dallin replied. "What I know is that the militia either thinks so or wants us to believe that they think so. Also, they want us to be suspicious of the Hrothmi. Thank God we've only got the minimum two guides from the militia with us. The road to FHQ runs right below the main Hrothmi settlement in Bakunin. The militia are too damned trigger-happy at their best for my peace of mind. With Hrothmi they make me sweat more than this filthy climate."

Five minutes past the railroad station they ran out of pavement and on to bonded earth. The road was just wide enough for two vehicles to pass if the drivers didn't blink an eye and everybody else held their breaths. The road curved sharply into a steep-walled ravine, then came out on the brow of a hill.

Suddenly Forbes-Brandon had a view across five kilometers of treetops to a range of broad-shouldered hills rising out of the valley mist. The railroad slashed through the trees—yellow-brown earth, silver-glinting metal, white plascrete—but everything else was green, more different shades of green than Forbes-Brandon had imagined could exist on any one world. The hills alone showed twenty different greens, and not the same twenty for two minutes straight. The mist eddied and swirled, brightening some colors, washing out others, sometimes reducing a hill to a dim, almost colorless shadow.

The sheer lushness of Greenhouse was too overpowering to be called beautiful, but it was certainly going to be hard to forget.

Dallin tapped the driver on the shoulder and the command car slowed, then turned into the first of what became a long series of switchbacks as the road descended into the valley. They went down with the driver riding the horn almost continuously, and began to find the turnouts at each curve filled with human-driven trucks and Hrothmi on foot or on bicycles. The militiaman in the back seat unslung his rifle at the sight of all the Hrothmi, but a glare from Dallin kept him from chambering a round.

Halfway down the hill they began to pass little clusters of sod houses with roofs of leaves woven into vine nets. Smoke rose from small brick ovens in front of each door. Hrothmi children ran back and forth, shoving twigs into the fire and carrying pots into the houses.

"My God, what wretched houses!" said Forbes-Brandon.

Dallin gave her a sharp look. "Don't ever say that around a local Hrothmi who understands Anglic. They build with sod, greenery, and handmade bricks so they won't have to beg or buy human-made building materials. Besides, for most of them it isn't worth the trouble of building fancy houses. They're waiting out the three local years for a Resident status that will let them homestead, or else waiting for relatives who've already home-steaded to send for them. No Hrothmi with the wits to find any-where else lives this close to any Utopian city."

This was a perspective on Greenhouse's Hrothmi community that the Group's briefing hadn't included. It was one that raised some interesting questions, too, considering that the Utopians were quite vocally militant against the Mountaineers and their large plantations and workshops employing indentured Hrothmi laborers.

Before the lieutenant could ask any questions of her own, the driver braked so suddenly that the command car swung sideways and rocked clear off its left-side wheels with a howl of abused tires. Forbes-Brandon was thrown sideways and her hat knocked down over her eyes. By the time she'd cleared her vision, Dallin was out of the car, patting the shoulder of a young Hrothmi who'd seemingly sprouted from the road. The other vehicles in the convoy had also stopped, the lead truck with its nose only half a meter behind the command car. The machine gunners were trying to look in every direction at once without knowing what they were looking for.

"It's all right," shouted Dallin. "Just a new kid in town who didn't understand blind curves."

The militia guide climbed out of the command car. "I don't trust . . . these people. That little *kukos* could be setting us up for an ambush."

From the look on the young Hrothmi's face, Forbes-Brandon knew that he'd just been called something particularly obscene. Human and Hrothmi faces and expressions were enough alike so that a glare was easy to recognize on either one.

Dallin shifted into the guttural Hrothmi language. When they knew they were going to Greenhouse, all the officers of Group Fourteen took sleep-tape lessons in Basic Hrothmi. Being relentlessly and irremediably monolingual, Forbes-Brandon had learned just enough to know that Dallin was asking the child where his parents were.

Finally Dallin turned. "He says his family lives at the bottom of the hill. They were packing for the move upcountry and wouldn't take him uphill to say good-bye to a friend who lives on the Fifth Terrace. So he decided to make the trip on his own.

"I've told him this was dishonorable behavior and I can't reward it by taking him to his friend. If he takes the punishment, his parents will give him with the spirit of a *jagrun*. I will have our next convoy bring his friend down to his parents' house."

The militia guide looked as if he'd been threatened with impalement. "You're going to send your people into a Hrothmi ambush. You can't take any chances with these (something unintelligible but obviously even more obscene than *kukos*)."

The young Hrothmi didn't bother glaring this time. He bared his teeth and grappled the militiaman around the left thigh, trying to get a good bite. The militiaman yelled, raised his rifle butt, and was about to bring it down on the child's head when Private Chaykin caught it by the muzzle. With no apparent effort he plucked it out of the man's hands and threw it away. Then he picked the man up by the collar of his shirt and the seat of his pants and swung him gently back and forth.

"Look, you little bastard," said Dallin. "Do you want to ride to the bottom of the hill with us or would you rather roll down?"

The militiaman grunted something that might have been the word "Ride," and Chaykin dropped him facedown on the road. He was brushing himself off and trying not to cry when the machine gun on the rear truck suddenly fired a short burst.

"What the—" began Dallin and Forbes-Brandon together.

"Sorry, ma'am," said the gunner. "But I thought I saw something moving up there in the trees, just below that terrace. Something with what might have been a weapon."

"Lieutenant, Chaykin. Go uphill and check. I'll man the gun to cover you, although I don't think you'll need it." Dallin ran back toward the rear truck. As she ran, she muttered something about, "If they'd wanted that schlemiel to think, they'd have issued him some brains, not just a trigger finger."

Ten minutes later Forbes-Brandon was able to radio that if anybody had been where the gunner aimed, they'd gone without leaving any traces she could see. "No damage to any of the Hrothmi homes either," she added. "Some of them have come out to see what's going on, but so far I haven't had to answer any questions."

"Good. Turn up the volume on your radio, and I'll explain to them what's happening."

Forbes-Brandon turned up her radio until the Hrothmi peering over the split-reed fences at the edge of their terraces could hear Dallin's words. With nothing to do herself, Forbes-Brandon had time to note that each Hrothmi house had a well-tended garbage and midden pit and a bucket of clean water standing by the door. Each door was also covered by a hanging of dried grass, some woven into intricate patterns which reminded her of the *Book of Kells*.

The Hrothmi themselves were no different from what she'd seen on three other planets, although most of them here wore no shoes on their broad feet with the four prehensile toes. With their leather-tough soles they probably had less to fear from burrowing soil parasites and fungi than humans, or else had smeared their feet with something that would have given a human being a second-degree chemical burn.

Otherwise they all seemed to be from . . . what *was* the nation where the dominant people had chestnut-brown fur and hair? The adults all stood 155 to 170 centimeters tall, but were so thick-bodied that the taller ones must have weighed nearly as much as Chaykin. Some of them were old enough for the tufts of fur in the triangular ears to be turning gray, but there were also a couple of children still being carried, and several more wearing only shorts.

One of the adults wore a dusty leather apron over his shirt and shorts, and the others seemed to be looking at him for their cues of how to respond to Dallin's speech. Finally he nodded, they all smiled, and he said something that made them all smile even wider.

"All right, Lieutenant. Shake hands with yourself, then come on down."

Mystified, Forbes-Brandon obeyed, but she could barely wait until the convoy was on the move again before asking what the Hrothmi leader had said.

"He was their brickmaker," replied Dallin. "That's almost as sacred as a blacksmith used to be in many human cultures. He said that since no harm was done by the shooting, no price would be asked. He also said that unless we were his enemies, he would not have asked a price even if damage had been done. He would wish only on his enemies the burden of trying to make the ruling-bond of Utopia pay a loss-price to the People."

"That wasn't quite the way our briefing had it."

"No. I think we're going to have to supplement the briefing with all the local intelligence we can gather."

4

THE TOE OF SERGEANT MAJOR PARKES'S boot caught a loop of creeper. He stumbled, started to fall forward, and twisted in midair, hoping to land on the trail. His martial-arts training and ten days' adaptation to Greenhouse's extra gravity kept him out of the worst of the flanking undergrowth. He still rose with a collage of mud, fungus, moss, leaves, and crushed insects on his trousers.

He started to brush it off, then drew his field knife and scraped himself clean with the back edge of the blade. That was probably an unnecessary precaution, but Parkes told himself he wanted to set a good example. He also hadn't forgotten the briefings on Greenhouse's vermin and parasites. They'd been detailed, including pictures of human victims, and left Parkes reluctant to touch any unknown Greenhouse life form with his bare hands.

Parkes knelt again to slash the loop of vine so it wouldn't trip any of the column behind him. It parted easily. At least blade-eater, which could dull the blade of a combat knife, didn't grow more than five hundred meters above sea level. The trail of today's route march had begun at eight hundred meters and was winding up toward a hilltop at eleven hundred, four kilometers ahead.

By now one of the Kabuele Company guides was coming back to see if Parkes was all right. Corporal Tsobo grinned as he saw the new camouflage pattern on Parkes's trousers, but said nothing. Parkes appreciated the tact, although he suspected that Major Kabuele and Captain Opperman had something to do with the unfailing politeness of their men. It made for easier relations between the Peace Forcers—who didn't care for mercenaries, but didn't know Greenhouse—and the mercenaries, who know what PFers usually thought of them, but also knew Greenhouse.

On this march the column was keeping the standard tactical

ten-meter interval between men. The man behind Parkes, Lance-Corporal Hagood, had just about closed the interval when Parkes heard a faint but distinct splash. He looked around, praying he'd be lucky enough to figure out where it came from before Tsobo's jungle-tuned ears did. If somebody back in the column had stumbled off the path and into a puddle—

"Sergeant Major. There. See, where the leaves have been broken. And is that not a Hrothmi footprint?"

It occurred to Parkes that tact could be carried to the point of silliness. Tsobo certainly knew Hrothmi footprints better than he did, and possibly what sex and nation of Hrothmi made them.

It also occurred to him that the Hrothmi who'd made the footprints and probably made the splash might be here for reasons that wouldn't stand close examination. The briefing on the terrorist attack on the University camp hadn't been quite as graphic as the one on Greenhouse jungle life, but Parkes hadn't forgotten any details of either. Not that junglewise terrorists would be likely to make loud splashes while laying an ambush for a Peace Force column, but still . . .

He decided to subject the splash makers to that close examination. "Hagood, hold up the column here. Message to Opperman and Vela: I'm investigating an unidentified Hrothmi contact with Corporal Tsobo."

"Yes, sir."

Any longer message would have wasted time, besides implying that Major Vela and Captain Opperman couldn't deploy the column tactically to meet an ambush or rescue Parkes and Tsobo —more likely, retrieve their bodies, because if somebody was lying in ambush off the trail, Parkes and Tsobo wouldn't be returning to it alive.

"Follow me, Corporal."

Tsobo "followed" in a way that let him sidle around into the lead before the two men had covered ten meters. Parkes let the matter ride. In heavy Greenhouse brush Tsobo was a better point man than Parkes would be, for a few more weeks at least. His last experience in this kind of jungle was ten years old. The knowledge remained, but the reflexes would have to be rebuilt.

Tsobo moved almost silently, giving hand and foot signals to Parkes so that the Sergeant Major could follow almost as silently. From the way Tsobo winced when he thought Parkes wasn't looking, Parkes suspected he sounded like a tiger lizard in the mating season.

Twenty-five meters, and the undergrowth had swallowed half

the light and all the fresh air. It wasn't as hot as it would have been in the true jungle lowlands, but Parkes still felt as if his uniform and pack were glued to his skin. It was like marching through a giant sauna, heated by a furnace burning a mixture of ripe garbage and raw sewage.

Thirty meters, and Parkes understood why the Kabuele Company's tactical interval in deep Greenhouse jungle was more like two meters. Any longer interval and you might lose sight of the man ahead of you, shortly followed by losing yourself, and that followed after some further interval by a painful death.

Parkes knew he'd have to ride everyone with a very tight rein, or Fourteen would be losing some people before the rest were junglewise. Peace Forcers were trained mostly against weapons that could take out a whole platoon with one round if they kept two-meter intervals. They'd have to unplug all their old instincts and plug in some new ones pretty damned fast.

Correction: he'd have to drop a hint to Chuck Voorhis, the Field First, about the new tactical interval. As Group First, Parkes was out of the Field Squadron chain of command. Not to mention that Voorhis was a bit sensitive about having the man he'd replaced looking over his shoulder. Voorhis was perfectly qualified for his new job, but he wasn't a decorated Bifrost veteran who'd been offered a commission twice, and he couldn't forget it.

Sooner rather than later he'd have to forget it. Otherwise there wouldn't be room for both him and Parkes in Group Fourteen and a nice headache for Colonel MacLean. That was one reason Parkes had refused a commission: beyond a certain point, an N.C.O. didn't have to face that kind of headache. He could always pass it on to an officer and let the officer spend his extra salary on headache remedies—

This time the splash sounded from ahead, a little to the left, and very close. Parkes had been carrying his rifle at high port; now he swung it down and chambered a round. With no communication except an exchange of glances, he and Tsobo separated. They would now come in on the splashmaker with a safe interval between them. Even if the enemy was waiting for one, the other should be able to get off at least a warning shot.

Parkes took a deep breath as he saw the foliage thinning out ahead. He took two more steps, pushed through the last curtain of trailing vines, and found himself on the bank of a small stream. Just upstream lay a round pool about ten meters in diameter, fed by a five-meter waterfall on the far side.

In the middle of the pool a small auburn-haired head was just breaking the surface. Freckled bare arms rose in a crawl stroke that took the head swiftly to the bank to the right of the waterfall.

Then the head's owner did a perfect imitation of Venus rising from the waves. She didn't have a goddess's height, but she had everything else. By chance or design, she'd stepped into a patch of sunlight falling through the canopy of trees. Every drop of water on her elfin face and tanned skin sparkled like a jewel, including the few trickling down across her breasts . . .

Parkes had the sensation of rudely interrupting something sacred. He was shifting his weight to his rear foot, ready to back away, when the woman turned to reach for a towel hanging from a bush and saw him.

"Oh, excuse me," she said. She sounded more concerned for Parke's possible embarrassment than for her own nudity. "I hope there's nothing wrong at the camp you couldn't—" She broke off, looked Parkes up and down, then frowned.

"You're not from the camp, or the militia either. Is that a Peace Force uniform?"

Parkes sketched a mock salute. "Sergeant Major John Parkes of Company Group Fourteen, at your service. You would be Professor Jean Grant, from the University of Scotia."

Grant smiled and started toweling herself dry. "Your briefing must have included a recognizable photograph of me. I didn't know there was such a thing."

"Peace Force Command is resourceful, sometimes. I apologize for having to ask, ma'am, but could you explain what you're doing here alone?"

"Call me Professor, if you can't call me Jean. 'Ma'am' makes me feel like a dowager noblewoman about ninety years old. I'm not alone either." She squatted down to dry between her toes, managing to remain decorative, even graceful in that inelegant position. "Kilaa, Tsigo. We have company."

"So have we seen, *Shedni-te,*" came a Hrothmi voice from Parkes's left. He looked that way but couldn't see anything. He also couldn't help thinking that the Hrothmi was in an excellent position for a clear shot at him, unless Tsobo had spied him out in turn.

"Could your Hrothmi friends come out and be seen?"

Grant pulled a robe out from under the bush and pulled it on. She also donned a rebellious look. In Parkes's opinion, neither improved her. An audible sigh from Tsobo indicated agreement.

"Professor, I came back here to interrupt your bath because we heard a splash."

"That was me diving. I come out here with Kilaa and Tsigo two or three times a week. The water's too clear and there's too much current for any of the water parasites. I know it's pulling rank, but I can't do a blessed thing in our new quarters except feel the mold growing on me as if I were a dead tree—"

"Professor, we—I wondered if the noise might be terrorists or bandits. There's a whole Peace Force rifle company going into tactical formation along the trail now, waiting for me to tell them what I've found."

The rebellious look gave way to the beginnings of an impish grin, then to a frown, and finally to a delightful smile. "I'm sorry, Sergeant Major. I didn't realize that I might be making trouble for the Peace Force. There haven't been any terrorist attacks around here. Kabuele's men don't know about this pool, and the militiamen seldom use this trail. Anyway, Kilaa and Tsigo could rout a whole platoon of militia before they knew what hit them if they did come around."

From what Parkes had seen of the Utopian militia, that was only a slight exaggeration. "Fair enough, Professor. But I'm afraid your secret is out now, as far as Kabuele's men are concerned. One of them is with me."

"Corporal Tsobo, I think," said the same Hrothmi voice.

Parkes took a deep breath and decided not to force the issue of the Hrothmi coming out into the open. "Could you please suggest that your Hrothmi friends give up lurking in the trees when Peace Forcers are around? We're not as trigger-happy as the militia, but we pack a lot more firepower. Our explosive rounds will go off, instead of being two thirds duds."

"Also, you are not yet junglewise, you and your Peace Forcers," came another Hrothmi voice from at least twenty meters to the right of the other. Parkes thought this one was a female. "We understand. It would be dishonorable to make you pay blood prices. You are only *jag-rufai*, not like the militia, who are *jag-hirmi*."

What Parkes knew was at least intended as flattery didn't make him more comfortable at being under the invisible eyes of doubtless well-armed Hrothmi and even worse, Hrothmi who knew one of the things about Group Fourteen that he'd been trying to avoid discussing.

Well, any Hrothmi who was enough at home with humans to be working for the University expedition was almost certainly an ex-*jagruni*. Allowing for differences of technology and species, any good soldier had a certain amount of knowledge in common with any other soldier. No doubt that included recognizing well-trained troops who still had a good deal to learn about the jungles of Greenhouse!

Parkes decided to try for a dignified exit from the situation, and pulled out his radio. "Fruit Merchant to Champion. Come in, Champion."

"Champion here," said Major Vela. "I was beginning to wonder what had happened to you."

"Nothing much." He didn't add "sir"—under field conditions salutes, sirring, and anything else that gave unneccessary clues to the identity and whereabouts of officers was proscribed. "I found Professor Grant from the University archeologists having a picnic by a little pond with a couple of her Hrothmi. They apologized for holding us up and will march back to their camp with us."

"Tell them that they can finish their picnic if they don't mind a little company. Is the pond pure?"

Parkes repeated the question to Grant. She nodded. "It comes from a spring about five hundred meters above the falls. We've been drinking it out of a standard two-liter filter jug for nearly thirty days with no trouble at all."

Parkes relayed the word to Vela, heard a minute of background conversation, then:

"We'll run a series of tactical exercises, including field replenishment of our water. Send Tsobo out to guide the water party into the pond, and look out for a good CP site yourself. Champion over."

"Okay, Champion. Fruit Merchant out."

Parkes explained the situation to Professor Grant, and was relieved to have her stop his apology in mid-sentence. It wouldn't help Group Fourteen's work on Greenhouse to start off on the wrong foot with one of the people they'd come to protect. There was such a thing as protecting people in spite of themselves, but that was another kind of headache, and one that the officers and N.C.O.'s took on share and share alike.

As soon as Tsobo vanished, the two Hrothmi appeared. Both carried well-worn shotguns as if they knew how to use them. Parkes suggested that they take over sentry duty. When they'd done so he unslung his pack, laid down his rifle, and started doing some limbering-up exercises.

The company was supposed to be aboard its vertis and on its way back to camp by nightfall, but that was six hours away. The landing zone was less than four kilometers away, maybe an hour and a half's march at most. That left four and a half hours for tactical exercises. In that time Major Vela's notions of exercise could reduce a rifle company to a collection of perspiring blobs of jelly.

A very fit man himself, Major Vela didn't always appreciate the limits of even Peace Force–trained flesh.

5

ONCE MAJOR VELA decided on improvised tactical exercises, the question of what kind remained. Also what level—the
whole column, individual rifle platoons, selected squads and
heavy-weapons teams, or what?

Parkes had his own opinions on the best mix, but kept them to
himself. Vela certainly had some ideas of his own. Voorhis probably had more. If Vela needed advice from a sergeant major,
Parkes decided, it would be better if he got it from Voorhis.

In two hours Vela ran the column through water resupply,
setting and detecting booby traps, marking L.Z.'s for medevac
and air resupply and D.Z.'s for orbital resupply, and a quartet of
short tactical problems. These involved a squad, a platoon, and a
heavy-weapons team chosen at random, plus a set-piece assault
with two platoons, one up and one back.

Everything went off as well as could be expected with elite
troops only semi-acclimatized and exercising on unfamiliar
ground. At least that was the picture Parkes assembled from
overheard radio messages and rumors. Vela left Parkes in charge
of C.P. defense and kept Voorhis in tow. Did the major have his
own doubts about Voorhis? Parkes didn't know, knew that Vela
would tell him if there was a need to know, and thought Vela was
doing the right thing for now.

As Group First, Parkes's presence would intimidate the junior
N.C.O.'s as well as Voorhis. The second lieutenants would also
find it hard to ignore him. There were only three officers above
that rank in the column: Vela himself, the Amazon, and Lieutenant Simmel, Third Company C.O.

In short, Parkes was neither fish nor flesh nor fowl nor good
red herring in a situation like this. Since he didn't really have any
business on this hike anyway, that was no surprise. Should he

show his gratitude to Vela by not inviting himself along on any more field exercises?

Sure, and if he did that he'd be so deskbound he might as well hand in his papers. Either that or apply for a transfer to a training unit, *if* there were any with vacancies for a twenty-two year Sergeant Major, *and* if Group Fourteen could spare him, which they probably couldn't. Breaking in a new Group First on top of a new Field First, and with no X.O. or adjutant—MacLean shouldn't have to face that headache.

Parkes's musings stopped there because the casualties started coming in. Leaf and grass cuts, insect bites, pigtail-sap poisoning—a baker's dozen in all, but only two who couldn't go straight back to their units after first-aid. (Parkes chalked up a point to Captain Laughton, the Group Surgeon: she was no more military than ever, but she was training her medics damned well.)

One was Corporal Tom Sykes from the launcher team; he knocked down a death's head nest, and was the only one in range of their attack pattern when the nest broke open. If he'd been a Greenhouse life form, he'd have been dead before the bearers brought him in. As it was, antihistamines and anticonvulsants let him quietly pass out, which was the best thing for him to do.

The other casualty was Katherine Forbes-Brandon. When the two-platoon assault moved out, she tried to move her D.Z. marking team out of their way on the double. Her navigation wasn't as good as her wind; she led them to a two-meter bluff masked in brush. Since she was taking point, she was the only one who actually went over. Her jump training kept her from more than a sprained knee, and the skin scraped off the back of her right wrist.

After the Amazon's injury, Vela cut the two-platoon exercise down to thirty minutes, then assigned bearers to the little cases and put everybody on the trail again. Parkes fell in behind the litter parties. He wanted to find some light remark to make to the Amazon, like, "Haven't we met this way before?"

The blue eyes were veiled, though, and staring straight up without seeing anything. The wide mouth was set in a hard line, and altogether the Amazon looked as tightly drawn as Parkes had ever seen her. Parkes suspected what was bothering her. She was a perfectionist, who'd not only failed at the on-the-double move but wracked herself up to boot.

At least she wouldn't have to wrestle with guilt over wracking up somebody else. What was left, she could probably work through herself. Parkes intended to let her try. He didn't know if she remembered falling asleep on his shoulder, vulnerable, maudlin, drunk, and at least temporarily purged of the demons she'd been wrestling with ever since Keith Holland and Rufus Garron died under the Game Master's rockets. He was damned sure she wouldn't want him reminding her of it, even by way of offering to help her with the wrestling next time. . . .

A light P.F. verti was circling over the hill when Jean Grant came out to the University camp gate for a breath of fresh air. This high, the evening actually had as much as a one-in-four chance of producing a breeze as well as a nine-in-ten chance of producing rain.

She'd just inspected the sentries and turned toward the bench beside the gate when two men in P.F. field uniform seemed to materialize in front of her. Their approach had been so silent, she started and found her hand halfway to her pistol before she caught herself.

"Sorry, Professor," said the leader. She recognized Sergeant Major Parkes's voice. "Corporal Dietsch and I were making an inspection of your camp perimeter. Your sentries need a little gingering up, I think. We weren't challenged once."

Grant smiled. "They had orders not to challenge anyone in a P.F. uniform."

"Was that a good idea? Terrorists have been known to disguise themselves as Peace Forcers."

"Not when you've only been on-planet ten days."

"What about thefts from our supply dumps?"

"Wouldn't it be insulting your security to suspect that?"

"We'd rather be insulted than have to bury you and your people. We're here to protect all of you, even Professor Carey."

The joke defused the exchange just before it grew tense. Grant laughed, and Parkes joined in. Dietsch seemed to have dematerialized again. Grant went to the bench and sat down. After a moment Parkes joined her.

"Would you care for a drink?" she asked. "It's Glen Parr Malt. Only the twelve-year, I'm afraid, but—"

"Thank you, but I'm still on duty."

"I thought the regulations only said you weren't allowed to make yourself unfit, not that you couldn't drink."

"If I fell asleep before I reviewed tomorrow's defaulters, I'd be unfit. Maybe we haven't been here long enough to have our uniforms snatched, but we've had time for a few people to step out of line. It's part of my job to review all their documents, then be bright and shiny-eyed in dress uniform tomorrow morning when the colonel hears the cases."

He blinked, as if seeing her for the first time. "But why the hell am I telling you this? I don't want to bore you with my professional headaches."

"You weren't boring me . . . Sergeant Major? Mr. Parkes? John?"

"Try Sergeant Major. It matches Professor."

"Very well, Sergeant Major. I hope I didn't embarrass you today by the pond."

"You didn't. Pleasantly surprised me, maybe, but embarrass?" He laughed. "By the time you've been in a combat unit for a year, you've seen damned near everybody in it the way nature made them, if not worse. You were at least as good if not better. That's a nice change."

"Thank you, Sergeant Major. Now, I hate to be pushy, but if you're tired and have some business—"

"You mean you don't suspect I was drawn here by a desire for your charming company?"

Something brittle in what ought to have been simply a feeble joke . . . She shook her head. "I suspect you're combining business with pleasure."

"I am. I wanted to discuss the security of your new camp. I know, you've copied us in on everything that's written down. I wanted to find out if there's anything else—that you want to tell us," he added hastily.

Grant hadn't realized how her eyebrows must have gone up. She gently laid a hand on Parkes's arm. "As Winston Churchill said when President Roosevelt found him in the same clothes you found me in this afternoon: 'We have nothing to hide.'

"Weapons—we drew our security gear from the University M.T.O. Their Weapons Officer is ex-P.F."

"That explains why you have ammunition that matches your weapons. Sometime you should offer Colonel MacLean a drink. He'll tell you about the time he was adviser to a Hephaestion militia brigade that thought they'd scored a big coup, buying fourteen thousand rifles at about twenty dollars apiece."

"What was wrong with them?"

"Half of them wouldn't fire. The other half—would you believe seven different calibers?"

"Yes. The Weapons Officer was there too. Donald MacCullum, from Group Six."

"Colonel MacLean will love you."

"In a platonic fashion, I hope."

"I don't think you'll have to seduce any of us to win our cooperation, Professor."

Grant couldn't help thinking about what that statement left unsaid. She thanked the twilight for hiding a blush, and hurried on.

"Weapons and ammunition—all right, unless there's heavy fighting. Leadership—Roger Carey is our self-appointed security officer. He knows enough to get by. The Hrothmi are mostly veterans who can fill in for themselves what he doesn't know."

"I've heard that he doesn't like Hrothmi."

"You've heard the truth."

"Well?"

"Well what?"

"What about Hrothmi loyalty and morale, with somebody like Carey throwing his weight around?"

Grant's eyebrows rose again, but this time Parkes didn't back off. Since he didn't seem like the kind of man to insult Hrothmi for no reason, or in fact at all—

"Our Hrothmi follow Kilaa M'ni Ifarn and her bond, Tsigo M'no Churaf. Both of them are oath-bound to the University and to me personally. They would probably kill Carey in a minute if I told them to, but what I'm telling them to do is ignore him as much as possible.

"Also, Kilaa at least sees the advantage of having a Hrothmi-hater giving the orders. It makes the local militia trust us. They think we believe in keeping fur-faces in their place." She couldn't keep the bitterness out of her voice, or keep her hand from tightening on Parkes's arm.

"I'd like to meet Kilaa."

"You can, if you'll arrange for Tsigo to meet your Major Vela. He was in Vela's battalion toward the end of the Akkwasi War. He'd been wounded early in the war and posted to a training depot, but finally pulled strings to get back into combat. There wasn't a vacancy in his local regiment, so he accepted a transfer, and a drop in rank as well."

"I'd like to meet them both."

"I'll see what I can do. Now—weapons, ammunition, officers, men. Anything I've left out? The site is well-watered, but we haven't had the labor to harden our buildings. If you think that's necessary—"

"The first thing I'd recommend is clearing the brush outside the perimeter. Then you can position sensors—What's so funny?"

Grant stopped her laughter before she had to wipe tears from her eyes. "I'm sorry, but have you ever seen how things grow on Greenhouse, even up here in the hills? We'd need half your Support Squadron to keep the perimeter clear, unless we used high-powered chemicals. That might contaminate the ground water, so that's out of the question."

"Okay. I'll defer to local knowledge. But short-range sensors, a missile detector hooked to an alarm system, and at least one hardened bunker—I think that's about the minimum. Support Squadron will have some hands to spare in a couple of days, once they've built our camp and before they go to work on the railroad. I'll ask Dozer. . . ."

Grant searched Parkes's long face with its oddly attractive beak of a nose, as if she could find the words she needed up his left nostril. "Sergeant Major, if you really wanted to help us—no, sorry. You do really want to help us. But the best way of helping us . . ."

"Yes?" His smile was quirky, almost lopsided, but it helped her over the barrier.

"Could you fly us out to the Survivors' Caves in your vertis? BAM has been promising ever since the raid wrecked our canoes, but promises is all they give us. If we could get on with our archeological work, we'd be out of your hair and out of the line of fire."

"What's so important about the caves? No, I don't mean that it's a silly whim, wanting to study them. I'm sure they're an immensely important archeological site. But are they important enough to risk getting all your people killed?"

"Sergeant Major, I don't quite follow you."

He took her through his reasoning and that of Group Fourteen in detail, without condescending to her as a civilian. He didn't even show irritation at any of her questions, as stupid as she knew some of them must be. In the end she had a clear picture of why Group Fourteen and the Peace Force Expeditionary Command thought the Survivors' Caves might be the terrorist base.

"They'd have every advantage," he finished. "Close enough to the border that either government might protest the other going in. Virtually detector-proof, and proof against anything much short of nukes if detectors did pick up anything. Roomy, well-watered, easy to secure against human intruders and local wild-life—what else could the terrorists need?"

"They'd be rather far from the railroad, at least by river. It's two hundred eighty kilometers as the verti flies, about four hundred by river."

"Oh, I'm sure they've got a base closer in, fifty kilometers out at the most. They could resupply it by air once every few days with a minimal risk of detection. Or they could have, until *Ark* deployed her surveillance satellites. That's our major objective now, finding their forward base and taking it out. That, and trying to find out if the terrorists are Hrothmi or have local Hrothmi support."

"Is that why you've been bothering Alexis Werbel? And is that why you want to meet Kilaa and Tsigo?"

"You sound as if you object."

"I sound as if I've lived with the Utopians' prejudices against Hrothmi for the better part of two local years. I also sound as if I'm tired of people harassing Alexis Werbel. She needs time to get over her father's death, not more interrogations!"

"It won't help anybody if we don't find out who's supporting the terrorists, whether they're humans, Hrothmi, or Grand Galactics."

"It will hurt a lot of innocent Hrothmi if you even hint that some of them might not be loyal. Or haven't you heard there's a faction in Utopia that wants to cancel all the Hrothmi homestead claims? Whose side are you on, anyway?"

"The Peace Force isn't on any side except against the terrorists. Or do you want them to kill the railroad? If that happens, a lot of your dear Hrothmi's homestead claims won't be worth the film they're recorded on!"

"No." The scholar in her responded to his appeal to facts.

"Then we have to consider every possibility, including some of the local Hrothmi helping the terrorists. If we don't investigate, how are we going to tell the guilty from the innocent? The whole Hrothmi community would be even more under suspicion if we let things slide."

"In other words, they're damned if you do and damned if you don't?"

"You know the Utopians better than I do. Isn't that about right?"

"Yes, but— Oh, the Judgment Lord take the Utopians! I don't like the situation, but there's no point in being angry at you. It's not your fault, and you are trying to make it better instead of worse. That's more than I've ever had from a Utopian."

"I should hope so. If the Peace Force can't do better than that,

we should all turn in our suits." He smiled again. The lights over
the gate had come on now, and Grant could see that the smile
made him look ten years younger. "We're supposed to be impartial between the Mountaineers and the Utopians, so I'd rather you
didn't quote that last remark."

"I won't. The Utopians were a nasty surprise to all of us
except Roger Carey. We thought that the Republic would be the
real hotbed of—"

A discreet cough from the shadows interrupted her. Parkes
turned. "Yeah, Dietsch?"

"Just came over the horn, Sergeant Major. Dallin's landing
and wants to pick us up and be out of here p.d.q."

"I'm on the way." Parkes stood up and held out his hand.
"Professor, it's been good talking to you. Now that we've cleared
the air, can I hope for some more of your company? I don't know
about mine, but your company really is charming."

"You certainly can." She squeezed his hand, almost tempted
to rise on her toes and kiss his cheek. From the look on his face,
he was sensing that near temptation and leaving the decision to
her. "Safe journey, Sergeant Major."

"Sleep well, Professor."

The noise in the verti's cabin drowned out Parkes's conversation with Dozer di Leone for anyone more than a meter away.
Parkes didn't much care if Dallin or Dietsch overheard; both
would keep their mouths shut. In fact, it might do Dietsch some
good to overhear how senior N.C.O.'s bargained. He was potential Sergeant Major material himself, if he ever wanted the torch
badly enough to give up arguing with field-grade officers.

Still, Dozer was a stickler for the proprieties of this sort of
thing. One of them was allowing the officers to pretend they
didn't know. (The good ones, anyway; the other kind you made
sure were *really* in the dark.) Parke didn't want to waste time by
waiting until after they'd landed to cut the deal. Now that he was
out of Jean Grant's company, the fatigue was hitting again, and
he still had those defaulters to settle up before his personal lights-
out.

"If you want everything installed before Support Squadron
gets shifted over to the railroad, you'll have to give me one full-
time security type from Field Squadron. At *least* one."

"Come on, Dozer. You gave me six people on a silver platter.
What's happened to Support's weapons training, that none of
them can do the security job?"

"They can't do it and test sensors, dig dugouts, or calibrate a missile-warning radar at the same time. You think my people have three hands apiece?"

"They didn't the last time I counted. Okay, two people."

"If one of them is Private Kennedy. I'll put two more of my own on the job. That should cut a day at least off it."

"Is that Jim Kennedy, from First Company?"

"The same."

"Jim Kennedy from First Company is up on charges for assaulting a civilian. You want a brawler standing guard?"

"When he'll be standing guard with Hrothmi, that particular brawler is just the right man. You know who he punched out?"

"A civilian who called him an obscene name."

"The obscene name was 'furballer.' The civilian had been insulting a Hrothmi waiter, and Kennedy told him to stop it. Kennedy's parents were Domiciled Humans on Hrothma."

"I see—I think." Being accused of having sex with Hrothmi probably hadn't triggered Kennedy's temper. With that background, it was something he could laugh off. Seeing some Utopian clown puffing himself up big by cutting down a Hrothmi, on the other hand . . .

"Okay. The civilian wasn't hurt, so the whole thing could be handled with administrative punishment. I'll have to get Vela and Voorhis to appeal for it, and hope Kennedy's not a barracks lawyer—"

"He isn't. Just a wet-behind-the-ears kid who'd rather deal with Hrothmi than with humans."

"You must have been going over his records."

She shook her head. "Just Mama Dozer's hunch, after meeting him a couple of times on the way out to Greenhouse."

That, Parkes thought, was an awfully tactful way of hinting that he should have gone over Kennedy's records himself long before this. Domiciled Humans were odd files everywhere, maybe a little less so in the Peace Force, but not enough to excuse not double-checking him. Of course, he was one of the replacements, but that was no excuse either. Or at least it wouldn't have been for Parkes in his days as Field First. Now . . .

Now, you're going to worry yourself sick if you make the same mistake as the Amazon, and think you can do everything. That won't do Kennedy or anybody else a bit of good. Relax, John.

"I don't suppose you'd mind if his punishment was a transfer to Support Squadron, would you?" said Parkes.

"No. If Vela and Captain Hansen don't mind losing one of their people—"

"And Voorhis."

"Of course."

The prepare-for-landing lights flashed on, and Parkes checked his harness. They'd pretty much wrapped it up, except for working out who would call on which of Kennedy's seniors.

Vela would be no problem. The major probably thought punching out anti-Hrothmi Utopians was worth a commendation. Hansen was a book soldier who wouldn't mind getting rid of a bad actor if he wasn't feeling short-handed. Voorhis—Parkes realized that he'd had to remind Dozer that the Field First needed consulting. Was there something Dozer wasn't telling him about, a personality clash or worse?

He could ask, and would. He doubted he'd get an answer until Dozer decided their friendship and the good of Group Fourteen required one. Before then, he'd have a better chance of prying secrets out of the Peace Force Commander.

6

COLONEL MACLEAN'S CHAIR creaked as he crossed one leg over the other and clasped his hands on the upper knee.

"Lieutenant, isn't this the fifth time you've tried to demolish yourself in the field?"

"No, sir," said Forbes-Brandon. "It's the sixth." Plus about twice as many occasions that weren't in her 82 File because they hadn't put her in the hands of the medics.

"I'm glad you're being honest."

Forbes-Brandon was tempted to ask, "Do I have a choice?" She suppressed the urge. Wherever MacLean intended to lead this conversation, he was at least conducting it informally, in her hospital room. Repaying this courtesy with insubordination could put the matter in the hands of Captain Cooper. *Ark Royal*'s C.O. could lean on her more heavily than MacLean, officially or otherwise.

She also suppressed the urge to reach inside her hospital gown and scratch. The hospital's air-conditioning ranged from the erratic to the nonexistent, in spite of Captain Laughton's protests and Support Squadron's best efforts. Laughton had been heard threatening to sacrifice the next technician who didn't fix the system to Murphy, God of Engineers.

"Has it occurred to you that Naval Liaison work may not be your ideal specialty?" MacLean went on. "I don't know whether it's physical limitations or attitude or maybe something else entirely. I do know you seem to be trying to compensate for something by consistently driving yourself to the edge. Sometimes over it, like today.

"So far you haven't taken anybody else with you. I want you to consider reassignment to ship duty before that happens. I hope I'm simply reminding you of something you've already considered yourself. I know I have to raise the question, or I'd be neglecting my duty. Neither of us wants an unnecessary death on our conscience, in training or combat."

"No, sir."

"Yes, sir" and "No, sir"—the universal cures for sticky situations involving superiors. Or if not cures, at least symptomatic relief.

Besides, what else could she say? That aboard ship she'd always be under the eyes of people Admiral Newton had told to watch out for her, but that with a Company Group she could stand or fall on her own? And that she'd rather fall than stand propped up by her mentor's network of well-intentioned, well-placed officers and senior petty officers?

Ten years of keeping silence on the matter kept her silent now. It was something she did without conscious thought, like brushing her teeth or polishing her boots.

Besides, the times she had broken silence, people seemed to think she was only fighting the rumors about her and Newton. It was a pity that Newton was "absolutely devoid of asceticism," to use a classic understatement she'd heard made about some Old Terran general. If he'd been as monkish as Commodore Zurger, for example—

"If wishes were horses, then beggars could ride." She would ride the mount fate led out of the stables for her, no matter how hard it might try to throw her.

"Sir, is applying for reassignment to ship duty an order?"

"No, Lieutenant. This isn't a matter for your next Efficiency Report either. It's—call it an appeal to your ethics, judgment, and conscience. You didn't get five commendations without all three, so I don't think I'm appealing in vain."

"No, sir."

"I understand you'll be fit for light duty in a couple of days. We're rather in betwixt and between as far as our mission is concerned. I propose to tie up a few loose ends before we start chasing terrorists and building railroads. I'll let you know what loose end I want to put in your hands."

"Yes, sir."

"Oh, before I go. Sergeant Majors Parkes and di Leone and Professor Grant sent this up for you." "This" was a two-liter thermos jug, its exterior misty with condensation. "It's Hrothmi homebrew. I'd recommend rationing it, in case Laughton can't get the air-conditioning working."

"Yes, sir."

Forbes-Brandon took the jug and tucked it under her pillow as

MacLean let himself out. When the door thumped shut behind him, she lay down, burying her face in the pillow. She couldn't stop the tears; maybe she could hide them.

Was this where ten years of silence and striving had brought her? To being told to run away and play somewhere else, because the big boys and girls didn't want her around?

Oh, MacLean had been the soul of courtesy. But it was the courtesy of the king who could also order her execution, or at least of the superior who could give her an E.R. downcheck that would force her to do what he wanted.

If that kind of courtesy was all she'd earned, had she earned anything at all in the ten years? Was she any better off than if she'd done as her father wanted, staying home to produce his grandchildren and eventually take his place on the board of directors of Olympus Machinery Limited?

At least she'd chosen a more intelligent form of rebellion than her brother. She was still alive, and those commendations had to be worth *something*. But could you make a career out of any rebellion without warping your judgment until you were a danger to the people you led?

MacLean was asking the question, but she had to answer it.

One of her sobs must have leaked through the pillow. An orderly came tramping in.

"Lieutenant, are you—"

"I'll be fine if you leave me alone."

"Lieutenant—"

"Get the hell out of here!"

The orderly fled. Forbes-Brandon turned her face back to the pillow, and for the first time since her brother's death, cried herself to sleep.

"You have a visitor, ma'am. Captain Hugo Opperman, of Kabuele Company."

After three days the orderly still seemed afraid that Forbes-Brandon would bite if not spoken to gently.

"Show him in."

She stood up, cautious about putting weight on a knee that still gave off an occasional twinge. At least the air-conditioning had finally yielded to either tinkering or threats. The robe she pulled on no longer felt as all-enveloping and uncomfortable as a malfunctioning E.V.A. suit.

Opperman came in with his usual bouncy stride. Was it an affectation, or did he really have that much animal energy? He grinned, laid his bush hat and a wrapped parcel on the side table, and at down.

"Good morning, Lieutenant. I'm your C.O. on the end-tying mission MacLean promised you. We're going to Ciudad Cervantes to study the records and security of their arms depots. The Council of Ministers wants to prove how clean their hands are as far as leaking arms to the terrorists."

"I suppose I can't march anybody over a cliff in a city of two hundred thousand people."

"Is that what you think, Lieutenant? If all you're doing is feeling sorry for yourself—"

"Captain Opperman, you can recommend that I be replaced or not, as you choose. I'm not going to beg."

Opperman took a deep breath. "I wasn't going to ask you to. I also wasn't going to discuss your personal problems. But if you're going to start by snapping my head off, I think I have the right to a few words."

Forbes-Brandon looked down at the floor, hoping her eyes would stay dry. When she knew they would, she raised her head.

"I'm sorry, Captain. I have had other things on my mind these past three days, believe me. It's just that it seems more than a coincidence, my being sent as far from the field as possible."

"It's not a coincidence that the mission needs somebody with a naval background. We need to look for leaks of anti-satellite systems, among other things. *Ark Royal* offered a Lieutenant-Commander Singer for the job, but I know MacLean specifically wanted you."

His tone left her sure he was telling the truth, and equally sure that she'd never find out how he knew. It didn't matter. If she'd been picked over one of *Ark*'s electronics wizards—

"The mission will be you, Captain Dallin, me, and Lieutenant Tegen from your Support Squadron. Security will be a half platoon from Kabuele Company, under Lieutenant Ngomba. We know Ciudad Cervantes better than you PFers, and they know us."

The mission was beginning to sound more and more like the genuine article. Maybe MacLean was also trying to give her some time to put her priorities in order, before she went back on field duty.

Maybe she even needed that time.

Opperman pulled his chair closer to the bed and unwrapped the package. It was a bottle of Mountaineer white wine, with two hand-carved wooden cups nested beside it.

"I understand your sentence is being remitted this afternoon, so I thought a toast was in order."

He broke the seal on the bottle and started to fill a cup. From close up, his eyes were a starling gray-green and his movements had a controlled grace. Maybe that bouncing step was natural after all.

Forbes-Brandon still felt a trifle underdressed, dealing with a man who'd so easily guessed or perhaps ferreted out one of her deep-buried worries. He also hadn't forced his knowledge down her throat, or stepped outside an official relationship in any other way.

She'd be just as happy if things stayed that way. Yet even within the frame of a purely official relationship, there could be such a thing as combining duty with pleasure. The mission to Ciudad Cervantes seemed to be offering that. How long was it since she'd been that lucky?

The raw wine bit her throat going down but she smiled as Opperman gave the traditional mercenary's toast:

"A good fight in company with good friends!"

7

FROM OUTSIDE THE far end of the ordnance warehouse, a submachine gun went *brrrrp*. Forbes-Brandon was already diving for the dusty floor when the warehouse rocked to an explosion.

The skylights shattered, dust swirled, and the piles of wooden crates with Mountaineer ordnance markings swayed gently. Forbes-Brandon swallowed both dust and fear. Those crates weighed fifty to a hundred kilos apiece. If one of them came straight down on her from two meters up—

Brrrp again, followed by several standard Mountaineer infantry rifles, a single pistol shot, and a Kabuele Company rifle shooting off a whole magazine on full automatic. From the other side of the aisle Hugo Opperman muttered something that promised no good to the rifleman.

Forbes-Brandon raised her head enough to see not only Opperman, but the three men who'd been escorting them through the warehouse. The Mountaineer sergeant looked as if the whole terrorist attack was about as interesting as an overflowing sewer, and somewhat less dangerous. A professional, that one.

Corporal Tsobo and a private whose name she didn't know also looked thoroughly professional, with the difference that they seemed to want to run down the aisle and join the fight. Opperman noticed the same difference.

"Hold it, everybody. If the terrorists penetrate the warehouse, we may be needed right where we are."

Tsobo nodded, rolled half over, and pulled two fresh magazines out of his belt. He'd just put them ready at hand when the sound of running feet gave them a few seconds' warning. Then a dark figure appeared at the end of the aisle, cradling a submachine gun.

Brrrrp!

Bullets sprayed the aisle. Two pistols and four rifles replied.

Forbes-Brandon's ears rang, and the dust kicked up by the bullets made her sneeze. She still heard someone's strangled grunt and the meaty *chunk* of a bullet hitting flesh. A moment later came the thump of the intruder hitting the floor, followed by the clatter of the submachine gun falling from dead hands. A final burst of firing from outside echoed through the warehouse, then silence settled along with the dust.

Opperman rose cautiously, holding his rifle with one hand as he brushed himself off with the other. Glass crunched under his boots as he bent over Tsobo. The corporal was contemplating a trouser leg rapidly turning dark, and fumbling for his medical kit.

"Lieutenant, could you see to Tsobo?"

"Certainly."

Forbes-Brandon knelt beside Tsobo, cutting away his trouser leg and slapping on the dressing the moment the wound appeared. It had both entry and exit holes, and was bleeding freely.

"Looks like a nice neat flesh wound," she said. "Unless it nicked a bone, you'll be back on your feet by the time the shooting starts."

"What do you call what that terr was doing, Lieutenant?" said Tsobo. "Playing tennis?"

Opperman and the Mountaineer sergeant rose from beside the dead terrorists. "It's a woman," the captain called. "Looks like a pretty rough character. First time you've ever been shot *by* a woman, instead of *over* one."

Tsobo grinned. Like most Black Star mercenaries, he was in a form of polite exile from his home planet. In his case it was for seducing both the wife and the daughter of the police chief of Kenyattaport. That was just his most famous achievement as a womanizer, not his only one. He'd even made an approach to Forbes-Brandon, so lighthearted that she couldn't resent it. He wasn't cutting notches, he was just bubbling over with animal energy—not unlike his captain.

When the reinforcements entered, Forbes-Brandon was looking down at the dead terrorists. Five bullet wounds didn't improve anybody, but the woman looked as if she'd been living rough for a long time. She was either naturally thin-flanked or else half starved. A shoulder bared in her last convulsions showed a couple of old scars that hinted of a life without access to modern medical care.

Peace Forcers often asked themselves the old question of professional soldiers: Why should I hate the man I'm paid to fight? They often made an exception for terrorists—"human vermin" was a term Forbes-Brandon often heard, but she couldn't hate this pathetic corpse, lying at her feet in a pool of blood already turning to mud in the thick dust. Whatever had driven the woman into terrorism, it couldn't have been a simple love of violence and death.

Major Dozo, their Mountaineer escort, entered at the head of his own squad. "There were four of them this time," he said. "One set off the explosives he was carrying. In the smoke the woman you killed fled into the warehouse. The other two got away, although I think one was wounded."

"That's the third attack since our mission arrived," said Opperman. "Do we have bad breath, I wonder?"

"We have exiles from a good many planets here in Ciudad Cervantes," said Dozo, shrugging. "I do not know what grievances they might have against the Peace Force. Certainly, though, you can see that they have grievances against the Republic and its citizens."

Forbes-Brandon's eyes met Opperman's. Lieutenant Tegen's check of the records hinted that three incidents in ten days was about five times the usual rate. More than Peace Force halitosis was involved here. Also, the incidents all followed the same pattern—nobody was left around to interrogate, even if the mission wanted to invoke Article Ninety-two and take them into Peace Force custody. The terrorists had either fled or died.

The corpse and the pieces of one all over the front of the warehouse might have been convincing, if Forbes-Brandon hadn't run the data through what her mother always called "your nasty, suspicious mind." It might not be easy to make people face certain death in a fake attack, but if they were convicts condemned to a slower death otherwise, or if you were threatening their families . . .

Speculating ahead of your data was always a waste of time. Forbes-Brandon would still have given a good deal to learn how the dead woman had acquired those scars.

Right now a more urgent matter was getting Corporal Tsobo to proper medical care. An ambulance must have been called the moment the attack started; it came careening through the gates of the arsenal as Forbes-Brandon stepped out the warehouse door. She stepped back almost at once, to avoid treading on the remains of the bomb carrier. For a moment she thought of Rufus Garron's similar death, and her stomach twitched.

Then two Hrothmi on either end of a stretcher were running out of the ambulance. Forbes-Brandon waved them inside as a battered six-wheeler whined up behind the ambulance and disgorged five exceptionally large and brawny Hrothmi. They wore sleeveless shirts, shorts, boots, and Hrothmi Police insignia, and carried both long and short sticks.

Major Dozo waved to them. "Thank you, my friends, for your sense of duty and honor," he began in Hrothmi. After that Forbes-Brandon caught only about one word in three. He seemed to be assuring them that the incident was over and no Hrothmi had been in danger. Descriptions of the escaped men would be circulated at once, so that if they appeared in the quarters where the Hrothmi Police had jurisdiction, they could be recognized and arrested.

Personally, Forbes-Brandon would have added a warning not to try arresting men armed with automatic weapons when the Police carried only clubs. Or would the Hrothmi have regarded that as an insult to their courage? The more she saw of the Hrothmi, the more she knew how little she knew about them. She also began to suspect that the pattern of human-Hrothmi relations in the Republic de las Montañas would be as complex as it was among the Utopians.

The ride to the hospital took them through the Hrothmi quarter, to the south of the Lepanto River. Most of the thirty thousand Hrothmi who did the unskilled and semi-skilled labor in the city lived here. The rest were indentured to farms in the area, and came into the city when work was slack.

Forbes-Brandon had expected that "indentured workers" would be ground down enough to break the spirit of the toughest Hrothmi. Reading the terms of the indentures, she'd been surprised that they actually offered a fair standard of living. At the worst it was above the subsistence level. At the best a Hrothmi bond-group pooling resources and saving money could give each group member a helping hand out into the world when their indentures were up.

Of course, "out into the world" usually meant either home to Hrothma or over the Mountains of Steel to Utopia. The Mountaineers seemed to prefer the Hrothmi in a safely subordinate position. Their good treatment in the Republic seemed to depend on their "keeping their place."

That was undesirable, certainly. Just as certainly, it was no worse than the open and sometimes bloodthirsty bigotry that ran around naked for all to see in Utopia. Whatever made the Populists think that Utopia was Paradise and should be supported to the limit against the Inferno of the Republic?

For the twentieth time Forbes-Brandon concluded that she did not understand politicans. She took some consolation in the fact that as a Peace Forcer she usually didn't have to and sat back to watch the Hrothmi quarter rattle and roll past.

Most of the houses were built of brick, stone, or salvaged industrial material. Even the last kind lacked the shanty-slum quality she'd seen on too many planets. Joints were mortared or caulked, doors swung on thongs if their material couldn't be drilled for hinges, and chimneys were either straight or deliberately crooked. One Hrothmi, with what she hoped was a skewed aesthetic sense and access to half a kilometer of plastic tubing, had festooned his whole house until it looked like a vine planter.

The houses were clearly built to last as long as Hrothmi came to Greenhouse. She remembered Major Vela saying, "That's one thing that helped the Hrothmi take the impact of contact almost in their stride. They always had a sense of being bonded to the future and the past the same way they are bonded to their kin. A Hrothmi who thinks history began the day of his or her birth is considered a madman, and used to be stoned to death. Still are, in some places that the missionaries haven't reached."

The ambulance and its escort had to run the gauntlet of small children, handcarts, and assorted domestic animals. Once they had to stop completely, until a soil cart drawn by six Hrothmi had finished collecting the pots from a whole street. Major Dozo stuck his head out the window and swore cheerfully at the Hrothmi; they swore back, asking him if he wanted to eat the soil, and if he didn't, would he let them get on with carrying it off?

"Most of the houses don't have sewer lines or water, so they use the carts," said Dozo as the convoy moved on. "As for bathing, there are many bathhouses with running water. Also, the Lepanto is unpolluted and never freezes over. Even in the winter a Hrothmi from the northern regions can take a fine bath in the shallows."

Forbes-Brandon nodded. With a sudden rush of cynicism, she decided to take advantage of Dozo's conversational mood.

"Major, we didn't come here to bother you with rumors. But there's one rumor that's been bothering us. Have you heard of any Hrothmi among the terrorists?"

Dozo's face set for a moment, long enough to notice, not long enough to be truly revealing. Then he shrugged. "As you have said, there are such rumors. We also have not thought them worth investigating. Certainly nothing has happened to make it worth insulting our Hrothmi by unfounded suspicions."

"Is there any way you could make a discreet investigation?"

"When dealing with Hrothmi, there is no such thing. If I could find a way, I would be fit to replace Colonel Limón as Chief of Intelligence, or become a Professor of Hrothmi Studies at any University in the Union. As I am, a simple soldier, I must bow to the way of the Hrothmi."

"Thank you, Major." She really was grateful; the little knowledge she had now was better than nothing. She also very much doubted that Major Dozo was anything like a simple soldier.

Forbes-Brandon and Opperman had left the hospital two hundred meters behind. Now they were angling down to the riverbank a hundred meters to the right.

Forbes-Brandon found that she had to step quickly to keep up with Opperman, even if he was four centimeters shorter. It wasn't just his normal energy either. He seemed nervous, and she didn't need words to know he was afraid of being tailed.

Finally they came out at the west end of a stretch of gravel beach. A path of clear sky showed stars above the buildings of downtown Cervantes. The Lepanto growled past, its level and current fed by jungles and mountain rains.

"This should do it," said Opperman. "We've shaken any tail, no pun intended. Distance and the river should defeat any eavesdroppers." He clasped his hands behind his back and turned abruptly toward her. "Do you think we're being given the runaround?"

"Yes." It was surprising how easily the answer came.

"So does Dallin. So does Ngomba. So do I."

"What about Tegen?"

"I haven't found a secure place to ask him yet. I'd rather let him make up his own mind, then tell me. The less the Mountaineers suspect him, the better. He's the one of us who operates with the least protection. An 'accident' for him would be easy to arrange. They wouldn't even have to fake a terrorist incident."

"Is Tegen a Command Intelligence Division man, by any chance?"

"If I tell you the truth, will you tell me how you guessed?"

"With that answer, I can guess the truth. And Lieutenant-Commander Singer is another?"

Opperman threw up his hands in mock despair. "Your mind's good enough that I could admire you for it alone. Yes. Singer wanted to run the mission. MacLean persuaded Cooper to let Tegen be our spy and keep command in the hands of the ground troops. Cooper's condition was that you not be told of either Singer's or Tegen's status."

Rage swept through Forbes-Brandon. She knew that part of it was reaction to the day's incident. The rest was shock, that Captain Cooper might not be willing to guard her back if she needed it to hold her position with Group Fourteen. She knew that she could explain the first to Opperman but not the second. Finally, she knew that if she let the rage out, she would have to explain both before she was done, or risk a breach with Opperman.

All that knowledge didn't do her a damned bit of good. Her mouth opened and the words poured out.

"What the hell does Cooper think he's doing? Did he forget that I might wind up in command of the mission if the terrorists got lucky? What the hell kind of cooperation with the Group does he think that is? Does he think the C.I.D. will back him for admiral if he kisses their bloody bums?"

"Lieutenant, calm down. We're—"

"Captain Cooper is an *ass,* and I don't care who hears me. Thank God I found out in time. He—"

"Lieutenant—" Opperman repeated, then gave up on words. He threw his arms around her and with more strength than she'd imagined he could have, bent her backward. His lips came down on hers and stayed there until he had to stop for breath. By then a good many parts of her body were shooting off small sparks.

"Lieutenant . . . Katherine—"

"Or Kate. Anything but Kathy."

"Well enough, fair Kate. I had to do something to quiet you down."

She laughed. The sparks were still shooting, and she felt anything but "quieted down."

"Was that the only reason? And this time will you tell me the truth without any conditions?"

"I don't recall that slowed you down the first time."

"Hugo—"

"No, that wasn't the only reason."

"Then why don't we try it again?"

The sparks were flying higher than ever by the time they broke apart. Both hands and lips were yearning now, and parts of Forbes-Brandon's body she'd been quite sure were adequately protected by her uniform.

"Damn," said Opperman when he'd caught his breath. "We're both in uniform—"

"Easily remedied. Not here, but—"

"To be sure. But we're still on duty, at least until Tegen finishes exploring the bowels of the Ordnance computers. That's not so easily remedied."

"Not without Dallin's and Ngomba's cooperation, I admit. Do we want to try to get it?"

"I don't mind admitting to good chemistry. Unless you think we should try to hide it?"

"I think it would be a waste of time. So promise me to make arrangements."

"Greedy woman."

"You mean hungry. Do you realize we haven't had dinner yet, and it's nearly 2100?"

Opperman looked at his watch. "So it is. I think we've just had a demonstration of Einstein's explanation of relativity. When a man is seated on a hot stove, a minute seems like an hour. But when he's with a beautiful woman, an hour seems like a minute."

8

COLONEL LIMÓN SLAPPED the screen control switch. The picture of the smoking warehouse and the odd assortment of armed men standing over the dead terrorist vanished. Shipo M'no Heru thought that the colonel looked satisfied, even complacent.

"So you can see, we have made every effort to persuade the Peace Force that the terrorists are active against the Republic. This should make them more willing to believe that any of our weapons found in terrorist hands were stolen."

Limón moved a file folder from his right to his left. "Of course, we cannot be sure that none of the Peace Force investigators will turn up anything compromising. To block every avenue of investigation would arouse enough suspicion to defeat our purposes. Yet even their intelligence man is unlikely to extract enough from our data banks to give unambiguous evidence."

"The word 'unlikely' does not please me," said Koyban M'no Shreen.

"It is not intended to please you," said Chabon M'ni Luurn. From many years' acquaintance and war-bond, Shipo knew that Chabon had nearly exhausted her usual philosophical acceptance of the outrageous. "I assume that it was intended to give us knowledge from which to determine our actions."

Koyban's ears went back and his nostrils quivered. One of these days someone would assume that he was really about to attack, instead of merely trying to frighten his audience. Shipo hoped that on that day either the someone would draw faster than Koyban or be one the Company could spare. He no longer greatly cared which.

"If I had the determining of our actions, I would have the intelligence man killed," said Koyban.

"Then thank all the Lords you do not," said Chabon. "Has not

the colonel said it is unwise to make the Peace Force certain we
have something to hide? Can you think of a better way to do so?"

"I could not, certainly," said Limón. "That is why we want
Lieutenant Tegen to go home alive and healthy. Remember that
the Peace Force ultimately must answer to the Expeditionary
Force commander. General Haskins is a fool. He must also answer to Ambassador Xia, who is cautious. He also is not wholly
his own master, in a matter so important as war against the Republic. As long as we do not spit in their faces, the Peace Force
should not quickly see us as enemies."

For a moment Koyban looked ready to continue the argument.
Then he spread his hands palms upward on the table. "Let it be as
you wish, for now."

Shipo stopped himself before throwing Limón a grateful look.
It was a tribute to Limón that with all his open hatred of humans,
Koyban would yield to the colonel as readily as to Shipo, and
more readily than to Chabon.

At least he had done so up to now. Thoughts of the future
made Shipo wish that he could light up his pipe. However, the
smell of *kasir* was even more offensive to humans than the smell
of tobacco was to Hrothmi. Colonel Limón, who loved a good
cigar, refrained from even carrying them when he was with
Hrothmi. The only honorable response to such courtesy was to
match it.

Limón was pulling another folder off the stack to his right and
opening it in front of him. "Now let us leave the Peace Force to
contrive its own fate. What do you think of the new draft of
recruits?"

Everyone looked at Chabon. As under-captain, training was
her duty. "In numbers, your recruiters have been generous. I had
not imagined that you could find seventy fit people without be-
traying the secret of where they were going."

"We have given out the story of a secret mining camp on the
edge of the jungle," said Limón. "The recruits' bond-kin will ask
few questions as long as they expect the recruits to return
wealthy, or at least earn fat death-bonuses."

"Then I rejoice in their numbers. I would rejoice more if I did
not fear it will take a good while to turn them into soldiers."

"You sound as if you anticipate some trouble here," said
Limón.

"Only ten have ever carried a rifle," said Chabon. "This is no
crime. Yet in days to come it may shape their fates in ways they
will not like, nor their bond-kin either.

"If my instructors and I could devote all our time to training the recruits, we could make them fit for battle soon enough. Can we hope to do this when we are also trying to move to a new advanced base and launch our first raids from it?"

"Do you wish to end the raiding until your recruits are fit to be out after dark?" said Koyban. It was almost a growl. "If they are full of zeal for the cause of the Alliance, is that not enough? It is time to see what such zeal can do. Perhaps it can do more than training by old captains too long in the company of humans."

Shipo wished again for his pipe. Also something to stun Koyban into silence, without caring greatly if the silence was permanent. Chabon was looking at the sweating rock of the ceiling, as if she hoped that the War Lord would descend through it and relieve her of listening to a fool.

Limón was looking anywhere but at the three Hrothmi. Shipo felt as if someone had just given him a hand grenade with the pin pulled. Well, there was always one way to muffle a grenade explosion.

"Colonel Limón, can we be moved to the new camp by air?"

Limón jerked his attention back to Shipo. A look of what seemed very much like calculation now ruled his face. "I suppose so," he said cautiously. "At least, we can if you are ready to evacuate the old camp within four days. After that, we can hardly risk open air movements so close to the railroad. They will have to be disguised as something legitimate. Otherwise we could draw the Peace Force Air Squadron, or even *Ark Royal*'s fighters."

Shipo nodded. The nearly permanent cloud cover of Greenhouse gave them a good deal of immunity for air movements. Peace Force rules of engagement in this kind of situation required visual identification of hostile targets. Electronic or thermal signatures weren't enough. If vertis were detected flying in and out of supposedly uninhabited jungle close to the railroad, however, the most foolish Peace Force general would not fail to order high-performance aircraft out to seek that visual identification. Then half the Company might be slaughtered as helpless passengers.

He looked at his comrades. "Can you be ready to move within two days?" Both nodded. "Good. Then why not move two raiding parties by air to where they can strike at the railroad? Meanwhile, Chabon can establish the new advanced camp with a mixture of trained people and recruits. The raiding parties can retreat to it overland, without crossing either too much open land or too much deep jungle."

"Two raids and setting up the new camp will still take more leaders than we have," said Chabon. "They will not divide like pond mites, though the War Lord himself blessed our cause."

"You doubt that he does?" said Koyban.

"I doubt nothing of the kind," said Chabon. "I only say that we have solved one problem—how to go on raiding. We have not solved the other—how to raise our new recruits until they are more than *jag-hirmi*."

"Would it help if a few humans came out to the caves, to free Hrothmi from training duties and setting up the new camp?" asked Limón. "I could not be sure of more than a dozen. They also might not be able to stay more than thirty days. Yet if they would be useful . . . ?"

"Do crackjaws bite?" said Chabon. She was trying hard not to smile, and not succeeding very well.

Shipo found it easier to look sober. As far as he could judge from Limón's face, the colonel felt that he had scored a victory. Even a dozen humans in the caves was a dozen more than there had been before. Where a dozen led, more might follow.

It was easy for Chabon not to fear this. She was a trusting spirit; those who showed her friendship received it unstintingly in return. She also was concerned above all else that the new recruits should not go into the field until they were battleworthy. That was enough for an under-captain, but Shipo had to see further.

Yet as far as he looked, he could see no good reason to refuse the colonel's aid. Indeed, if it was refused, Limón might suspect that the Hrothmi in the caves wished to hide something from their human allies. Then the humans in turn might refuse something. Once begun, such a quarrel could go on until everything here on Greenhouse ended in waste and failure, if not defeat and disaster.

"We will accept the colonel's offer with thanks," said Shipo. "Will the people be able to fly out with the aircraft? That will free yet more of ours for the raids. . . ."

Limón shrugged. "I cannot conjure radio operators and ordnance technicians out of the air. What can be done, I will do."

They settled down to planning the raids on the basis of no human replacements and insertion by air. Shipo's hopes that this would go quickly and peacefully were disappointed almost at once. Koyban's other obsession at once rose, like scum in a broached barrel.

"We must start gaining support among the People who have homesteaded along the railroad," he said. "I have urged this more times than I have fingers and toes. How much longer does it make sense to put it off?"

"Until we can protect those the Utopians will try to punish, or rescue those they take hostage," said Chabon. "That is the answer I have given just as often. It is the answer I will go on giving."

"As long as you go on giving it, there will be no peace between us," said Koyban. "Also, there will be suspicion in my heart. Do you trust the humans too much to be truly one of us?"

"Your plain words are honorable, Koyban," said Shipo. "They show your courage. They do not show your wisdom. Even with ten times the strength we have, we could not help those among the People exposed to Utopian punishment. All we could do was be sure that we would face the Peace Force itself. I hope you do not despise them as you seem to despise the militia?"

"I do not."

"You are wiser than I thought." Ill-spoken, doubtless, but Shipo was growing weary of these wrangles between Chabon and Koyban. The less either relied on his continued patience, the more they might seek peace. Either that, or one of them might resign—and shameful as it was, Shipo was almost past caring which one.

"Also, remember that the Peace Force is much more disciplined than the militia," put in Limón. "If the militia were turned loose on the homesteaders, they might drive so many into our arms by sheer brutal stupidity that the homesteaders could protect themselves. The Peace Force will not be so witless."

Shipo wished Limón had kept silent. It was not well done to put new ideas into Koyban's ears. Those ears were attached to a head overfull of lust for blood, particularly that of traitors to the People, and not too well-furnished with scruples.

"Do you, then, forbid trying to raise the homesteaders?" said Koyban.

Shipo pressed his hand to his mouth. *Never give an order you know won't be obeyed* was something he'd learned from his father and grandmother before Koyban was born.

"No. You may speak to anyone who will listen, if you can speak to them secretly. Do not give out weapons. Take no recruits except those who have no bond-kin or friends who can be held hostage."

"That is asking us to quickly learn much about total strangers."

"That is also the only way we can avoid giving the militia an excuse for a massacre. And it *is* an order."

"It shall be obeyed," said Koyban. His tone held every shade of respect that Shipo had ever heard. Why, then, did he also hear mockery and feel so uneasy that the hair along his spine was rising?

If he could not grasp the reason for it, then perhaps there was no response. "Well and good," he said.

The discussion turned again, to whether the University archeologists' camp should be a target. If so, what forces should be sent against it? By the time they had settled those questions, Shipo was satisfied that at least this time his fear of Koyban's hungry heart was only imagination.

9

THE ROAR OF the mole at the tunnel face two hundred meters ahead battered at Jean Grant's ears even through her ear protectors. As she tried to keep up with the two Sergeant Majors, a patch of loose gravel shifted under her feet. She staggered. Parkes turned and held out an arm, letting her grip it to steady herself.

Another twenty meters took them around the last bend, past a section of wall braced with heavy beams and cocooned in fiber wire. That must be where the fault that had forced the bend in the tunnel came closest, she thought.

Now the roar of the mole attacked Grant's ears like a club. It seemed the voice of the mountain itself, fighting against the men driving their tunnel through its bowels. Grant wanted to turn on her radio and ask a few questions, but her jaw wouldn't move to work the switch. She was oddly afraid that if she opened the circuit, the mountain itself would hear her.

Odd indeed, because she'd been far deeper in natural caves more than a dozen times. Of course then she and her fellow cavers had been moving gently along paths nature left for them, not assaulting the rock around them with machines the size of houses.

Had the Gaean teachings of her old biology professor struck deeper than she'd realized? Or was this just a new form of her case of nerves over when the terrorists would strike next? If so, maybe she'd better accept the fact that her nerves were taking charge a little too much, and seek medical assistance. The Peace Force medics by preference; they could be relied on not to discuss her case anywhere it might reach the ears of Roger Carey. . . .

But wasn't that trying to maintain her authority by telling a lie? She had a potentially disabling condition. Shouldn't the peo-

ple who might have to take over be warned in advance, whatever
this might do to her authority?

Maybe. And maybe the potentially disabling condition wasn't
her nerves. Maybe it was a lingering remnant of a Calvinistic
conscience leading her into overscrupulousness. Keeping Roger
Carey from making trouble might justify bigger and worse lies
than she was thinking of telling—

Parkes stopped so abruptly that Grant bumped into him. She
stepped clear and saw a wall of more fiber wire rising across the
tunnel. Strips of armorcloth were woven into the fiber. A heavy
curtain of armorcloth was tied in place over the one opening in
the wall, a square about two meters on a side. Through the opening Grant saw one end of the housing of the mole's power generator. It was as motionless as the walls of the rock, though it was
putting out enough power for a small city.

Four armed soldiers guarded the door. They wore sensor packs
and helmets and carried submachine guns. Two were from Kabuele Company and two from Group Fourteen's Support Squadron. All four came to attention and saluted as the two Sergeant
Majors approached.

Parkes also straightened into a subtly different form of the
same stance. More relaxed? That would be true but oversimpli-
fied. He certainly wore his authority lightly. Maybe he could
advise her on how far to go to keep Roger Carey from making
trouble.

While Grant considered this, Parkes and di Leone made a
quick inspection of the sentries. Then Parkes came on the radio.

"This is as far as we go. BAM won't be responsible for our
safety if we go beyond the frag wall."

"I thought the Peace Forcers were running the mole now."

"Holy Mother, no," said di Leone. "We've got exactly two
people in the whole Squadron who can run that monster. They're
both refreshing themselves on the stimulator so they can spell the
BAM people starting next week. Our job is to guard the BAM-
mies while they dig."

The soldiers exchanged salutes again, and the two Peace
Forcers turned back down the tunnel. Grant took an overlong step
to keep up, and again felt gravel sliding underfoot. Parkes held
out his arm again. She took it, but this time didn't let go.

The little train rattled out of the tunnel and into Greenhouse's
surrogate daylight. With a bang the passenger car uncoupled
from the tail of the loaded hoppers. Under its own power it rattled

across a switch and off to the right, while the rest of the train stayed on the main track to the left.

Di Leone jerked a thumb the size of a sausage at the disappearing train. "If we'd stayed with the train, you'd have seen one of our projects. We've set up a crusher near the refuse dump. We grind rock and set it in bonder/sealer to make slabs for hardening up all the exposed equipment sites."

Grant looked around as the car began to slow. When they'd come up this way earlier, mist and clouds had swallowed most of the early-morning light. Now she could make out the details of machines that had only been hunched shapes like Old Terran dinosaurs an hour ago.

"Is that the crusher?" she asked, pointing at a plume of dust shooting out of the mountain.

"No," said Parkes. "That's our own tunnel. We're putting the explosives, bonder/sealer, fuel, anything else that can make a secondary explosion or a fire, underground. It'll make for some extra work hauling that stuff around, but we're also extending the rail spur to the cave. Meanwhile, it'll be a lot safer all around if there is an attack. Anybody who starts shooting rockets at the camp will have to hit something directly. They won't be able to wreck everything with a lucky hit."

"Yeah, *if* we get the (something obscene in what sounded like Italian) tunnel dug in time," said di Leone. "BAM won't let us blast, and there's not enough water for hydroboring. So we're stuck with lasers and mechanicals against some damned tough rock. BAM says blasting might trigger faults farther inside the mountain."

"That's what I've heard too," said Grant politely. Di Leone was transparently fishing for information. Maybe also for a promise from Grant to use her connections with BAM to get at the truth. She didn't have those "connections," but she'd be damned if she was going to admit it to the Peace Force. As for the information . . .

"We did a fairly thorough review of Greenhouse geology when we were planning the trip to the caves," Grant said. "With the heavy rainfall, there's a lot more minor faulting than you'd expect. We knew we'd have to allow for a couple of tons of shoring in our airlift if we wanted to go really deep in the Survivors' Caves."

"That's a hell of a lot of airlift," said Dozer.

"We weren't planning on flying it in until we knew we needed it," said Grant. "Even then we'd have done it in stages. For all we know, the caves could have completely flooded in the last couple of centuries."

The car reached the end of the spur and stopped abruptly, throwing Grant against her seat belt. As they climbed out, Parkes put a hand on her arm. She doubted it was her imagination that gave the touch a new quality. She knew it lingered longer than strictly necessary.

After the stuffiness and continuous roar inside the cave, the open hillside seemed like Paradise. Grant jogged in place, un-kinking her legs and sucking in great lungfuls of air. She was aware of Parkes's eyes on her, and glad that her slacks and shirt flattered her figure without being inappropriately snug. Parkes wasn't the sort of man to be attracted by impractical clothing, no matter what it showed. More likely the reverse.

Of course, this assumed that she wanted to attract Parkes *and* had a chance to do so. . . .

A six-wheeler loaded with yellow and red drums grumbled past, filling the fresh air with dust. When the truck was past, Grant saw the two Peace Forcers studying the side of the hill. Parkes had pulled out binoculars and started reading off the ranges of key points all the way down to the edge of the forest. Dozer recorded them on a belt computer. To both of them Jean Grant might no longer have existed.

Grant wondered. *Did* she want to attract a man who could turn his attention to her on and off like a computer scan? If she wanted to risk it, what were her chances? Without any dirty tricks, either, because if Parkes was at all like what he seemed, he'd either run or laugh if she tried any.

After about ten minutes Parkes slung his binoculars and seemed to let the rest of the world back into his consciousness. "Professor, you said you were up here to pick up three vehicles from the BAM park. Do you need any help?"

"No. Tsigo and Kilaa both drive. In fact, Tsigo's better than I am. He'll load the trucks onto the train." She told herself she was only licking her lips to get the dust off, then hurried on.

"If I do have a chance to talk to any BAM people, about your tunnel—it would help if I knew how much danger of attack there really was. I assume this end of the tunnel will be the main target?"

The two Peace Forcers exchanged unreadable looks. Dozer nodded. "Yes. The other end's too far from any possible terrorist base."

"Unless the terrs have put a base on the south side of the Gran

Carlos River," Parkes added. "We'll be making random airmobile
sweeps through the area as soon as the Mountaineers give permission for operations so close to their border. Somebody might
have slipped across the Villa Segunda Bridge before security
tightened up, but there's not much cover south of the river. Even
if our sweeps don't flush them out, they should be too busy
ducking to terrorize anybody."

A gesture of aversion Grant didn't recognize accompanied
those last words. The scholar in her made a mental note to ask
him about it the first chance she had.

"And at this end of the tunnel?"

Di Leone's response to Grant's gentle prod was a wholly read-
able look. It said, "Should we be telling this civilian so much?"

Grant was suddenly determined to attract Parkes, and not only
because she now knew she wanted him. Di Leone had annoyed
her, first trying to pump her, and then to keep her from being
informed—in short, treating her like a cow to be milked. Grant
wanted to pay di Leone back a little.

She didn't expect that keeping company with Parkes would do
the job all by itself. The relationship between the two Sergeant
Majors was clearly straightforward military comradeship with
overtones of big sister-little brother. Sexual jealousy over Parkes
wasn't in di Leone. If it had been, Grant would have stayed
kilometers clear of Parkes.

Keeping company with Parkes would tell di Leone very
clearly that Grant could tell when she was being pushed out of the
picture—and could retaliate. If di Leone had the wits her stripes
suggested, she wouldn't have to be told more than once.

"Why don't we discuss this over lunch?" Grant said. "I don't
know what the Support Squadron mess is serving, but the BAM
commissary might be persuaded to do better. Maybe they could
even produce a picnic lunch. I could spend the rest of the morning drawing and testing the vehicles. Then we could take them
out someplace clear of the dust and noise, unless that would be
too far from the safe area. . . ."

Dozer shrugged. "Go uphill to the south of the railroad, and
we'd be as safe as in church. I'll have to take a rain check,
though. This is my day to sample the food in the Support Squadron mess. If I find anything that's fit for a picnic, where should I
send it?"

"The BAM vehicle park, at noon?" said Grant, looking at
Parkes. He nodded.

"Can do," said di Leone. "Now, can we give you a lift to the vehicle park? We can borrow a scouter. . . ."

"Thank you, but I'd rather walk. A kilometer or so will be enough to flush the dust out of my lungs so I can argue with the commissary people."

"All right," said Parkes. "See you at noon, Professor." They shook hands all around, then the two Sergeant Majors jogged off uphill toward the Peace Force cave diggers.

A lift would have been nice, but Dozer di Leone deserved some reward for her unexpected tact. Or was she just quicker to recognize a losing fight? Either way, she'd seen at once that three would be a crowd on any picnic. It would be just as much a crowd when she said whatever she wanted to say to Parkes, and wanted to say *now*.

Grant took a long swig from her canteen, corked it, then turned onto the same path, but downhill.

10

"Is THAT THE best BAM could do for you?" said Parkes. He hoped the question wasn't purely rhetorical. The all-wheel light truck Jean Grant had just driven up looked as if it had been dropped off a cliff, then bombarded with rocks.

"They only promised us surplus equipment," Grant said. "We're not planning on using them deep in the field."

"The Wise One be thanked," said Parkes.

"That's the second time you've made that gesture of aversion," said Grant. "What does it mean?"

Parkes opened the door. Once he was sure it wouldn't come off in his hand, he climbed in. "It asks the Wise One to set aside fear so that I can do my duty. Right now, that's riding in this truck."

Grant wrinkled her nose at Parkes, then cautiously fed power to the wheels. The motors whined angrily; three of the four wheels began to turn. The fourth was slow to start turning, making the truck slew uncertainly before it lurched onto the road.

Parkes tried to tighten his belt, to have it snap under the strain. He cast aspersions on the ancestry of BAM's transportation people and risked a look backward. One of the Hrothmi was trying to push the other's truck into motion. As Grant reached the turn toward the gate, Parkes saw the Hrothmi in the stalled truck leap out, basket in hand, and jump into the other one. The driver must have opened the motors wide; the truck shot after Grant's and nearly rear-ended it at the gate.

Grant stopped and climbed out. "Kilaa, I think we'd all better ride in your truck. This one will run, but I'd hate to try climbing a hill in it."

"As you wish, *Shedni-ti,*" said the Hrothmi woman. "But I fear this one as much going downhill. It has no brakes worthy of the name."

76

This time it was Grant's turn to discuss BAM's transportation people. Her fluency made Parkes regret that he didn't understand Scots Gaelic. Finally she subsided and returned to Anglic.

"I'll be damned if I'll let some inanimate metal and plastic spoil my first holiday in Lord knows how long! Sergeant Major, do you know of any nice quiet place around here we can reach without going uphill or down?"

Parkes wondered how quiet she meant. If she wanted the seclusion of her forest bathing pool . . . Parkes forced his mind away from the line of thought to conjuring up a mental map of the area.

"There's a stand of forest at the foot of Jogan's Spur, with a natural spring," he said. "That's about seven klicks southeast, on the road all the way and mostly level. The only thing is, it's right on the edge of a Hrothmi homestead. If the bond's touchy about human strangers—"

"If they are inhospitable, we will make them otherwise," said Kilaa. "We have guestbonds to every greatbond in this land. All we must do is remind them of it."

"Kilas, I can't understand how you manage to get any work done at all, spending so much time partying. Or are you a new form of Hrothmi, who doesn't need sleep?"

Kilaa's pursed lips were the Hrothmi equivalent of a broad grin. A Hrothmi grinning like a human was issuing a challenge to fight or at least argue, by exposing all his teeth.

"Then since Kilaa has volunteered to be—point?"

"Right."

"—Let's get on the road."

Grant's truck bowled along well enough on the level. Parkes suspected that it was suffering from nothing worse than long immobility and overaged wiring. He said so to Grant.

"Maybe. I suspect the best thing for us to do would be to cannibalize all three trucks into one that works. Among us, we should be able to scrape up enough mechanical talent. It's too bad that Roger Carey will have to be one of the foremen, because we'll need the Hrothmi—"

"Jean. We've got a Sergeant Guslenko in Transportation Company. Resurrecting dead machines and healing sick ones is his specialty. Right now he has a light workload. We've got the camp set up and we aren't putting much wear on our vehicles. If I could persuade him to look over your trucks, you might get all of them running. Even if he did have to cannibalize, the job would go a lot faster with him on it."

"What would your price be, John?"

The exchange of first names took some of the sting out of Grant's question. "Did Dozer get your back up that much?"

"At first she did. Then she let me carry you off, so I'm not really angry at her. I'm not accusing you of anything, either. I just wonder if you Peace Forcers would really like me to talk to any BAM higher-ups about that tunnel. I don't guarantee that I'll be meeting any, but if I do . . . Well?"

"And if you do, you'll need to be briefed on the military situation this side of the mountain?"

"Would they listen to me if they thought the Peace Force didn't trust me with a little intelligence?"

Parkes grinned. "I'll concede the match." He would also concede, not for the first time, that faculty politics were good training for any kind of bargaining. *Unworldly professors, my left big toe!*

"I'll show you on a map when we stop, but here's the situation in brief . . ."

Parkes took Grant through the factors involved in calculating the risk of terrorist attack on different parts of the railroad. The factors included distance from probable enemy bases and defending units, cover for the approach and withdrawal, and target vulnerability to light-infantry weapons.

At that point Grant interrupted. "Are light-infantry weapons all we have to worry about?" Parkes frowned. "If I'm asking what you really can't tell me—"

"No, I can tell you that we don't know very much. Other than light-infantry weapons, there'd be four threats. One is long-range missile attack. Another is a tactical air strike. Both can be ruled out, unless and until the Mountaineers simply declare war on Utopia. They're not stupid enough to give the Union a perfect excuse to buy off the Populists by stamping the Republic flat."

"What's left?"

"One is air attack disguised as an 'accident.' A verti 'crashing' into some vital equipment could make a nice mess. The other is infiltrating saboteurs. That's the one that gives the best chance of getting charges right into the tunnel itself. The saboteurs wouldn't have much chance of getting out again, but we can't be sure we aren't dealing with fanatics."

Parkes turned to Grant. "I'd rather not tell you about what we're doing against those two threats. If anybody suspected you knew, that could make you a prime target for kidnapping and the roughest kind of questioning."

"Thanks. I don't need to know everything. What about attacks on the University camp?"

"Light-infantry weapons only, and maybe not many of those. We have a mission in the Republic now, trying to find out what the terrs may have snatched and when. If the mission gets lucky, we should have a better idea of what we're facing."

He did not add that it would have to be very lucky indeed to persuade General Haskins and the ambassador to take any precautions or recommend any action against the Mountaineers. That fact was depressing enough for the Peace Forcers; why add it to the load on Jean's mind?

"One thing you could do, to make an attack on your camp less likely. . ." he added. "Move Alexis Werbel—"

"Into Peace Force custody?"

"Look, if she really knows something about the terrs, she's a prime target for a termination. That makes your camp a prime target for whatever it takes to terminate Alexis. You could be endangering your own people!"

"I've asked them, and they all say the same thing. Alexis needs to recover among friends. We're the closest thing to friends she has on Greenhouse, a damned sight closer than the Peace Force! We're willing to run the risks."

"All right." Parkes was pretty sure that Grant wasn't telling the whole truth. He'd also be damned if he'd ally himself or the Group with Roger Carey to save a young woman who might not be in danger. Not to mention breaking up a promising friendship with Jean Grant. The one time he'd met Carey, he'd felt like taking a long hot shower afterward, with plenty of strong soap to wash off the slime.

"I'm sorry, Jean. I wasn't trying to prod or pressure you. I was just finishing the threat estimate you asked for."

"I won't buy that story, John. In fact, I won't even have it as a gift."

"Jean—" He felt perilously close to apologizing.

"No. I forgive—no, there's nothing to forgive. You had your duty and you did it. I know that, and you know that I know it. So there aren't any lies between us, and you don't have anything on your conscience."

"My conscience isn't that delicate, but thank you." Or was it? How many times had he avoided important decisions because they involved something that gave his conscience twinges over deserting his father to help his sister?

"I don't care if your conscience is armor plated. I still don't want putting any loads on it on *mine*."

He reached over and laid an arm across her shoulders. She squeezed his free hand, then pointed to a stand of trees about a kilometer ahead.

"Is that where we're going?"

"As far as I remember."

White-painted boundary stones with Hrothmi letters on them crept almost to the edge of the trees. The nearest cultivated field was three hundred meters away. Between the stones and the field was a knee-high wilderness of purple-gray boulders and scrub in half a dozen shades of green. A few stumps and one pile of boulders told where the homesteaders had begun clearing the wilderness. In most places a whole rifle platoon could have found both cover and concealment.

At the edge of the trees a spring bubbled up from the bottom of a hollow, to form a stream that flowed off into the trees. Grant ran to the edge of the hollow and waved good-bye to the two Hrothmi as they also vanished into the trees. Then she ran down to the spring.

Parkes followed more sedately, loaded as he was with their picnic basket, both shotguns, and his own rifle. With luck the rifle wouldn't be needed for anything except his own piece of mind, but he'd learned not to despise that. A soldier worried about his back was poor company.

Grant was pulling off her boots as Parkes reached the spring. She dabbed her bare feet in the water as he spread out the table-cloth and started unpacking the basket. The BAM commissary hadn't bungled their job as badly as the Transportation Section. Ham, beef, smoked snakebird, three kinds of salad, two kinds of rolls, a whole baker's window full of desserts—

"If I eat half of this, you'll have to call the Hrothmi to roll me back to the trucks!" said Parkes, hefting the package of snake-bird.

"Don't worry. You'll have to fight me for the snakebird and the salad at least. Oh, and you overlooked—wait a minute, that's two flasks. I put in the whiskey, but—"

"I know. I put in a flask of Brezek's moonshine. It may give you a poor opinion of Peace Force taste in liquor, but—"

"I'm feeling reckless today. Let's start with that."

Parkes unscrewed the top of the flask, poured out a healthy slug, then filled his own canteen cup. "Try a sip first. It's pretty raw, but if—"

Grant took the whole slug at one gulp. Her face turned the color of her hair, then darker red; her eyes gushed tears and her breath stopped entirely for a moment. Then it turned into a coughing fit. Parkes threw his arms around her and began patting her on the back. By the time her breath turned into tortured wheezes, her head was resting on his shoulder. By the time her breathing was normal, she had her arms around him.

"Jean, I don't really want to let go."

"I wasn't asking you to." She tightened her embrace.

She also lifted her face to be kissed. Kissing her seemed very simple. Everything that followed was almost as simple. The only awkward moment was when Parkes suggested that they move up to the lip of the hollow. Grant made a noise halfway between a contented sigh and a frustrated grunt and pulled his hands back to her breasts. Parkes didn't fight too hard. Those breasts looked much more in proportion bare than they did covered, and they were delightfully firm and sensitive.

"No, seriously," he said somewhat later. "If somebody did show up looking for trouble, we'd be sitting targets at the bottom of the hollow."

"That depends on the position we were—"

He moved a hand down her body to distract her from further efforts to grapple him to the ground. "Come on, Jean. Bonnie Jean. Sweet Jean. It's only a minute, and the longer we wait—"

Grant's strangled sound resembled the word "Men!" but she stood up, slipping off her trousers as she did. They marched up to the lip of the hollow, Grant completely bare and Parkes wearing nothing but the tablecloth over his shoulder and the rifle in his left hand.

After that it was another simple matter to spread the tablecloth and lie down on it together. It didn't take long for Parkes to answer the question filling his mind. Did all of Jean Grant feel as good as she looked?

The answer was an unqualified "Yes."

In fact, Grant felt so good, that Parkes was inspired to heights he'd seldom reached since he was a teenager. "You know," he said after a while, "this shouldn't be happening. We shouldn't be at all compatible—"

"You weren't worrying about that ten minutes ago. Are you the kind of man who insists on philosophizing between bouts?"

"May the Wise One take my manhood if I do!"

"If the Wise One doesn't, I will." She pulled him down onto her again, this time to cuddle rather than couple. The cuddling felt so comfortable that it was a while before Parkes realized he was ravenously hungry.

"Jean, I hate to sound like a man of nothing but appetites—"

"You've already ruined your image there, John. But I take your meaning." They untangled and sat up; Grant began laying out lunch. "Could you get some water, to cut the liquor? You were right about that moonshine. What's in it, by the way?"

"That's Brezek's secret, and he wouldn't tell me if I was the Commander-in-Chief. The only person who knows is whoever takes over the still if Brezek buys it. I don't know who he is either."

"I was just curious. One of the family businesses is a little distillery. I watched the mash being tested when I was four."

"Sorry. I'd have more chance of getting permission to show you a circuit diagram of a fusion warhead than getting Brezek's formula." Parkes rose and started downhill.

Not secret, but something he preferred not to talk about, was the role Brezek's still would play in turning Sergeant Guslenko loose on Grant's trucks. Guslenko owed Brezek for half a year's moonshine, and the stillmaster was about to cut off his supply. Parkes would persuade Brezek to cancel Guslenko's debt in return for Guslenko's work on the trucks. That way everybody would benefit—including all of the people who might have to handle a Guslenko cut off from a regular supply of low-priced liquor.

Parkes had filled two cups with water when he thought he heard a faint new sound beyond the lip of the hollow. He set the cups down, unslung his rifle, and listened. It sounded like pebbles shifting under moving feet, with a hint of Hrothmi voices.

Parkes lunged up the slope, snapping off the safety and signaling frantically to Grant as he moved. He went to ground behind a moldering log, poor concealment and worse cover but better than nothing. As he thrust his rifle over the log, three Hrothmi came tramping blithely over the lip of the hollow.

Parkes grunted with relief. They were Kilaa, Tsigo, and an exceptionally tall and elderly Hrothmi man Parkes didn't know. They were not only friends, they weren't looking downhill to see Parkes making a spectacle of himself.

Jean Grant waved, making no effort to cover herself. The elderly Hrothmi replied, in a dialect that almost completely defeated Parkes' hypnoed knowledge. Grant thanked him for his good wishes and what appeared to be an invitation, then the three Hrothmi vanished.

"What was he saying?" Parkes asked once the Hrothmi footsteps had died away. The embarrassment he hid put an edge on his voice.

"His name is Ribon M'no Berus, and those are his boundary stones. He offers us the hospitality of his house, bond, and land, at our need or wish."

Parkes knew that was one of the more generous formulas of Hrothmi hospitality, most often extended to bondkin or as repayment of similar hospitality. "I'm grateful, but why . . . ?"

"You may not like this, John, but—"

"I'll like not knowing even less."

"All right. He owes us hospitality for our rites to the Lifegiver, seeking Her blessing for his land."

"Our . . . rites to the . . . Lifegiver. Ohhhhh . . ." Parkes put his head in his hands. "Is that the Hrothmi . . . sympathetic magic for fertility?"

"Yes. At least it is among the Frenuli. Among the Akkwasi, they practice abstinence in order to save up life force."

A thought struck Parkes. His first impulse was to jerk on his pants, as rude as that might be as long as Grant was naked. Instead he picked up the Scotch, opened it, and swigged a mouthful. When he'd wiped his mouth with the back of his hand, he said very slowly:

"Jean, how long were they listening to us?"

"I suppose long enough to know what we were doing. I didn't ask, and Ribon wouldn't have told me. He wouldn't want to embarrass us."

"He wouldn't—" Parkes drowned wild laughter in another gulp of whiskey. "Jean, you must have heard the theory that the Hrothmi are really disguised Grand Galactics testing the human race?"

"Of course. Some archeologists make a point of pretending they haven't, but that's just pompous. Why?"

"I'm beginning to believe it. I'm also beginning to believe that when the Grand Galactics disguised themselves as Hrothmi, they really did it as a practical joke." He took another sip of whiskey. "Let's eat."

11

KATHERINE FORBES-BRANDON contemplated with mild distaste a day spent in either idleness or busywork. Wasted, in either case.

The intelligence mission to the Republic was over, or so Lieutenant Tegen said. She was willing to take his word for that, although he refused to explain why he thought so. Intelligence spooks and computer people seldom apologized and never explained; Tegen was both.

She'd risen early, run six kilometers on the paths around the firing range, then showered. After breakfast, catching up on her personal correspondence took almost half the morning. She made it do so, recording letters to people she hadn't written to in more than a year.

If she'd had any official filework along, the rest of the day's work would have been handed to her on a platter. The C.O. had prohibited any of the intelligence mission from bringing official files along, though. Forbes-Brandon had been annoyed at the time. Now she had to concede that MacLean had been taking a sensible precaution.

She made cleaning her room last until lunchtime. The housekeeping in the Fort San Martín Transient Officers' Quarters helped; it was a long way below Peace Force standards. By the time she was done, the room would have passed a white-glove inspection by three generals or one sergeant major.

She ate lunch in the fungus-green Officer's Mess, even though she wasn't hungry. Then she went to the post library and pretended to be searching out their holdings from Little England Media. By the time the librarian corporal started looking suspiciously at her, her lunch was settled enough to let her run again.

She got only half a kilometer into the run when the skies opened in a too familiar Greenhouse downpour. By the time she

84

returned to the T.O.Q., the water on the front walk was halfway up her shoes and she was drenched to the skin.

She'd finished her shower and she was waiting for the orderly to deliver a hair dryer when someone knocked.

"Who is it?"

"Orderly, señora."

The accent didn't sound quite Mountaineer. Forbes-Brandon moved to where she could see the door without being seen by anyone coming through it, chambered a round in her pistol, and released the lock.

"Hullo, Kate. Expecting unwelcome company?"

It was Hugo Opperman, carrying the hair dryer. Water dripped off his raincoat, puddling on the scarred plastic floor.

"Nor any other kind, actually," she said. "But I'm glad to be surprised." She took the dryer and began playing it over her hair while Opperman hung up his raincoat. He was wearing a civilian tunic and tight trousers that displayed his attractive build better than any uniform she'd seen him wear.

"Actually, what I came to do was invite you out for dinner tonight."

"Who's got the duty?"

"Dallin's taking it until midnight, Ngomba after that until morning."

That sounded as if Captain Dallin had run through the local supply of sushi bars and compatible pilots in the past week. Nothing short of a direct order from the Commander-in-Chief could have made her take the duty tonight if she'd still had new fields of either to explore.

"You're on. Where are we going?"

"La Principesa del Mar. Unless you don't like seafood . . . ?"

"I do, and even if I didn't, I'd go. It'll be a month before I can look a steak in the face again." Mountaineer cuisine seemed to consist of eighty-six ways of doing each of forty different parts of beef cattle. Not to mention that half the cattle were fed on seaweed and their meat tasted like something from an aquarium.

"Good. They have a couple of Hrothmi cooks doing specials, and I'll put in for one of those. Were you going to wear civilian clothes?"

"No, but I can squeeze in a shopping trip if we're not—"

"Hey, uniform's fine. Besides, it's pouring down rain, and I don't think you want to be wheezing—"

"You don't have to be protective."

"I'm not being—well, maybe I was, a little. But you don't

have to be so eager to please either. Besides, I have to warn you. The average Mountaineer woman is ten centimeters shorter than you are and, ah . . . differently configured. You'd get soaked, and you might not find anything for your trouble."

"All right. Blue undress?"

"Fine. And your sidearm."

"Will they let us . . . ?"

"The restaurant won't mind. As for the other Mountaineers—if they object, that's one more piece of data we can use."

"Do you always combine business with pleasure?"

"Whenever I can. But tonight I'm more interested in pleasure."

He hadn't touched her, but the tone of voice made her feel as if she'd been caressed in several moderately intimate places. She thought of asking him if he wanted to put this rainy afternoon to one of the traditional uses for them, then decided no. The chemistry had been right from the beginning; it didn't need to be rushed. When they were both ready. . .

"Pick you up, or will you call?" she asked.

"Meet me down front about 2030," he said. "I've rented a car."

"Until tonight, then." They didn't get farther than a hand-shake, but the feeling of being caressed came over her again. It stayed long after Opperman's footsteps had faded away.

Koyban M'no Shreen refused to carry night-vision binoculars. He preferred to rely on his own night sight, keen even among the People. In spite of the darkness and the misting rain, he saw the approaching figure while it was barely halfway across the un-cleared ground.

He rested his rifle on one of the boundary stones and waited as the figure grew slowly larger. At last he was barely able to re-strain a cry of delight. It was the Frenuli homesteader and Hair-less-lover, Ribon M'no Berus. He must be making a final inspection of his boundaries before evening rites.

Koyban chambered a round. The One Squad leader put a hand on his shoulder.

"The captain's orders were not to attack any homesteaders unless they acted against us."

"Ribon may come close enough to see us, unless he is half blind. Will you wager all our lives on that?"

Both the fact and Koyban's tone forced the squad leader to incline his ears forward. "I am not going to run among the farm buildings, tossing grenades into the buildings and warning the whole bond and the Peace Force besides," Koyban went on. "I will take Ribon from where we lie. By the time he is missed, we will be approaching our firing points."

The squad leader made a gesture of aversion, which Koyban chose to ignore. The leader had the heart of a *jagrun,* even if his tongue was sometimes that of a *jag-rufai.*

The homesteader would be an easy target. He was passing no more than fifty *shirhi* away. In daylight Koyban would have wagered on taking him down with a pistol, let alone a rifle! He also had the air of someone doing a duty that had long since ceased to interest him, but which could not be abandoned. His eyes were aimed at the ground, and mostly in front of him instead of to either side.

Had this old fool truly ever been an honored *jagrun?* Perhaps, but even the best of *jagruni* could lose his cunning with age. Look at Captain Shipo, who could not be more than two thirds Ribon's age, and how caution had infected him. Perhaps that also explained why Ribon was so disgustingly intimate with the Hairless Ones. He could no longer guard his own back or those of his kin, so he had sold himself to the Hairless Ones in return for what he hoped would be protection in his last years.

He was about to find out how worthless that protection would be. The lesson would not quickly be lost on all like him—and when it was learned, Captain Shipo would also have learned something he did not seem to know.

Ribon was in the sights of the rifle now. Koyban sucked in a breath, then let it out slowly as his finger closed on the trigger.

In the silent darkness the crack of the rifle sounded like an explosion. Koyban felt rather than saw the squad leader flinching. What he saw was Ribon M'no Berus throwing up both arms, then falling. The thud of his striking the ground came clearly.

Koyban listened for any sign that Ribon was alive and conscious or that the sound of the shot had reached the farm buildings. Only the expected silence replied.

Shot in the head, Ribon would not talk soon, if ever. Koyban had enough faith in his aim to believe his bullet had gone where he'd sent it. As for the rest of Ribon's bondkin and workers, the best remedy for them was a light, swift foot.

Koyban chambered another round and slung his rifle. "Move out, single file, Objective Two." He heard acknowledgments from both squad leaders, then only the sound of *jagruni* rising to their feet and picking up their launchers and sacks of rockets.

Ribon's death had been necessary and would be useful, but tonight's real work was not yet even well begun.

Forbes-Brandon ladled more *zarzuela* onto her plate and attacked the largest pieces. Greenhouse's oceans offered comparatively few edible fish, but most of those few were delicious. Shellfish also abounded, and Greenhouse crabcakes were a delicacy on most human-inhabited planets.

Opperman took her hand gently. "Kate, they're not going to take the tureen back if you don't break the house record for emptying it."

"I'm hungry."

"So am I, but—Kate, do you mind if I get personal?"

"Would you stop if I said yes?"

"I think you know me well enough not to have to ask that."

"I'm sorry, Hugo. I . . . well, the food's delicious, the wine is better than I expected, and the company is marvelous. So I shouldn't be so prickly. I'm sorry."

"You haven't done anything that needs an apology, Kate. So why not try slowing down instead?"

"Slowing down?"

"Kate, you want to fill the unforgiving minute with sixty-seven seconds' worth of distance run. Then when you can only manage sixty-two, you feel guilty. Who will you be letting down if you don't try for the impossible? Who's going to use the failure against you?"

"I don't ask myself those questions, Hugo."

"Afraid to?"

"Hugo, this is beginning to spoil what could be a pleasant evening—"

"If you allowed yourself to relax and enjoy it, yes. Otherwise . . ." He shrugged. "Besides, I'm thinking beyond this evening. Kate, you can only go so far on trying to be Superofficer. Maybe you think you owe it to Vice-Admiral Newton—"

"Who told you about Newton?" She saw Opperman's face trying to be unreadable but not quite succeeding. "MacLean? Or was it Sergeant Major Parkes?"

Her fork went *sploosh* into the tureen. Bits of shellfish and vegetables splattered across the tablecloth. Opperman's face now showed that her long shot had hit the mark.

"Did Parkes also set up my going on this mission?"

"Well, I think the initial suggestion to Colonel MacLean may have been his. . . ."

"Initial suggestion, Pontius Pilate's left ball!" She snatched up her wineglass and emptied it at a gulp. A slow smile crept over Opperman's face.

"That's a good start, Kate. Let's get drunk. Or maybe you want to have a fight? This is a Latin-temperament planet, so nobody will mind. They won't even notice if you wait until the Hrothmi dancers come on. They've got two drummers who could drown out anything short of a tactical nuke."

Forbes-Brandon didn't know whether to laugh or cry. She bit her lip hard enough to prevent both. Opperman used the silence to signal the waiter for another bottle of wine.

When she knew her voice would be steady again, she smiled. "If I waited until the drummers started up, I could scream myself hoarse and you wouldn't hear a word. So maybe your other suggestion is better."

She reached across the table and gripped both his hands. "Only—Hugo, don't play 'let's strip her naked and see if that solves her problems' games with me. They don't help with anything. They just make me more suspicious the next time."

"I don't see how you could be more suspicious. You were about ready to throw something at me." Mischief joined the smile on his face. "Word of honor, Kate—we'll both be naked together."

"And not ashamed."

"I bloody well hope not!"

The wine arrived, a local white. Forbes-Brandon didn't bother sipping; she poured her glass full and gulped it down. She also managed to avoid gagging. Her father would have not only sent the wine back, but abused the sommelier as well.

And since when did you care what your father did, except maybe as a horrible example, Katherine Forbes-Brandon?

Her glass had been refilled while she asked herself that question. She drank more cautiously, feeling the alcohol begin to hit her. Another glass and she wouldn't care what it tasted like.

The Hrothmi dancers were filing onto the stage, doing their warmup numbers. Opperman moved his chair around to her side of the table, so they were both facing the stage. By the time the drummers started up, they had their free arms around each other. They were also drinking from each other's glasses, but it didn't seem to matter.

In fact, a lot of things didn't seem to matter any more. How long had it been since she was that drunk?

Just maybe too long.

• • •

Darkness had fallen on the University camp more than an hour ago. Now a thunderstorm was moving in, and the rain was doing the same. Jean Grant stood at the entrance to Alexis Werbel's tent, water dripping off her raincoat. She wondered if it was really worthwhile, dragging Alexis to the mess for a dinner of broiled snakebird, basketfruit, Peace Force ration bread, and tea. The Hrothmi cooks were good; they weren't miracle workers.

Behind her Private Jim Kennedy sneezed. He'd done such good work helping build the camp defenses that he was being transferred to Support Squadron. Until Major Kuzik and Dozer di Leone agreed on his own assignment, he was on Detached Duty for University camp security and maintenance. Everybody liked him except Roger Carey, who couldn't really be expected to like anyone who knew exactly how much the Hrothmi disliked the metallurgist.

"Who is it?" came a weary voice from inside the tent.

"Jean Grant, Allie. It's time for dinner."

"I'm not hungry."

"You don't have to eat much."

"Then I can eat it just as well here."

"Allie, you can't sulk in your tent all the time."

"Who's sulking?"

"What else would you call it?"

Silence. Grant decided it was time to do something about Alexis's keeping completely to herself. Even barging into her tent and shaking some sense into her, or nonsense out of her, was better than leaving her to the nonexistent mercy of the Peace Force medics. She suspected that they wouldn't actually violate their Hippocratic Oaths by making a false diagnosis. She was sure they would shade a diagnosis enough to get Alexis out of the University camp and into P.F. custody.

Damn it, Alexis wasn't in danger! Or at least she wasn't in so much danger that she needed to be surrounded by uniforms and guns. They had their place in the Universe, but right now for Alexis Werbel, they would be just the frying pan instead of the fire.

Lightning flared overhead; the puddles reflected it until the ground seemed to be on fire. Thunder followed, a roar at first, then fading through a rumble and a growl into silence. The silence lasted only moments before another thunderclap broke it, without lightning. The thunder seemed to be going on, too, with little pops and cracks—

"Down!" screamed Kennedy. Grant stared in confusion as a black ovoid the size of a hen's egg hit the tent roof and rolled down into a puddle.

"Get down, damn it!" shouted Kennedy, his voice a little more under control. "That's a grenade!" Grant dove for the ground as Kennedy lunged for the grenade. She buried her face in her arms, not wanting to see an act she'd heard described several times—a man throwing himself on a grenade to muffle the explosion with his own body.

No explosion. Instead she heard a long sigh, followed by the sound of a man pulling himself out of the mud. She risked lifting her head. Kennedy was standing over the grenade, wearing a thick layer of mud and a sheepish look.

"A dud?"

"Guess so. We'd better clear the area, though. It still might go off. It's just a light-case concussion round, but—"

Something that emphatically wasn't a dud exploded near the camp gate. The gate dissolved into flying chunks and splinters. Kennedy shouted, "Take cover! Fire on the gate! Unarmed people, stay down!" Grant prayed the last was an unnecessary piece of advice.

Now something went *pffump!* instead of *boom!* Smoke swirled up from the gateway. Kennedy's rifle snapped up and his hands danced across the selector and trigger. A burst ripped into the smoke, the first rounds kicking up muddy spray.

From inside the smoke a rifle and a pistol replied. Someone in the camp cried out—a Hrothmi, Grant thought. She bit her knuckles to keep from screaming. If she'd only had her own shotgun, or even a pistol—

Alexis Werbel burst out of the tent, barefoot and wearing only a bathrobe. Five meters from the tent she stumbled and fell. As she splashed into the mud, something hammered her tent flat in a cloud of smoke. Shreds of fibercloth and bits of her personal gear pattered down with the rain.

Kennedy fired again, a long burst that drew more fire from beyond the smoke, then a crashing explosion. Debris that had just settled into the mud flew back into the air. The smoke lifted just enough to show Grant several dim figures dashing for the trees, while a couple of others writhed on the ground.

What seemed like half the Hrothmi in the camp dashed past, firing their shotguns from the hip. Several humans followed, waving pistols. Mercifully, they all seemed to have the sense not to shoot with the Hrothmi between them and the enemy.

Natural thunder and lightning exploded overhead as Grant forced herself to her feet. Alexis was lying in the mud, pounding her fists into a puddle and whimpering like a wounded animal. Grant knelt beside her and decided she'd need a sedative before anything else would help. The camp medical kit had plenty, but Jim Kennedy's first-aid kit was closer. . . .

Except that Kennedy wasn't going to be giving anybody first-aid again. He wasn't going to need it, either, not with one temple smashed in by a rifle bullet. The rain was already washing the blood off his head. The puddle forming around him shone red in the next lightning flash.

Grant threw back her head and gave the high-pitched Hrothmi mourning keen. Kennedy would have plenty more of those before his ashes were packed off to *Ark Royal*. Grant thought her seniority entitled her to give him the first one, before she forced herself to count the casualties and get on the radio to Peace Force Headquarters. . . .

12

THE STAIRS UNDERFOOT let out a sepulchral creak. Forbes-Brandon started, nearly missing a step. Opperman's arm at her back kept her upright.

"Parts of this building must be close to two hundred Standard Years old, if the owner's telling the truth," he said. "I'm not surprised that it's a little arthritic."

At the moment Forbes-Brandon wouldn't have said she was feeling exactly limber. Her head was light, her limbs heavy, and her internal organs somewhere in between. "Is the owner telling the truth?"

"He has been, every time Ngomba checked him out," said Opperman. "That's twenty times over the last three years. So I suspect we can believe him about the privacy and the discreet guarding."

Still not a clue whether he'd taken other women here. Forbes-Brandon told herself that she was overstepping the bounds dividing curiosity from jealousy. She really had no right to either. At least Opperman didn't behave like a polished seducer, although she'd never had the—call it chance—to meet one. . . .

"Here we are."

The arm at her back propelled her to the left, toward a solid varnished wooden door. The time it took to open after Opperman thrust his card into the ID slot suggested rather comprehensive security equipment.

The room was of a piece with the rest of the compact hotel. One narrow window, looking out on the park that separated Hrothmi and human quarters on this side of the city. A bed that certainly looked large enough, with controls set into the headboard for the screen on the opposite wall. A closet, two chairs, a desk, and a small refrigerator.

As Forbes-Brandon stepped back from the window, Opperman punched the curtains shut and the lights on low. "I'll wager the only way anyone could get at us would be a bomb or shooting their way in. Nobody's going to risk either, or so Ngomba says."

"The owner has political connections?"

This was no time for small talk, even if they did have all night. She braced herself for his telling her so, then for his dismay or anger when she told him that somehow the chemistry was gone. Was it the wine, or had a year of celibacy skewed her system? Going to bed with Hugo now seemed such a cold-blooded proposition that she doubted she'd be able to warm up. That would hit him harder than a flat refusal.

"He has connections that the politicians will respect. At least all the politicians except the Radical Liberals. They're not in power now, anyway."

To Forbes-Brandon's ears, the description of the hotel owner's probable underworld connections sounded like a dismissal of her curiosity. Damn! A beautiful friendship had about two more minutes to run.

Not wanting to meet Hugo's eyes, she went to the closet, opened it, and dropped her traveling case on the floor. Then she took off her tunic and hung it up neatly. "Always take care of your clothes and they'll take care of you," had been one of her nurse's messages. It had helped at the Academy, and now it was helping keep her hands busy.

She knelt to pull off her boots. The floor creaked behind her, and she felt warm breath on the back of her neck. Two muscular arms slipped around her form behind.

"Kate, you didn't make any promises. At least none that I'll hold you to." He kissed the back of her neck, then started to pull away. Whatever she wanted, it wasn't that. She caught his hands and drew them against her shirt.

"Thank you, Hugo. You don't have to be that much of a gentleman."

It began as a polite formula, but ended as the truth. The chemistry hadn't spontaneously returned, but perhaps they could rediscover it together. Certainly it was worth a try—more than worth fighting down her fear that she wouldn't be a perfect partner.

She pulled her boots off, stood up, and began peeling off layers of clothing. As each garment came off, it joined the tunic, hanging neatly in the closet. She was bare to the waist when she heard a half growl, a half laugh behind her.

"I see you don't hurry with everything." She felt herself being embraced hard, by a man who'd clearly gone considerably further than she had in the matter of undressing. His hands stroked her neck, glided across her shoulders, and settled onto her breasts.

They stayed there for what might have been seconds, minutes, or hours. Forbes-Brandon found the urge to be precise deserting her. Eventually the hands slipped farther down, inside the waist of her trousers. She turned and ran her own hands down a back as beautifully muscled as she'd anticipated, nibbled ears that she'd thought stuck out too far but now seemed ideally placed for being nibbled on. . . .

"Ready when you are!" shouted Corporal Brezek.

Dozer di Leone looked over her shoulder. Brezek had positioned the self-propelled pallet right under the tailgate of the six-wheeler. She slapped the driver on the shoulder. Her hands danced over the controls. Barrels of bonder/sealer and insecticide began to slide aft, to be caught by the grabs on the tailgate and lowered onto the pallet.

Only eight barrels this time, and that was the last load for tonight, thank God. A couple more hours' work tomorrow morning and they'd have everything that could make a secondary explosion locked up in the cave.

A particularly sharp thunderclap sounded, then another. At the third, Dozer realized she wasn't seeing any lightning flashes. Bracing herself against the rain, she flung the cab door open and jumped out into ankle-deep mud. If the grabs were dropping those damned barrels instead of lowering them—

Something that was unmistakably an explosion hammered at her ears. Mud, stones, and fragments swept over the truck. One of the tires wheezed and sagged, the windshield showed stars, and a barrel of bonder/sealer erupted in blue flames.

Brezek was already backing the pallet toward the cave mouth before Dozer yelled at him to do so. Dozer leaped back into the cab.

"Hey, Sarge, I've got to get this truck—" began the driver.

"Correction, young lady. *I've* got to get this truck moving."

"But—"

"R.H.I.P., *bambina*."

In Dozer's case, Rank also Had Its Muscles. Dozer had the build of her Sicilian father and the height of her Milanese mother, besides pumping iron. The driver found herself flying out of her seat in a trajectory resembling a mortar shell's. Before she landed, Dozer was feeding power to all six wheels. The truck felt as if more than one tire was punctured, but they were run flats. They should hold up long enough to get the truck a safe distance from anything vital.

The best place for that—where? Dozer scrolled a mental map of the area. By the time she did, the truck was doing forty kilometers an hour and the burning barrel was trailing flame like a miniature comet.

Down the hill, then turn right at the junction. The turn would take her along the hillside, where the truck could burn out without anybody being too much the worse for wear. Bonder/sealer burned like dilute IC 52 in liquid form, and even a biodegradable insecticide wasn't healthy to breathe before it degraded.

By the time Dozer reached the junction, a second barrel was on fire. The rear window was beginning to deform from heat that Dozer could feel breathing down the back of her neck.

A hundred meters past the junction the rear window sagged and collapsed in a hot, runny mess. Dozer felt her skin blister from searing drops, and knew that her hair would catch fire in another moment. She turned the wheel hard left with one hand and opened the right door with the other.

As the truck swerved off the road, she flung herself out of the cab, tucked into a ball and holding her breath. A wave of heat worse than before enveloped her, then passed. She heard metal scream and plastic shatter, then raised her head to watch the truck roll down the thirty-degree slope. It shed barrels as it went, reaching the bottom nearly empty.

Dozer patted her head and felt hairs singed to brittleness crumble under her touch. She went flat in the mud as another explosion erupted on the road fifty meters back toward the junction. Both her rifle and the driver's had gone downhill with the truck. Her pistol was no good against the appalling feeling of nakedness that comes from being caught on a battlefield without an effective weapon.

She counted three more explosions and something that could have been either an explosion or a thunderclap before the bombardment ceased. The silence only made her feel even more naked. The end of the rockets could mean the attackers had shot themselves dry and were breaking off. It could also mean that assault squads were moving in on foot, and the rocket teams had ceased fire to avoid hitting friends. . . .

In the bed, Hugo Opperman and Katherine Forbes-Brandon made a new pleasure from the old discovery that everyone is the same height lying down. They discovered a number of other things as well. None of these were particularly new, either, but some of them also gave so much pleasure that they felt an urge to try them over and over again.

After a while Forbes-Brandon's head was swimming with something much stronger and more pleasant than the wine. Her stomach, on the other hand, was sending emphatic warnings about being jounced and bounced anymore. She stretched out full length against Opperman, savoring the quieter pleasures of his warmth and his arms around her. His breathing was steady, and she wondered if he was falling asleep. No doubt he would apologize afterward if he did, but from where she lay, she couldn't see he had anything to apologize for. Come to think of it, going to sleep might be the best thing for her too. Her stomach—

The door alarm went *dongdongdong* furiously.

Forbes-Brandon bruised both knees and set her stomach churning by leaping out of bed and snatching her pistol from under the pillow. Opperman was doing the same on his side of the bed when the screen lit up. He hastily slapped the switch to make the vision one-way and stared at the face of Lieutenant Ngomba.

"Sorry to disturb you, sir, ma'am, but the terrs have hit the tunnel and the University camp. Nothing really bad, but the mission's been ordered home on the double."

Opperman groaned and stood up. "Fine. We'll be right down. You can ride back in my car—"

"Sir, we thought that might have been traced, Captain Dallin and I did. So we scared up a couple of motorcycles. A friend of a friend of the owner here loaned them. I'll run the car back to the agency and meet you at the field."

"Well done, Lieutenant."

To Forbes-Brandon it sounded as if Opperman was saying that because he couldn't think of anything else to say. As the screen darkened, their eyes met.

"Motorcycles?" she said.

"Motorcycles," repeated Opperman. "At least that's what I think he said. Did you hear it?"

"Yes."

"Then either we're both having the same hallucination or

else he really did come up with a couple of motorcycles." He started dressing. Forbes-Brandon suppressed a pang of frustration at seeing that splendid body covered up. She walked to the closet, followed by intense green eyes filled with the same sentiment.

"Actually, it makes sense," said Opperman as he pulled on his boots. "We don't know if the Mountaineers have anything to do with the terrs. If they do, traveling in a known car along a known route could make us sitting targets. Even if the terrs are independent, they could still be making a coordinated push. No sense in being easy meat either way."

"But . . . motorcycles?" She started buttoning her shirt.

"Chalk it up to Ngomba never doing things the orthodox way. That's why he's with Kabuele, by the way. He's not in exile, it's just that he won't ever get promoted in the Black Star regular army again. He made monkeys of about half-a-dozen high brass in an exercise a couple of years back, with foreign observers present. That sort of thing gives generals long memories.

"In fact, Kyril's a lot like you. Both of you are absolutely determined to show that you're the best, and the devil take anybody who gets in the way. You do it by the book, he writes his own book, but otherwise . . ." He shrugged. "At least you haven't stepped on too many high-brass toes."

"Yet? Is that what you're leaving out?"

"Damn! Only one night together and already she knows my innermost secrets?"

"Not the innermost. We didn't— *mmmfff,*" as he kissed her, starting on the lips and ending up on the bare skin exposed by her open shirt.

"No. But it wasn't a whole night either. It's not even 0200 yet."

"Is that a promise for the future?"

"Yes—as much as any soldier can ever make one."

She hugged him until he grunted in protest, which didn't stop him from hugging her back until her stomach was churning again. Not just her stomach either—a wide-awake hangover was coming on. Well, even if nothing happened between them beyond this night, it had been worth it.

13

THE SKY WAS dark and silent, the rain fading to a drizzle. For lack of anything else that seemed to need doing, Parkes was standing guard over the bodies on their stretchers.

One body was human. Jim Kennedy hadn't been at home in the Field Squadron, or so Dozer said. Now he'd gone where either nobody or everybody was at home, depending on your religion. The lodges of the Wise One opted for everybody, although Parkes couldn't help wondering if there was a special place for soldiers. They were likely to be odd volumes in this world, and probably would be in the next. It should still count for something—that if Jim Kennedy hadn't died like a soldier, a good many humans and Hrothmi in the University camp would have died like sheep.

The other three bodies were Hrothmi—the camp's second cook and two terrorists. Every time he looked at those two, Parkes could hear the sizzling of fat in the fire. By morning word that the terrorists were or at least included Hrothmi would be all over Utopia. Even comparatively level-headed Utopians (if that wasn't a contradiction in terms) would be hitting ceilings in record numbers. As for what the bigots would be doing—

Parkes told himself firmly to worry about only six things at a time, at least until he could get something hot to drink. News of the attack had dragged him out of bed and on to a verti before he'd really reached full sapience. Any properly programmed robot could have done as well as he had for the first half hour at the University camp. Now he was about to be left in charge here, with Lieutenant Simmel taking her company into the field and Major Vela flying on to join Kuzik and MacLean at the tunnel. He had to at least simulate knowing what he was doing.

". . . can't embalm them, with the equipment available?"

Major Vela's voice sounded indignant, just short of angry. He also seemed to be wanting to make himself heard all over the camp—particularly, Parkes suspected, by Anglic-speaking Hrothmi. Vela's partisanship for his beloved Hrothmi went beyond the bounds of discretion, or even saw discretion as disloyalty.

The tone of Captain Laughton's reply bordered on insubordination. "It's not a question of equipment, sir. It's a question of people. We've got nine casualties here and fourteen more up at the tunnel. We'll probably have more before the night's over. Do you want me to let some of the wounded—Hrothmi wounded, maybe—die to embalm corpses as evidence for God knows what?"

Parkes clearly heard Vela's indrawn breath. The big vein on the side of his neck would be throbbing now. *Wise One grant that Laughton knew what this meant.* . . .

"Captain Laughton, if you can't handle twenty-three casualties and still spare a couple of people for embalming the terrs, you don't know how to run your company. I mean it. Either those Hrothmi are embalmed or I'm going to Colonel MacLean about this."

"Sir!" Captain Laughton's tone would have turned the rain into hail if she'd spoken louder.

"Of course, I think we can pull a few aid people from First Company to lend a hand. They're the reserve, and if we get even two companies engaged tonight, it will mean either we're very luck or the terrs are very dumb. I'm not betting on either, so if you do need a little help . . ."

The surgeon's reply to Vela's olive branch was lost in a belated roll of thunder. Parkes sighed. One of these days Vela was going to leave the olive branch until too late, and somebody was going to be court-martialed for telling him what to do with it. Parkes hoped it wouldn't be tonight.

When she could be heard again, Laughton sounded mollified. The rest of the conversation was too quiet for Parkes to hear, so he checked the bore of his rifle and made a quick circuit of the bodies. He didn't think anybody could have slipped up and booby-trapped one, but Bifrost veterans were all accustomed to looking on the dark side.

At last Vela appeared. "All in order, Sergeant Major?"

"Yes, sir."

"Good. We have to have those bodies autopsied, to find out what they've been eating. If they've been on issued rations, they can't possibly be local Hrothmi."

"And if they've been eating the local diet?"

The silence lasted until Parkes began to brace himself for another Vela explosion. "Then we tell the truth and hope to God that we can keep the militia from broiling Hrothmi babies like chickens!" Parkes noted that Vela's hands weren't quite steady.

"I suppose it won't be that bad," Vela said finally. "But it's not going to be the sort of thing either of us signed on for. At least we'll have a bigger gun than we expected in our battery."

"Has . . . is Haskins taking action?"

"Not that I've heard of. Nor the ambassador either. We're getting General Duchamp as the new Expeditionary Force C.O. *Macbeth* just brought the word."

Macbeth was a sistership of *Ark Royal*'s normal transport partner, *Ivanhoe*. She'd reached the Greenhouse system four days before, bringing a full load of supplies and equipment to extend Group Fourteen's capabilities. Until then the Group had been relying on the prepositioned stockpiles on Greenhouse plus *Ark Royal*'s Basic Tactical Load.

"Too bad it didn't bring Duchamp himself. When's he coming?"

"Ten days, give or take two. He's traveling light, in *Artemis*, but he still needs to pull together a staff."

Parkes wished it could be otherwise, but knew the wish was futile. With a proper staff Major-General Jeanpierre Duchamp was worth ten of Haskins. Without it, he'd have to work through Haskins's staff. They would be loyal to Haskins, worthless as he was, unless Duchamp was both ruthless enough to try turning them and lucky enough to succeed.

Duchamp was both, as his record proved, but fighting with your X.O. for staff loyalties was a piss-poor way to start a command. Not to mention a good way of getting people killed by the enemy while you and the X.O. were fighting each other.

"Any word of reinforcements?"

With two stars, Duchamp could command a division-sized Expeditionary Force. Parkes felt an irrational resentment at the idea of Group Fourteen being swamped by such a mob of late arrivals.

"No. I think they want Duchamp in position just in case, so he'll be familiar with Greenhouse. Then they can be sure he'll slot any reinforcements into the right place. Meanwhile, he can help us out with the militia if we can just hold the line for a few days."

Parkes knew the tone an officer uses when he wants help that he doesn't dare put into an order. "What do you want me to do, Major?"

"Keep the lid on here. That means arresting Roger Carey if he starts pimping for the militia. I'll authorize you to invoke Article Ninety-two in the absence of an officer."

That authorization would need approval by MacLean and Haskins. Parkes expected no trouble from the colonel and little from Haskins. He still found himself thinking that if he were an officer himself, that would be one less headache for Major Vela, who had enough already. He also found that the thought didn't bother him as much as it once would have.

"Anything else?"

"I . . . well, I can't ask you to exploit any personal relationship you have with Professor Grant—"

I hope to kiss a pig you can't was the reply Parkes suppressed.

"—but I hope you can talk some sense into her on the subject of Alexis Werbel. They aren't lovers, are they?"

"No, I think the Professor's preferences are quite hetero. She just likes taking lost kittens in out of the rain."

"Well, maybe tonight's convinced her that's a good way to get clawed."

"Maybe." Parkes would have liked to sound optimistic.

"All right. I know you'll do your best."

"Thank you, sir." *Now, if I could only promise that my best would be good enough.*

The verti banked sharply, throwing Forbes-Brandon against her harness. Involuntarily she grunted, as the belt dug into a tender stomach.

"You all right?" said Opperman.

"I have to be," she said, trying to grin. "There's nothing left in my stomach."

"I have some Analgo if you want it."

"Thanks, but on an empty stomach that always makes me loopy. I have a nasty feeling there's going to be work to do from the moment we land."

Opperman grinned, somewhat more successfully. "I'd say that you were up to your old compulsively-ahead-of-everybody self, except that you're probably right. Even if nothing else nasty's happened, you may have to plot a supply drop for Simmel's people."

The verti settled into what would have been level flight except for the rough mountain air. Dallin, an expert at nap-of-the-earth flying, was taking them through the passes to make the mission's homeward flight hard to track and even harder to hit. Not that anybody necessarily wanted to do either, but just in case. . . .

Forbes-Brandon relaxed as much as the seat and harness would allow, thinking of the last two hours. The motorcycle ride from the hotel to the airfield had been worse than any combat experience she could recall. Her driver looked more Semitic than Negroid and drove as if *afreets* would snatch him the moment he dropped below sixty kilometers an hour—on the narrow, winding streets in the Hrothmi quarters.

Thank God or Somebody most of the Hrothmi were at home in bed, and the few on the streets alert enough to jump out of the way.

The wild ride hadn't killed anybody, but halfway to the field she knew her stomach wasn't going to last the course. Pummeling the driver on the back with one hand finally got his attention. He slowed down, but she couldn't wait for him to stop. She flung herself into the ditch and got rid of what felt like everything she'd eaten in the last three days.

When she rose, her uniform soaked to the knees and elbows, Opperman was ready with a canteen and a handkerchief. She wiped her face and hands and rinsed out her mouth, then climbed the bank, muttering what she would do to Lieutenant Kyril Ngomba if she ever had the chance.

"Let me tie the noose, Kate," Opperman said. She'd bristled, all her reflexes against unsolicited protectiveness awake. "He's *my* officer, not yours."

"Sorry."

"Nothing to be sorry for. But there will be if we don't get to the field before Dallin smokes her last cigarette."

She'd smiled and let him help her back onto the motorcycle. It was easier to survive the rest of the trip; she'd kept her eyes resolutely shut until she felt the cycle hit the smooth plascrete of the airfield's runways.

The floor tilted as the verti began to climb steeply. Dallin came on the intercom.

"Last of the mountains, people. I'm going up to five thousand meters. That should be clean out of range of anything the terrs are carrying. If not, it'll still give us a chance to maneuver and fire decoys."

They'd had only a sketchy description of the two attacks, since HQ hadn't been sure if the Mountaineers were reading P.F. code or not. If they were, they shouldn't get free intelligence. If they weren't, they shouldn't get a long message to feed their code-breaker programs.

From that sketch Forbes-Brandon knew that Dallin was doing the sensible thing. The attack on the tunnel had been launched by three or four squads carrying light rockets. Fired as anti-aircraft missiles, they probably couldn't reach four thousand meters.

The University camp, on the other hand, had been hit by one large rocket, set for an airburst. Undetected because of the effects of the lightning on the radar, it rained down concussion grenades all over the camp. Fortunately most of them were duds. This left enough University people, human and Hrothmi alike, to back up Jim Kennedy in defending the gate against the ground attack.

The whole attack had the smell of a possibly improvised hit-and-run affair. Two separate forces, probably, and traveling light almost certainly. The University's rocket had been the only crew-served weapon involved. Otherwise it had been strictly individual weapons, well aimed with I.R. sights but still no more than light infantry.

The problem was, the limitations of the enemy hadn't kept them from doing a good deal of damage. On that the reports weren't just sketchy, they were damned near silent. Forbes-Brandon hoped that didn't mean what it too often meant, which was more damage than it was wise to talk about where you might be overheard.

Even if the physical damage wasn't great, the second attack on the University camp was bound to raise a political storm. Neither the ambassador nor Haskins sounded up to the job of keeping the storm from blowing around Group Fourteen while it was trying to come to grips with the enemy. Not that either had enough rank to fend off, let's say, the Scotian Populist Labor Party if it started asking Questions in Parliament . . .

Forbes-Brandon rubbed her throbbing temples and managed not to groan. She'd expected to see dawn breaking over Ciudad Cervantes while she and Hugo had a leisurely breakfast and other things in bed. Now duty had laid them both by the heels and was dragging them back to their posts.

It was an age-old dilemma for soldiers, or at least as old as armies of both sexes. Form your attachments with your own breed so that there's twice the chance of duty tearing you apart? Or cultivate civilians, who as likely as not won't understand you?

Forbes-Brandon knew she had no solution to that problem. The only problem she could hope to solve right now was her hangover.

"Hugo? I think I will have that painkiller. But could you dissolve it in something first, so it goes down easier?"

"That bad, eh? I'll ask Ngomba. He usually has some herb teas in his kit, and I think he's feeling guilty about making you sick on the motorcycles."

"Just get the tea, and I'll call it even."

"You really killed him?" said Shipo M'no Heru. It was a stupid thing to say, but he hardly cared. It seemed that if he somehow broke the silence in the clearing, what he had heard Koyban say would not be true.

"I may not have killed him outright. Yet I am sure that he died of his wound, unless he was found almost at once. It was a rainy night, and he was old."

Shipo wondered if Koyban's brutality was genuine or an act. Had he crossed the border between the soldier and the butcher? Certainly he had broken through the barrier that divides the man of independent opinions from the rebel.

And what to do about this rebellion? Shipo had ceased to be merely indifferent to the prospect of Koyban's death in battle. He was beginning to have to fight the urge to draw his pistol and shoot Koyban himself.

Which would give only a moment's pleasure, solve nothing, destroy his company, and perhaps end his own life. Shipo could hear the voices of all of his tutors and teachers uniting in a grand chorus to assure him of that. He wished he could be deaf to them.

Wishing would not solve the problem, however. He could do little or nothing against Koyban here and now. Of the *jagruni* who'd reached the rendezvous before dawn, two out of three were in Koyban's squads. They had a victory to report, too, or at least a good many explosions and fires in the construction camp at the tunnel.

Shipo's attack had damaged the University camp, or so it seemed. He did not know if he had killed Alexis Werbel or indeed anybody except, perhaps, one Peace Forcer. In return he'd lost four of his *jagruni*, and left behind two of the bodies. He'd done well to break free of the pursuing Peace Forcers, but a successful retreat was not the sort of victory of which tales were made, if it was a victory at all.

Shipo leaned back against a tree, stuffed *kasir* in his pipe, and lit it. Then he began to reload the five remaining magazines of his rifle, wiping off each round as he inserted it. The steady rhythm of puffing and wiping restored some measure of calm to his mind. His thoughts flowed smoothly again, instead of foaming and boiling over the rock of his anger at Koyban.

The death of Ribon M'no Berus made little difference now. The bodies of the People left at the University camp would be all the evidence the would-be persecutors of the homesteaders could ask for. It might even convince the Peace Force that their main enemy was close at hand. If it did not, they would still have a busy time of it, keeping Utopian militia and homesteading People from each other's throats.

Had he been wrong to discourage Koyban, giving him orders he had not obeyed and which might indeed have been hard to enforce? (The chorus of tutors and teachers broke in briefly to remind him of the folly of giving orders that could not be enforced.) Or was he simply trying to avoid a confrontation with Koyban, by telling himself that Koyban had not done so much harm after all?

He needed no chorus in his mind to remember that too many scruples can lead to too few decisions. Certainly the homesteaders now faced a danger not of their making, against which they could not be defended by those who had put them in danger. Just as certainly the cause of the Alliance would gain from this.

The Judgment Lord could afford to mull over the question until the end of time. Captain Shipo M'no Heru could not. He would hold his peace and lead his *jagruni* home for the battles yet to come.

As Shipo slid the last magazine into its loop on his belt, a Peace Force verti droned overhead. Shipo tracked it by sound, judging that its course would take it close to the old camp. It was as well that he'd decided against leaving a single squad behind there, to ambush at least the first Peace Forcers to stumble on it. They could never have been extracted by air from a place that now lay almost between the enemy's teeth, and they might not have reached safety on foot or by river. At best they would have been useless for all the time it took them to retreat to safety.

Also, Colonel Limón would surely have made extracting the squad into a favor to be repaid. In Shipo's mind the thought grew firmer every day: it was not wise to be too much in the colonel's debt.

Three kilometers away a camouflaged parachute blossomed, dark against the yellow-gray clouds. Parkes focused his binoculars and saw the cargo pod swaying underneath the 'chute.

The Amazon was on the ball as usual. Now if the verti could just make the snatch . . .

The duty verti shot up from the mesh landing pad that linked the tops of four trees the color of unripe lemons. It shot across the river, climbing as it went, the retrieval hook trailing out behind. Two circles around the descending pod, then the parachute was collapsing as the hook drew the pod up against the belly of the hovering verti. Parkes slung his binoculars and headed for the Amazon's O.P. The pods could be landed on the landing pad then winched to the ground, but why go to all that trouble when there was a stretch of riverbank available?

Beside a bush the color of a seasick albino, Parkes stepped into a patch of soft ground and nearly tumbled headfirst into the Amazon's lap. She was leaning back against a tree, watching the radio with eyes nearly as red as some of the indicator lights.

"Sit down, Sergeant Major, and join me for lunch. Or is it dinner? I'm afraid I've lost track."

So he wasn't the only one for whom time seemed to have been flowing into one endless moment ever since last night's attack. It wasn't as bad, now that he knew Dozer di Leone wasn't even seriously hurt—"just sore enough to be mad as hell," she told him over the radio.

In fact, it wasn't really bad at all. Simmel's people hadn't caught the terrs, but recon flights supporting them had turned up the terrs' old camp. Vela, Parkes, and Voorhis had been on the second verti into the L.Z., just before noon. The terrs were long gone, but they'd left a prepared, well-located camp behind them. Scrounging from friends was an old Peace Force tradition; scrounging from enemies was even older.

The autopsies on the two dead Hrothmi terrs had proved they weren't local homesteaders. That plus the natural incompetence of the Utopian militia just might keep things from getting too hairy too fast. Certainly the knowledge that the militia would have to go through two of the Group's rifle companies to get to any homesteaders might cool the hotter heads.

None of this would bring the dead back, or even speed up Jim Kennedy's medal. It did mean that Parkes was about ready for a nap, in the knowledge that things wouldn't have completely fallen apart before he woke up.

"Here."

The Amazon was handing him an entire can of self-heating stew and a package of crackers.

"Save some for yourself, why don't you?"

"Thanks, but I suddenly realized I'm not hungry." She opened her canteen and took a generous swig.

Parkes started scooping up the stew with the crackers. The Amazon must still have a bit of the morning-after-the-night-before feeling inside. Considering how she'd looked when she got off the verti eight hours ago, she was doing pretty well to be on duty at all.

The Amazon corked her canteen and set it down. "Sergeant Major, I think I owe you . . . something for a suggestion you made. I think you know which one."

Parkes did. It was enough of a repayment to know that Forbes-Brandon wasn't the type to resent an N.C.O.'s trying to do her a favor. However, she probably wouldn't see it that way.

"If you can—what did you dig up on that mission? That you can talk about now, anyway?"

"That would be paying you in counterfeit money. The colonel's called a Command Group meeting for tomorrow morning. Dallin, Tegen, and I will be briefing everybody at once inside of twelve hours. Think of something else—after you get some sleep."

Parkes finished the stew and all but two of the crackers, spread his poncho on the ground, and lay down with his rifle across his knees. As he did, a half platoon of Kabuele Company trotted out of the trees and started unloading the pod. The verti, Parkes noted, had returned to its perch while he was eating.

A compact blond figure broke away from the work party and headed toward the Amazon. She gave him something that was more than a wave and something less than blowing a kiss. Parkes lurched to his feet, poncho in one hand and rifle in the other.

Parkes had a gut feeling that Opperman and the Amazon had spent at least part of last night a damned sight more pleasantly than he had. His talk with Jean Grant in the small hours of the morning hadn't led to a fight, but she was as stubborn as Scotia granite about not turning Alexis Werbel over to the Peace Forcers except for medical treatment, at least without a direct order. He rose to find another sleeping place. Talk between officers wasn't necessarily privileged; talk between lovers certainly was.

Halfway around the perimeter of the clear area, Parkes found a patch of fallen leaves that was only damp instead of soggy. His poncho finished it off. He was drifting into sleep before the verti was half unloaded.

His last waking thought was odd enough to surprise him, even through the haze of oncoming sleep. He hoped Hugo Opperman would give the Amazon something more than just a good time in the sack. Sleep took him before he could even begin to think what that might be.

14

MacLean debriefed Parkes and Vela personally. Parkes expected pointed questions about his dealings with Jean Grant. Instead MacLean's questions let him paint a charitable picture of the professor's ethics and judgment (except where Alexis Werbel was concerned).

"It's nice to know that we'll be dealing with at least one civilian who doesn't have a heavy finger on the panic button," MacLean finished. "All right, gentlemen. Command Group meeting at 1030 tomorrow."

Major Vela looked a question. MacLean flicked crumbs from a late dinner out of his beard. "We're meeting at such a sybaritic hour because I want everyone to get a good night's sleep, me included. I hate to sound like a prophet of doom, but I suspect it may be the last one we have for quite a while. Well done, both of you, and dismissed."

They saluted and headed for the mess.

A good night's sleep and two meals eaten at a table instead of gobbled out of cans did wonders for Parkes. He reached the meeting five minutes early, showered, shaved, dressed in a clean uniform, and ready to beat twice his weight in terrorists or guerrillas.

(At least, twice his weight if they were human. If they were Hrothmi, a combat-trained Hrothmi was more likely to beat twice his weight in Sergeant Majors. Or her weight—a crucial fact about the Hrothmi was that sexual dimorphism among them was minimal. The average Hrothmi woman was as combat-capable as the average man. This nearly doubled their potential recruits and considerably more than halved their rate of sex crimes.)

No Order of the Day about uniforms had come down, but everyone was in fatigues, the Amazon included. Parkes couldn't help noticing, however, that hers were the neatest in the room. Makeup, hair, and nails also looked ready to stand inspection. He'd already listened for complaints about her putting too much work on the Command Group orderlies, and heard only silence. Did she put in a lot of time on "the appearance of an officer and a lady"? Or was she one of those lucky people who radiated a local field repealing the Second Law of Thermodynamics, keeping their persons and clothes in impeccable order with a minimum of effort?

(Maybe not so local either. Parkes recalled Forbes-Brandon seated at the radio, long legs tucked neatly under her, maps, calculators, and everything else laid out even more neatly within easy reach. No simple Lieutenant Rich-Bitch she—which didn't mean that she was going to be able to cope with the other problems she had. . . .)

But on to the problems of Peace Force Company Group Fourteen—not to mention 31 Squadron and Kabuele Company. Both were represented at the meeting. The air man was a Major Stephen Hughes, who greeted Dallin like an old friend, while Major Kabuele spoke for himself. The Major was so black that he had a bluish sheen to his skin, and so impeccable even in fatigues that he made the Amazon look dowdy.

MacLean opened the briefing with a summary of the attack and events since. He used full visuals but didn't give Parkes much news. One bad note: Mike Guslenko wasn't going to be fixing anything for a while. He'd also be hoisting whatever bottles the doctors allowed him with his left hand until he got out of the regeneration ward.

Not getting her trucks fixed would annoy Jean Grant, who hardly needed more annoyances. She'd not been happy with the news that University movements would be convoyed until further notice. She'd be even less delighted at having to hitch rides with the Peace Forcers on a regular basis. The professor had few prejudices against the Peace Force, but her commitment to keep Alexis Werbel out of their hands was doing the same job.

MacLean ran down, then turned the floor and the screen over to Mediator Arthur Goff. Goff was a former professor of sociology, whose only explanation for his change of careers was, "I was tired of enjoying the leisure of the theory class." He was tall, thin, wore mostly leisure suits in more different shades of green than the forests outside, and had a resolutely academic manner of speaking.

His subject still kept everyone listening out of more than sim-

ple courtesy. He summarized available intelligence on the
Hrothmi political movement known as the Alliance, dedicated to
a Hrothma more independent of "the Hairless Ones." He went on
to describe the key factions, ending:

"There are about sixteen more factions with recognized
names. There are also many splinter or beginning groups, probably at least half a dozen in each organized Hrothmi nation, city-
state, or tribal confederation. The ones I've described are the
ones most likely to have off-planet connections.

"So you can see that there's nothing inherently impossible
about the Alliance supporting off-planet terrorism among local
Hrothmi. There's also little chance of its being done without at
least the tacit consent of at least one local human political authority. They'd need a blind eye to arms deliveries, or at least a
nearsighted one.

"One of my jobs is going to be judicious inquiries in Mountaineer commercial circles." Which should have been left to the
commercial attaché at the Union Embassy, except that the Union
had no ambassador to the Republic. A Populist majority in the
Union Senate had yanked the embassy for some Montañan piece
of political thuggery two years before Parkes joined the Peace
Force. Populist pressure had kept the embassy from being re-
opened ever since.

"Any corporations with business or hopes of it on Hrothma
might be a channel for arms shipments," Goff continued. "They
would expect economic privileges in return, which might be quite
valuable."

Parkes couldn't see any "might" about it. The total Hrothmi
population of Greenhouse was well into six figures. Being the
main link with their homeworld for all those Hrothmi would be
impressively profitable by Greenhouse standards—profitable
enough to overcome more scruples than Parkes suspected most
businessmen of any planet or race had. Not to mention the possibilities on Hrothma itself, in those places where the Alliance had
support among the governments or the merchants.

"However, this intelligence gathering will have to take a back
seat for the time being. My overriding priority is keeping the
peace between the Utopians and their Hrothmi homesteaders.
That has to be done, whether the terrorists are being locally recruited or imported. The alternative does not bear contemplation."

It might not bear contemplation, but Major Vela certainly
looked as if he were contemplating it. He also looked as if he

were suffering from a bad case of blister fungus and trying desperately to hide it.

Parkes sympathized with Vela. The major's commitment to the Hrothmi—with whom he'd soldiered, sweated, and bled for fifteen years—was one of the most admirable things about a generally admirable man. Even if he hadn't been so worth his rations, Parkes would have preferred him ten times over one of the Utopian bigots.

At least Parkes now understood where the bigotry came from. By and large, the homesteading Hrothmi were doing a better job of keeping their houses in order (not to mention building them in the first place) than the human Utopians. Nobody likes being shown up, least of all by a different species.

In this case, to understand all was to forgive even less than before. Parkes knew that his oath would keep him from committing any actual crimes to help the Hrothmi against the militia. Anything short of that, however...

"Thank you for your attention," said Goff. "I will now turn matters over to Lieutenant Tegen."

Tegen was undersized and slightly overweight, with a neat red beard and eyes at least temporarily the same color. His voice was so low that Parkes had to strain to hear it.

"Exhibit One." A table of statistics flashed on the screen. "The losses of Mountaineer arms and equipment to 'terrorist' raids." Parkes clearly heard the quotation marks. He also saw that the losses were enough to arm and equip a light-infantry battalion for medium-intensity action.

"I'm sure you all know that Hrothmi are anatomically sufficiently different from humans to require modification in some weapons and much personal gear. All of the items listed here appeared to be for human use.

"I say 'appeared' because the Army also has control over storage and shipment of Hrothmi-modified items produced in the Republic. There's quite a lot of those, more than half of them manufactured by Armas Dozo y Cerrar. Major Dozo, son of the senior partner in the firm, is an Army officer attached to Intelligence. He was one of our guides during our mission.

"By methods I'm not at liberty to discuss, I obtained certain codes. I was also able to penetrate files containing data on Hrothmi-modified items stored in the warehouses raided by terrorists. This data is displayed in Exhibit Two."

Tegen slapped a switch. After a moment Parkes frowned. In the categories where items needed to be modified for Hrothmi use, more than sixty percent of the missing material had been modified.

"Your conclusions, Lieutenant?" said MacLean.

Parkes knew the colonel was testing Tegen. MacLean loathed people unwilling to commit themselves to decisions or conclusions. If Tegen waffled, like so many Intelligence officers did, neither Lieutenant-Commander Singer nor Captain Cooper nor the chief of Intelligence herself could save him from being barbecued on the spot and served up for the Command Group's lunch.

"As long as you don't mind a tentative one, sir..." MacLean's stony stare was enough answer. "Then the Mountaineers are arming at least a couple of companies of Hrothmi, recruited in the Republic, for unconventional operations in Utopia. Main target—the railroad; secondary targets of opportunity include the local Hrothmi homesteaders. I won't speculate on the amount of support they may enjoy among the homesteaders."

Major Vela's expression suggested that was a wise course of action. The X.O. looked torn between sheer relief and a desire to descend on Mountaineer GHQ with a rifle company of *jagruni* and clean it out to the bare walls.

"Thank you, Lieutenant Tegen," said MacLean. "From the intelligence you've provided, I conclude that we need most of our rifle platoons available for field service. This will force Support Squadron to double up for security and escort duty as well. Major Kuzik, do you see any critical problems with that?"

"Not critical, no. Serious, maybe. I can also see a way to our having no real problems at all. Major Kabuele, I know that your company isn't currently air mobile. Would you be able to take over most of the local security work?"

Kabuele carefully looked at a spot on the opposite wall that kept him from having to meet anyone's eyes. "I would be delighted to give you an unqualified yes. Unfortunately, local security work may now involve fighting more than terrorists. It may involve standing between the Hrothmi homesteaders and the Utopian militia. Kabuele Company can afford only a very limited involvement in such a confrontation."

Parkes acknowledged Kabuele's courage in making such a frank admission of his Company's political constraints in the presence of so many people who traditionally had no love for mercenaries. The Black Star government wouldn't let Kabuele or any of his people come home if they were involved in shooting up Hrothmi homesteaders. Old prejudices from the days of Terran colonial empires died hard.

On the other hand, Barron, Allison, & McNeil wouldn't appreciate soldiers who were technically their employees shooting Utopian militiamen. Their ability to finish the railroad depended on good relations with both governments. If their mercenaries disrupted those relations, they would not get a good recommendation when their contract was up. Without such a recommendation, Kabuele Company's chances of a new contract as a unit would be slim. That could finish their chances of earning their way home.

Even the best mercenaries had their limitations, and both Kuzik and Vela should have known better. Dozer would undoubtedly tell Kuzik that respectfully but firmly as soon as the meeting was over. Voorhis should also have been alert to Vela's short fuse where Hrothmi were concerned. If he wasn't, it was another downcheck against him. Now how to find out . . . ?

"This doesn't seem to be a situation for invoking Article Ninety-two," said MacLean. Not to mention that General Haskins might not back up the Group if MacLean did invoke it. "But I think I see another way out. Major Kabuele, will BAM object if we give your Company refresher training in airmobile operations? If we cycle them through a couple of platoons at a time, we should have them ready to deploy with our rifle companies within a few weeks. That would let us use our reserves for security work."

This would be giving Kabuele Company a new capability at Peace Force expense. If Kabuele Company did engage the terrorists in the field, it would give both them and their employers a nice political credential as well.

MacLean had devised what might look to some people like a bribe, but one that would be profitable to both briber and bribee. Parkes decided that Vela and Kuzik would have to get up very early in the morning to make trouble MacLean couldn't handle. That meant less need for him and Dozer to lose sleep, and that was pure good news considering how little they were likely to get anyway. . . .

The meeting wound up with a discussion of deployments (unchanged for now), use of air assets (which would be stretched thin), and routine matters (kept to a minimum, because everyone knew MacLean didn't like officers who needed his permission to blow a lance-corporal's nose). Parkes and Dozer added an unofficial discussion of Major Kuzik in a corner just outside the room.

Voorhis would have been invited to join in if he'd been around to invite. Instead he disappeared immediately after the conclusion of a meeting at which Parkes now realized the man hadn't said a single word. Parkes told himself for the tenth time not to prejudge Voorhis. He also had to admit that on Group Fourteen's next operation, he'd be happier if there was either not a single Hrothmi within light-years, or a different Field First. MacLean couldn't do all the work of keeping Vela from going off like an instantaneous-fused grenade at any threat to Hrothmi.

After Dozer left, Parkes remembered he hadn't picked up his briefing printout. On the chance that the printouts hadn't been cleared away into the secure locker, he went back into the room. The printouts were gone, but the Amazon was standing by the main display, contemplating the general A.O. map.

She turned and smiled as Parkes approached. When the smile reached her eyes, Parkes realized she was even better looking than usual. If Hugo Opperman was giving her more than usual to smile about . . .

"Sergeant Major."

"Ma'am?"

"How critical are we going to be, for air assets? That's assuming we commit some to a training program for Kabuele Company."

"Captain Dallin—"

"Isn't here. Right now, I'm asking you."

"Very critical, if we're using only our organic vertis. If we can draw on 31 Squadron, a lot better."

"I trust Major Hughes. The problem is, drawing on 31 needs Haskins's permission."

Parkes jerked his head, acknowledging what Forbes-Brandon wasn't putting into words. Criticizing a general was as dangerous as throwing yourself on a grenade, mostly less useful, and almost always less generously rewarded.

"Duchamp's on the way. He's more field-oriented."

"Yes, but he's not here. What do we do in the meantime?"

That didn't sound like a rhetorical question. "I was thinking that in a combat situation we could limit the vertis to troops and medevac. That would dump most of the resupply load on you, but . . ."

"But . . . ?"

"Ma'am, you're the best judge of *Ark Royal*'s capabilities in this area."

"Very true. And my judgment is that the Group shouldn't rely on our ability to produce miracles on demand. At least not when we may have to drop some of the loads into quintuple canopy."

"Quintuple?"

"I know. I didn't think there was such a thing, either, until Hugo—Captain Opperman—showed me. We could use up the whole Engineer Company without finding half a drop in that sort of jungle."

Also probably not without provoking Kuzik and Dozer to just this side of mutiny. Parkes decided to bet that what the Amazon wanted was what would make sense if he were in her place. This was betting on his knowledge of someone who put in a good deal of time being mysterious, but what the hell, they didn't give out torches for taking the easy way out.

"Lieutenant, if you want to arrange some informal ways of increasing our air assets on short notice, I think I can help."

The answering smile made Parkes feel he was warming his hands at a fire.

"I appreciate your offer, Sergeant Major. Don't commit yourself or anybody else to anything until I've, ah . . . examined the situation aboard ship. That should take a couple of days. After that I can deal with Captain Dallin and Major Hughes. You can take Sergeant Major di Leone and the appropriate people in 31. What do you think we need, in vertis or equivalent capacity?"

"Giving you a S.W.A.G.—I'd say two heavy and one light more than we can guarantee out of the Group's organic air."

"Very good, Sergeant Major. I say again, I appreciate this, even if nothing comes of it." Forbes-Brandon tucked her printouts under her arm, turned off the map, and strode out.

Parkes waited a discreet few minutes before following her. Maybe the Amazon was trying to cover her shapely rear, making sure there wouldn't be any resupply failures to kill PFers, or even be a black mark on her record.

More likely, she was leveling with him. Parkes was surprised how much he wanted to believe that—not just wanted to believe it, but *did* believe it. Far from covering her posterior regions, she risked laying them on the line with her Navy superiors. They'd be reluctant to admit that there was anything they couldn't do by way of resupplying their Embarked Group, and eager to downcheck a naval officer who blew the whistle on them. Parkes hoped the Wise One would give Forbes-Brandon some discretion in "examining the situation" aboard *Ark,* or she might be in something of a situation herself before she got to square one.

Not a damned thing he could do about it, either, if she did get herself into one. No, there was something he could do. He could buy two bottles of whiskey and give one to Captain Opperman, so they could both get drunk in memory of the career of an officer and a lady.

15

"THE NEW AIR base will also be underground?" asked Chabon M'ni Luurn.

Colonel Limón did not reply immediately. He and his guards were crossing a rough and slippery patch of floor in the down-sloping tunnel. When he seemed sure of his footing, he nodded.

Chabon and her three *jagruni* dropped back to within hand-signing distance of Shipo. Her hands sketched a question: "Dare we ask where and how large?"

His hands replied: "Not here."

Chabon made a sour face. Shipo knew why. Two days ago Limón had told them that eight armed vertis were being assigned to support the Company. He had told them nothing else, except that they would be operating from a separate underground base.

Koyban and many others chose to behave as if this were good news. Chabon was openly torn between hope and doubt. It would be good news *if* the humans did not force the Company into action against the Peace Force before her new recruits were fit for battle. Otherwise it meant only danger for them, as well as shame for her that she could not protect them from that danger until they could face it as true *jagruni*.

The party passed through Human's Stoop, where only Shipo had to duck his head, and around the last bend in the tunnel before Yellowsand Cave. As they approached the mouth of the tunnel, Shipo heard the voice of an officer lecturing recruits. Speeding their hearts too—Shipo heard shouts and hands thumping knees.

Then he stopped abruptly, and Chabon did the same. The lecturer was Koyban. They looked at each other, then had to hurry to catch up with Colonel Limón before he reached the open sand.

About twenty of the recruits were sitting beside the pool in the middle of the cave. Most were squatting or kneeling to look at a map Koyban had drawn in the sand. A few were staring at the rock ceiling. None were obviously catching up on their sleep.

Koyban saluted. "Permission to continue, Captain?"

This was a breach of both regulations and manners. The recruits were in bond to Chabon before any other officer. Koyban should have asked her permission, not just to continue but to speak to them in the first place.

Nothing to be done about it, either, without publicly reprimanding Koyban in front of the recruits. That was never wise. It would be doubly foolish now with Koyban, whose hero's aura from the raid still clung to him.

Shipo nodded. Koyban's voice rose again.

"The Hairless Ones ran about like *iskupi* from a kicked nest. Even the Peace Force cannot stand against the attack of a band of *jag-tsari*. Remember this when you are told lies about how much training you will need. The warrior's spirit is either born in you or not. All of you have it, so do not listen to—"

Chabon stamped forward, spraying sand from under her boots. "Do not listen to this *steki*-wit!" she shouted. "He cares nothing for the warrior spirit in you, nor for your lives and the tears of your bondkin! He cares only for having more people listen to his lies and be turned away from—"

"A liar, am I?" said Koyban, turning to face her. "Do you truly doubt that I have done what I said I did at the tunnel, while you huddled in the caves leading these warriors astray?"

Shipo strode forward to stand beside Chabon. Drown in dung the unwisdom of reprimanding Koyban! He'd just forfeited the right to have his breach of manners and regulations ignored. He'd best be silenced before he forfeited more.

Chabon would have to be corrected too. Death duels had been fought over milder accusations than lying and cowardice. But first Koyban—

"Look out, *cuirna!*" cried Chabon.

Koyban's pistol cleared its holster as Chabon flung herself in front of Shipo. The next moment her pistol was drawn, too, and she was falling on top of him, slamming him down into the sand.

Where her shot went, no one ever knew. Everyone knew where Koyban's shot went. It struck under the point of Chabon's jaw and tore its way out the back of her head. Shipo was so thoroughly spattered with blood and brains that for a moment he was blind.

For another moment he prayed that he would remain blind.

That was not granted. He scraped his face with one hand, drew
his own pistol with the other, and stood up.

What he saw drew a worthier prayer of thanks, that the mad-
ness had burned itself out with two shots. All his own and Chabon's *jagruni* were gripping Limón and his escort, to keep them
from shooting Koyban.

Not that Koyban deserved anything less, but his summary execution at the hands of humans would have ruined the Company
in a moment. Shipo would have held authority only as the
humans' puppet. That was not authority worth having, no authority to make the Company fit to face the Peace Force.

Koyban had thrown his pistol muzzle first to the sand and was
kneeling out of reach of it, hands clasped behind his back. A
couple of the recruits looked as if they'd have taken up the fight
on his side, if two of their comrades hadn't been sitting on their
chests. Shipo looked at the two quick-witted ones, and saw that
they were twin sisters.

"You two, sitting on the *steki*-wits. Your names?"

"Piera and Nina M'ni Simas," they said, almost together.

"Very good. You are now both squad leaders in the Recruit
Platoon. I will recommend that the new Recruit Leaders confirm
those promotions."

"We thank the captain." Again it came out almost as if a single
woman were speaking.

Thank the captain, yes. Thank the captain who gave Koyban too
long a leash, and so brought death to a warbonded friend of twenty
years, whose last word to him was *cuirna*. Thank him for what?

For seeing that the Company had to go on, or Chabon's death
was wasted. For starting to do what must be done, to keep the
Company alive and battleworthy.

For being what he should have been an hour ago, in time to
save Chabon.

Despair swept into Shipo. It nearly swept him away, to make
him then and there start keening and kicking up the sand in Chabon's death dance. Instead he forced himself to look at Koyban.

It was some comfort that the Company would now go on
without Koyban M'no Shreen.

Koyban at least had the sense to meet his captain's eyes. Otherwise, Shipo knew, he would have shot the man down on the
spot. That was his right, for mutiny and murder were both de-
serving of the extreme penalty.

"Do you wish a chance to die with . . . some honor?" he said.

"Need you ask, Captain?"

Koyban had always behaved like a *kukmar*, but perhaps that was only his manner. Perhaps there were indeed bondkin who were innocent of his folly but would know shame if he were shot down to mingle his blood with Chabon's.

"Then will you swear the True Oath of the *jag-tsari?*"

"What do you wish me to do?"

"Kill Alexis Werbel."

Shipo was not too intent on Koyban to miss the grin that spread across Colonel Limón's face. Shipo had chosen that particular deed almost at random. It was a blow that could be struck only by someone prepared to die in the act. Yet Limón looked as if his firstborn had just won the Star of Honor. What did he know about Alexis Werbel that he had not told Shipo?

Koyban cleared his throat. "By steel and fire, by the sky and the wind, I swear to hold my own life as nothing if I may end the life of the Hairless One called Alexis Werbel."

"I witness that he has sworn," said Shipo.

"We witness it," said the Simas twins.

"We witness it," said the six *jagruni* of Shipo's and Chabon's escorts.

"He has sworn, and it is witnessed," said Shipo. "Now go draw whatever equipment you think you will need. Come back when you are ready to leave. Colonel Limón and I will arrange transportation for you."

The colonel nodded. His face was blank again. Except for the momentary grin, he'd had the wits to keep silent and blank-faced throughout the whole affair. Even being restrained by *jagruni* had not ruffled him.

That was the behavior of a man with more wisdom than Shipo had expected. Or perhaps it was the behavior of a man playing for such large stakes that his dignity was a small matter?

Shipo wondered if he would ever know, and knew he would not even ask here.

"Now, you are all dismissed."

"Captain—" began the colonel.

"I cannot order you, *Jagrun-te* Limón, but will you go on as wisely as you have begun and *leave me alone?*"

Limón saluted. "Certainly."

Shipo knelt and closed his eyes until the sound of boots shuffling through sand died away. He kept them closed for a further moment, listening to the faint murmur of the spring that fed the pond. Then he opened his eyes, clasped his arms across his chest, took a deep breath, and began to keen for Chabon M'ni Luurn.

16

THE THUNDER ROLLED louder. The rain would begin soon, f Koyban knew anything about Greenhouse weather. Rain would low the feet and dim the vision of the Hairless Ones, improving is chances of success. Probably not of escape, not with a full latoon of Peace Forcers plus a militia outpost ready to bar his ath. He was sworn not to be concerned about escape, but could ot be so indifferent to the possibility of outright failure.

Lightning again, more thunder, and the first pattering drops of ain. The clouds were thickening overhead. Soon it would be as lark as twilight, though perhaps not for long. "Quick come, uick go" was the rule for such storms.

Koyban examined himself. The rough shorts, sleeveless tunic, alf boots, and pouched belt could be those of the itinerant ped-ller he claimed to be. Then he examined his basket of squashes nd nuts. In the rain and dimness the line where one squash had een cut open to hold the grenade should be invisible. A metal letector would show nothing; the grenade was plastic and ce-amics. Even the weight of the squash was hardly affected.

With a prayer to the Lady of Fortune, Koyban strode forward. The militia sitting around their truck stopped glowering at the 'eace Forcers at the University camp gate and glowered at Koy-an instead. He ignored them, walked up to the corporal of the ;uard and presented his peddler's license.

The corporal looked at both sides and all four edges, then ran is scanwand over it. Koyban managed not to hold his breath. The wand purred like a contented *feyos*, and a green light glowed t the upper end.

"Pass, friend," said the corporal. "There's a tent to the right of he gate, set up for travelers. You might want to sit out the rain in hat."

"Thank you. The hospitality of the *Shedni* is honorable."

"We got no complaints, I'll say that much. Hey, is that Lutt-wak's squash you got there?"

The corporal was pointing at *the* squash. Koyban's heart turned over in his breast. "I do not know the . . . human name for the kind," he said, forcing himself to speak slowly. "I know that most of the ones I have are not yet ripe."

"Oh, hell. I was thinking of a break from rations tonight. What about the nuts?"

Every nerve in Koyban's body shouted an urgent command to have no more to do with this corporal. His brain refused the command. Refusing would awaken suspicion; selling some nuts should send it into a deeper sleep.

"Eight pesos a dozen."

"Eight? You got hair on the brain too? Those are nuts, not jewels. Five."

"You would doom me to starvation. Seven and a half, if you respect a man's right to live."

"I don't have that bad a quarrel with you. I also have just a corporal's pay. Six."

The bargaining ended with a price of six and two-thirds pesos for a "baker's dozen" of nuts. It also ended with each side convinced they'd got the better of the bargain, which Koyban knew was half the pleasure of bargaining. Having had this pleasure, the corporal would be less alert now.

"Thank you, *Jagrun-te*."

The corporal nodded and waved Koyban through. He turned right, walked through the hospitality tent and continued out the back. None of the People waiting out the rain on the benches paid any attention to him. Confident that everyone saw just one more peddler too eager to sell to stay in from the rain, he turned down the path toward Alexis Werbel's tent.

Or at least where the tent had been. Perhaps it had been moved; just possibly she was no longer even in the University camp. But he had to start somewhere. As long as he was unsuspected, he could also ask a few questions. Too many and suspicion would come, but probably not soon enough to save the woman.

Jean Grant watched Alexis Werbel brushing her hair with slow, desultory strokes. She knew that her presence was annoying the girl. She also couldn't bring herself to leave without at least one more effort to get Alexis to the mess hall. She hadn't had a proper meal since the night of her father's death, and was beginning to look like a famine victim.

A thought sparked. "Alexis, would you eat something if I had a tray sent over?"

"Wouldn't that be asking somebody to come out in the rain?"

"Look, Alexis, half the humans and all the Hrothmi in the camp would swim the Lepanto River to get you a meal! If going to the mess is like sticking your head into a borer's nest . . ."

Grant's voice trailed off as Alexis gave her a faint, tentative smile. Had she accidentally guessed the girl's problem? Did she think of the University people as friends who would protect her? Or did she want to run away and hide, maybe even among the Peace Forcers? If so—

"Excuse me, *Shedni-te*," said a Hrothmi voice from outside. "There is a peddler—"

"A peddler?" The drumming rain must have distorted the last word. What would a peddler be doing in a storm like this? "We don't want any—"

Grant heard the thud of a club on bone and the splash of a falling body. Then a hairy arm darted through the tent flap and a hairy hand let fly an egg-sized green object. Grant lunged for Alexis, to knock her to the floor, but missed and went sprawling on the other side of the girl's cot.

Alexis Werbel was still sitting on her cot when the grenade exploded.

Behind Koyban the sound of shooting was fading into the rain. He said a prayer of thanks to the War Lord and the Lady of Fortune. The rain and the skirmishing between the Peace Force and the militia had let him come this far. If they went on, he might win free, wounded leg and all.

He didn't know if it was a wild shot from the militia or an aimed shot from the Peace Force that tore through the flesh of his thigh fifty *shirhi* outside the camp. It would be more honorable to be shot by Hairless Ones who did, after all, rank as warriors. It was more encouraging to think that the witless Utopians were shooting so wildly that they might kill a Peace Forcer. Then there might be the next thing to war between the two. . . .

The pain was spreading from his thigh up and down his leg. Each step seemed to twist a knife in the wound and send cold fire up into his belly and down into his lower leg. It was as well he'd had a change of disguise ready. Snatched from the bottom of the basket, the soiled blue smock now made him look like a poor homesteader's farmhand. A drunken farmhand, anyone would say if they saw him staggering down the road.

In a new disguise he might hope to stay on the road. Otherwise he would have had to break away across country, difficult if he'd been unhurt, near to impossible as he was.

He'd come almost a whole *demashirhi* from the camp. Two more and he could leave the road for a while. Long enough to properly clean and bandage his wound, drink water, take the strengthening pills, and complete his new disguise by trimming his hair and sidewhiskers. He would still be doomed if anyone stopped him and discovered his wound, but if Peace Forcers and militia were too busy watching each other to watch the roads—

"Hssst. Brother *Hygar*."

The salutation startled Koyban even more than being called at all. "Brother *Hygar*" was the mode of address among the Frenuli members of the Alliance. Had the death of that *kukos* Berus brought them forward into the open? Not yet to openly attack the Hairless Ones, perhaps, but at least to aid those who did?

"Brother *Hygar*, what seek you?"

"A chance to aid a brave *jagrun*."

Was the voice quite steady? No, it was not, but then if the speaker was not himself *jagruni*, he might well be frightened. With good reason, too, considering what the militia or even the Peace Force might do to him and his bondkin if they learned of this night's work.

That would be one more cause of discontent among the homesteaders, one more victory for the Alliance. *If* this offer of help was real. Could the voice be trusted?

Koyban decided it hardly mattered. The blood was flowing again, around the cloth he'd stuffed with agonizing care into the wound. He'd be fortunate to cover one more *demashirhi* and still have the strength to turn his knife against himself. Better die fighting against *kanai* than be found a bloodless corpse on the road at dawn.

He turned and lurched down the embankment, into the bushes. Two *shirhi* beyond the first bush, he saw three of the People facing him, a fourth with his back turned. Koyban staggered as the three came forward, almost falling into their arms.

The first thing that broke his sense of relief was realizing how tightly his arms were gripped. The second was hearing one of the grippers say, "We have him, Tsigo." Koyban was already tensing, ready to break free, when the one addressed as Tsigo turned around.

He wore workman's clothes, with a wide leather belt. From that belt hung binding thongs and an ivory-hilted *cheeness*. On his face was a smile, the smile of a triumphant *kukos*.

Koyban broke free and lunged at Tsigo, wanting to smash that smile if it was the last thing he did in this life. It nearly was. If he'd had his own knife drawn, he could have thrust it into Tsigo's ribs. Instead, Koyban rammed his head up under Tsigo's chin and at the same time tried to knee him in the groin.

Tsigo's head snapped back, but both arms clamped around Koyban's back like iron bands. Koyban felt himself being dragged down as Tsigo fell backward. If the fall knocked the breath out of Tsigo, he still had a chance to take one last enemy with him—

Incredibly, Tsigo was rolling over, still gripping Koyban and now crushing him into the mud. Koyban kicked, clawed, bit, and cursed, but it was his lungs that now fought for breath. His curses rose to a scream of rage, ending only when thunder exploded in his head as someone kicked him.

The last thing he heard before the second thunderclap was Tsigo's gasping, "Don't kill the *kanai*." Koyban had no time to resent the insult before the second kick ended his hearing anything.

Outside, the evening rains were starting. The weather had lifted enough to speed up casevac from the University camp and let Parkes fly in from Advance Camp One to be with Jean Grant. He couldn't stay long, because he was now the quick-reaction reserve for the Command Group, likely to be thrown in at the next trouble spot. However, "debriefing" Jean Grant was a plausible excuse for spending some time privately with her.

"You look like you've been to the wars," was the first thing he could think of.

"Or the wars came after me," she replied. "I didn't think they would. If I had, Alexis would be alive now, and—"

"Jean, it's easy to punish yourself for . . . using your best judgment and still having somebody under you get killed. Every soldier goes through it the first time he leads a squad in combat."

"That doesn't make it any easier, does it?"

The intensity of her face and voice would have forced him to be honest, even if he hadn't wanted to be. That was the only way to go with Jean. Neither of them expected more than a pleasant affair, but Parkes had learned the hard way that even affairs wouldn't stay pleasant without work.

"No, it doesn't make it any easier. Not the first time, not the hundredth. All I'm saying is that it can be lived with, or all combat officers and N.C.O.'s would be crazy. Or crazier than we already are."

"You're not crazy, John. Weird, maybe. A little fey, almost certainly. But not crazy."

She held out her arms, and he gripped her hands gently. That was as far as he felt like going. The right side of her head, her right arm, and right leg had all been sprayed, sealed, and bandaged, after having about a dozen grenade fragments dug out of them.

"Jean, you may not want to talk about it. But I—we'd like to know what was wrong with Alexis Werbel. If you know yourself, that is. The medics said she shouldn't have died of her wounds, particularly since you managed to get a tourniquet on her leg."

"It's . . . as if she didn't want to live, is that what they're saying?"

Parkes nodded, suddenly sure that Jean had the answer, and equally sure he was going to be sorry he'd asked for it.

"She didn't. You see, John, she killed her father, the night of the attack. He was going to join the terrorists, to establish communications between them and somebody called the Game Master. She—John, what is it?"

Briefly, the little cubicle danced around Parkes. He forced himself not to stare at Jean like a frog staring at an unbelievably succulent fly.

"Did she leave anything in writing, or is this just . . . ?"

"She told me to look under the bottom of her green footlocker." Grant reached inside her hospital gown and undershirt and pulled out a wafer-thin white packet four centimeters square. "She said the code was File Minotaur. At least that's what I thought it was. It was the last thing she said before she passed out."

"Jean, I'm going to get a secure viewer. It's breaking a whole bunch of regulations, but I think we'd better read this over together before passing it on."

She threw both arms around him, wincing at the pain but kissing him at the same time. Parkes kissed her back, then stood up.

"I shouldn't be more than fifteen, twenty minutes if I can find anything at all."

• • •

He was back in a minute less than his minimum predicted time. The first officer he'd found was Dr. Laughton, which let him jump the whole chain of command. Laughton was the most civilian-minded officer he'd ever known who could still function in the field with a Company Group. She'd also been around Fourteen long enough to know what it meant when Sergeant Major Parkes appeared with a face like one of the Horsemen of the Apocalypse and asked for something.

The disk clicked into place, the screen lit up, and Parkes's fingers danced over the keys. FILE MINOTAUR flashed on the screen, then:

This is the confession of Alexis Miriam Werbel, of why she murdered her father, Julius Werbel. He was an agent of the Game Master—

Grant gasped. Parkes swallowed and watched the words march past in grim array. When they told of Werbel's plans to make the Mountaineer-backed terrorists the Game Master's agents on Greenhouse, Parkes found his voice.

"Jean, we could both do ten Standard Years on Davout for accessing this stuff. You haven't any clearance at all, and I don't think they give Sergeant Majors a clearance for anything this hot. It's 'Burn while reading,' at least."

"I hope so. If it stays secret, there won't be scandal following Alexis to the grave."

"Not to mention keeping the Game Master from knowing—did Alexis have any family?"

"Her parents were divorced when she was six. She was an only child. She—John, her father was everything she had in the world. And she k-k-killed—"

She broke down completely at that point, and Parkes knew his own eyes weren't dry. He held her as closely as he dared, knowing that it helped both of them not to be alone now.

He also couldn't help remembering the Durgin twins from his high school. Keith and Sam were as close as two fingers of the same hand growing up. After leaving school they went separate ways. Keith started on a drinking problem, Sam started as a rookie on the county police. One night Keith was driving drunk, ran down a boy on a bicycle, and tried to escape.

It was Sam Durgin who arrested his brother, subdued him, and testified at the trial. It was Sam Durgin's evidence that persuaded

the jury to sentence Keith Durgin to death. It might have been
Sam Durgin on duty at the prison the day of Keith's execution, if
he hadn't resigned from the force a week before. Where he was
now, or even whether he was alive, nobody knew.

Alexis Werbel had found a more complete solution to a far
worse problem. Maybe she was the luckiest person on Greenhouse tonight. It was easy to quote the old Foreign Legion motto,
to yourself or people you thought needed encouragement:

"You can live down anything except death."

As you got older, it wasn't always as easy to believe it.

Tsigo M'no Churaf turned away from the blanket-shrouded
corpse of Koyban M'no Shreen. The movement sent sharp pains
through strained muscles and joints. He'd proved that he was still
fit for hand-to-hand combat, in spite of Kilaa's doubts. He also
had to admit that there was reason in her doubts. The next time
he fought barehanded against someone as young and fit as Koyban, he might not escape with nothing worse than aches and
pains.

"What do we do with him now?" said Kufsa M'ni Tersa.
She'd earned herself a good name tonight, stunning Koyban and
then acting as scribe after he began to confess. The second was
the harder of the two tasks. By the time Koyban confessed, he
had been screaming so long that he had little voice left.

Or trying to scream. They'd had to gag him tightly, lest his
screams attract human attention. The Peace Forcers might have
understood even while they disapproved. Their ways of war were
not the ways of the People, but they did not think theirs were the
only ways in all the worlds.

The militia were another story, wearying to tell or even think
about. They found it hard to believe well of any of the People.
Had they come upon Koyban's interrogation, they would doubtless have believed he was an innocent victim, being tortured to
hide the tracks of the real killer.

Tsigo spat into the mud at the thought of the militia.

"That is all he is worth, true," said Kufsa. She sounded wear-
isomely like Kilaa. "Yet more must be done. What shall it be?"

"We will bury him two *demashirhi* into the jungle. All except
for his head. That we will bear to the bondkin of Ribon M'no
Berus. They have the best claim to it. If they yield that claim to
us, then we will bear it to the Peace Force along with your scrib-
ings."

Kufsa spread her hands. "Honorable in the best old way. But

to carry the head through militia-ridden lands . . . ? The Shedni-te Jean M'ni Grant would doubtless help, but is she even alive?"

"All the more reason to make the journey, Kufsa. If Jean M'ni Grant is dead, we must earn the right to go with the Peace Force when they strike the nest of *kanai*. We owe her their blood, shed with our own hands."

Tsigo drew his *cheeness*. Tonight its name in human speech, "debt-payer," seemed more fit than usual. "This is not a matter for argument, Kufsa," he said, kneeling by the body. "It is a matter of what must be done."

"Yes, Tsigo," said Kufsa. The slightly mocking note once more reminded him of Kilaa.

"Any sign of dawn yet?" asked Vela.

Parkes shook his head as he sat down. It would have taken too much effort to speak. Automatically he unslung his rifle and checked the bore, unhooked his webbing and hung it over the back of the chair, and undid his boots to check his feet for blisters or fungus infections.

Vela waited until Parkes was done, then reached into his desk drawer and pulled out a flask. "Carlos Quinto, fifteen-year old. Help yourself."

Two swigs restored Parkes's powers of speech, if not his energy. He capped the flask and handed it back. "It's stopped raining, if that helps."

"Some. How's Jean Grant?"

"Hurting, but she was asleep when I left her. Dr. Laughton's practically sitting by her bed. Our other people aren't seriously hurt except for Mackenzie, and she's stabilized. Laughton will operate tomorrow."

"What about the militia casualties?"

"An ambulance arrived with a major in charge while I was sitting with Jeannie—with Professor Grant. He took all the wounded, including the two Laughton said shouldn't be moved."

Vela said something that Parkes suspected questioned the major's ancestry. "Gillam's body too?"

"Of course."

"What the hell did those *hijos de putas* think we were going to do with him? Boil him up for soup for the People?"

"I suppose they've got some right to be pissed—"

"Pissed? They're damned lucky they lost only one dead and six hurt. After they'd winged four of ours, I'd have a clear conscience about sending the whole damned outpost section back in bodysacks!"

Vela sounded as if the brandy flask had been emptied at least once already tonight. Not that Parkes blamed the major, but Voorhis had bunked up without telling him about Vela's mood. If Voorhis was carrying his suspicion of Parkes to the point of depriving him of essential if unofficial intelligence—well, he could have picked quite a few better times for it.

Alexis Werbel's confession was a pretty good jolt to the circuits all by itself. Throw in the firefight the militia outpost caused when they panicked, and its one dead and ten wounded, and there was going to be hell to pay by dinnertime today.

At least *Artemis* should be arriving any day with General Duchamp. Then the Peace Force would have a big gun to turn on any locals who made too much trouble. Bigger than Haskins, and one that would *shoot* too.

Abruptly Vela stood up. "Sergeant Major, I've got some bad news for you. *Artemis* hit orbit an hour ago and her first shuttle is coming down. She's got Colonel Lindholm aboard, but Duchamp's still on Union."

"Oh, shit."

"And we're in it." Vela pulled out the flask again; they both drank.

There goes our big gun, thought Parkes. Now what?

Maybe Voorhis hadn't been so sloppy after all. He'd probably needed his sleep, and hit his bunk just before this news arrived. If that was what had Vela sweating—

"Lindholm either doesn't know or won't say why Duchamp was held up. I've served with her; I know she'll do what she can. Let's hope that's enough."

Parkes had also known Duchamp's famous chief of staff from Bifrost. She probably knew what was holding up Duchamp, but wouldn't discuss it except face to face. She almost certainly would do what she could to keep things from getting out of hand, but she'd still be facing a superior officer. Duchamp would have been facing a junior.

Not to mention that Duchamp just might have given Lindholm orders not to stick her neck out this time. It was strongly rumored that Duchamp badly wanted a third star, which meant a division command. His best chance for one of those rare slots was having Lindholm still in tow, with few enemies and no court-martials to her credit.

Group Fourteen and 31 Squadron had a bigger gun than they'd

had before. It might not be big enough, and it might not fire at
all.

"Sergeant Major. Lindholm, the C.O., Commander Dubignon
from *Ark*, Forbes-Brandon, and I will be meeting with Haskins
and the ambassador tomorrow evening. We want to work out
plans for calming things down generally, protecting the homesteaders, and taking the offensive.

"I'd feel better with answers to a couple of questions. I'm not
ordering you to answer either one. I'm just relying on your good
judgment.

"First question: how reliable is Alexis Werbel's confession?
It's the only evidence we have that the Game Master might have
stuck his finger into the pie."

"I know."

*Stall for time, wonder how Voorhis is going to cope with being
cut out of the circuit—oh, to hell with Voorhis! It's not his fault
you and Dozer have been tight for ten years, or that you're
sleeping with Jeannie! Answer the man and then get some sleep
yourself!*

"Professor Grant trusted Alexis and believes she's telling the
truth. Professor Grant is capable of making mistakes about people. I don't think she'd fail to recognize a pathological liar or a
planted piece of disinformation. That's as far as I can go."

"Thank you. And thank Professor Grant the next time you talk
to her. We owe her one already, and I have a feeling we're going
to owe her more before this is over.

"Second question. This is *really* one you don't need to answer
if you don't think the time is right. You and . . . certain other
officers and N.C.O.'s have been arranging for some extra air
support for the Group. Nonorganic support. Correct?"

*Just the kind of question it's always fun to answer when you
haven't had any sleep for thirty-six hours.* "May I ask how you
learned, sir?"

"When I think you need to know, I'll tell you without your
asking. In return, will you do one thing?"

"What, sir?"

"Keep your arrangements quiet for the time being, but go on
making them. My guts are telling me two things. One is that I've
drunk too much brandy on an empty stomach. The other is that
we may need your underground air support procurement system
very badly very soon. Dismissed."

17 ══════

THE PARTITIONS IN the HQ building were thin, and the
X.O.'s office wasn't one of the few rooms with additional sound-
proofing. Parkes could hear enough of Vela's argument with Colonel Macomber of the Utopian Militia to have a pretty good
notion of the parts he couldn't hear. Vela was enjoying himself,
maybe too much.

One of the Macomber's men had been killed and six wounded.
It was mostly their own damned fault and that of the people who
hadn't trained them properly, including their colonel. Still, asking
the man to admit that to Vela might be asking a little too
much. . . .

"Colonel, I will *not* authorize your investigators to enter this
camp or interrogate any of our men. I have no authority to do so
without orders from Colonel MacLean or General Haskins."

Mutter, mutter, mutter from Macomber. It was a pity he was
doing a better job of keeping his temper or at least keeping his
voice down than Vela. Parkes had a feeling that things were about
to happen that it would be useful for him to hear clearly. Guesses
about what must have been said weren't evidence you could offer
under oath at a court-martial.

Vela's voice rose again. "That accusation against Colonel
MacLean is outrageous. He has gone to Thomasport to confer
with General Haskins. One of the subjects of their conference is
an impartial investigation of the incident we are discussing. Colonel MacLean is not opposed to seeing justice done, sir. He is only
opposed to a witchhunt."

Mutter, mutter.

"Sir, I will maintain that description of what you are proposing under any circumstances, including a court-martial."

Vela wasn't bluffing. From the long period of inaudible mut-
terings that followed, Macomber must have realized it too. With

134

nothing to listen to, Parkes turned his attention to the big wall map in the guardroom. There was no such thing as looking at a map too often. It might be the tenth or the twentieth time before it told you what you wanted to know. If you didn't keep looking, you'd never learn at all.

The main land feature of the Peace Force Area of Operations on Greenhouse was the Sierra del Sur. On the contoured map it resembled a four-armed starfish, a *shuriken,* or—to Parkes's jaundiced eye—an old-fashioned swastika. Yes, a swastika, tilted about forty-five degrees to the east of true north.

The northwestern and southwestern arms of the swastika were only marginally important for P.F. operations. The southwestern arm (known to the Utopians as the Mountains of Steel) was the major natural barrier to the railroad; the tunnel was the key to penetrating it. Once through the Mountains of Steel, the railroad looped away, across the Altiplano and down toward the sea to the west. It wound through the foothills at the seaward end of the northwestern arm and on into the heartland of the Republic.

The northeastern and southeastern arms were more critical. The Survivors' Caves were on the northeastern arm, just above the center of the swastika. The northeastern arm ran off into impenetrable jungle which stretched a thousand kilometers until the land began to rise into the Sierra del Norte.

The southeastern arm created a solid barrier to a land approach to the caves except by the Academy River and Henry Canyon. Vertis approaching the Survivors' Caves from the south would have to either zigzag through the valleys or come over the crests, easily detected and perhaps easily hit. Vertis approaching from the east would first have to swing clear around the end of the southeastern arm, cutting payload or else needing a secure L.Z. en route for refueling. They would also be detectable from both the southeastern and northeastern arms as they approached the Caves.

Parkes knew he would very much like it if the Caves turned out to be of no interest to anyone except the University archeologists. He also knew that all the evidence was against this easy way out. The Wise One seldom arranged the Universe in such a way as to make tactical problems so conveniently simple.

The argument in the office reached audibility again. Some of the bad temper seemed to have faded. At least Macomber wasn't accusing MacLean of deliberately making himself unavailable in order to sabotage an investigation of the P.F.-Militia fight. Parkes still wished that MacLean instead of Vela could have taken Macomber. MacLean had a little bit more rank and much more control of his temper where Hrothmi were concerned, even if he would have been just as stubborn—

"Sergeant of the Guard! Sergeant of the Guard! Intruder alert!"

The alarm gong instantly reinforced Corporal Sykes's frantic voice.

Parkes vaulted over his desk to retrieve his rifle, spraying papers. He vaulted back, knocking the desk's terminal to the floor. With his rifle at high port, he charged out the door so fast that he nearly fell over someone kneeling on the doorstep.

Skidding to a stop, Parkes saw that the someone was an elderly Hrothmi woman. She was kneeling in the posture of a supplicant to a superior who was obliged by law and custom to hear her petition. What that petition might be, Parkes had no idea and for the moment didn't care. He was facing other, more urgent matters.

Sykes and the two sentries had their rifles leveled at a squad of militia from the HQ outpost. The militia had their rifles leveled at six Hrothmi. For the moment the Hrothmi were standing with their arms out and hands spread, their shotguns slung and their pistols holstered. From their bristling ruffs and stiff ears, Parkes knew it wouldn't take much to make them lose control. With the militia already having the drop on them, the result would be a massacre.

"Corporal Sykes. Report!"

"Sergeant Major, we are trying to arrest these Hrothmi on suspicion of—" began a man at the rear of the militia squad. Parkes started to tell him what to do with that idea, then noticed he was wearing captain's bars.

"Sir, with all due respect, I would prefer to hear Corporal Sykes first, sir."

"Sergeant Major—"

"Sir, this case is now under Peace Force jurisdiction. I am obliged by Standing Orders to hear Corporal Sykes first."

Sykes took his cue and launched into his report before the captain could open his mouth again. "Sir, these Hrothmi came to the HQ gate five minutes ago. They asked to see the C.O. I told them that he was unavailable and asked their business. The leader"—he pointed at a Hrothmi Parkes recognized as Tsigo M'no Churaf—"said it was a matter of a blood-debt they had paid."

Sykes swallowed. "I asked them to explain. The leader

showed me a . . . severed Hrothmi head. He said it was the head of the terr who killed Alexis Werbel."

"He's lying, of course," said the captain.

"*Who* is lying, sir?" said Parkes. He drew his sidearm to add weight to his rifle. The captain looked at both, then realized he'd been ambiguous when he needed to be explicit.

"This . . . Hrothmi," said the captain, pointing at Tsigo. "He's obviously a leader of the terrorists. That head belongs to some innocent homesteader they've killed to cover their tracks. We have to arrest them, interrogate them, and find out who—"

"Sir, I would not advise making such arrests in a Peace Force camp. If you would care to wait a minute, I will guarantee that these Hrothmi will not leave the camp while I call Major Vela. He is Acting—"

"That damned furballer!" snapped the captain.

The captain's corporeal existence nearly ended in the next moment. It would have ended, except that Parkes grabbed Sykes and Tsigo grabbed one of the guards. She was a rather small woman, and he lifted her clean off her feet. Setting her down with a muttered apology, he turned to the captain.

"*Kukos,* captain over soapboilers—if you wish to die, have both the courtesy and the courage to ask me first."

With a sudden attack of prudence, the captain neither spoke nor moved. Parkes was still making mental bets on how many of the people here would be alive in another two minutes, when Major Vela came out. He took one look at the scene and stopped so abruptly that Colonel Macomber bumped into him from the rear.

"Sergeant Major, I think an explanation is in order."

Parkes nodded to Sykes. This time the corporal went through his explanation too fast to let anyone interrupt. The captain seemed to have lost the impulse to do so, and maybe the power of speech as well. Colonel Macomber, on the other hand, was the color of a ripe clubfruit by the time Sykes was finished.

"Major Vela! Your men are interfering with mine in a matter clearly within my jurisdiction. I must, respectfully, request that these Hrothmi be released into my custody for proper investigation of their crimes—"

Vela made a short, explicit suggestion for disposing of Colonel Macomber's custody over Hrothmi or anybody else. The colonel's face couldn't get any redder; instead he started to gasp. This let Vela continue.

"Sir, by my authority as Acting C.O. of Group Fourteen and

Senior Peace Force officer present, I declare that these People are under Peace Force Protective Custody until further notice. I am prepared to make an exception for this woman"—with a look toward the still-kneeling figure—"for reasons of health or family duties."

"*Jagrun-te* Vela," said Tsigo. "The lady is the bond of Ribon M'no Berus, murdered by the traitor Koyban. She has the greatest reason of any of us to wish to aid the Peace Force. Let her stay among you, and we shall see to her care."

Parkes now understood Hrothmi tones and expressions enough to realize what Tsigo hadn't wanted to put into words. Translated, it went:

"The captain is a little man. He has been humiliated. He wants vengeance. He won't dare take it on the Peace Force, but he might take it on Ribon's widow. She needs your protection more than any of us."

Vela nodded. "As you wish."

"Major—" began Macomber. Vela interrupted him by drawing his own sidearm.

"Colonel Macomber, you and your men have had the privilege of entering Peace Force territory on simple presentation of ID's, without stating your business. Today you have abused that privilege, harassing Peace Force sentries on duty and threatening persons in Peace Force custody.

"Under the authority of Article Ninety-two of the Peace Force Covenant, I declare that such access is a danger to Planetary Union security. I therefore revoke the right of such access, effective on all posts of Company Group Fourteen as of one minute from now."

Vela grinned like a wolf seeing a fat lamb within easy reach. "That means, Colonel Macomber, that if you and your bullyboys aren't out of this camp in one minute, I can arrest the whole bunch of you. If you resist arrest, I can use lethal force to subdue you."

"You wouldn't dare!"

"Colonel, you may think I'm bluffing. How much are you willing to bet on that notion?"

Macomber's higher faculties still seemed to be functioning well enough to let him make a threat assessment. The correct conclusion showed on his face as plainly as if it had been a monitor screen: Vela wasn't bluffing.

"You'll hear about this again, Major," said Macomber as he turned toward the gate.

"I sincerely hope so, Colonel," was the reply. "Corruption, bigotry, and poor training on this scale are a matter that deserves investigation at the Planetary Union level. I will be very happy if an opportunity arises to testify before an investigating committee."

The final exchange didn't accelerate the militia retreat into a rout, but did keep it from slowing down. The sentries at the gate presented arms as the militiamen marched out, turned right, and vanished from Parkes's view.

Major Vela sat down so abruptly that Ribon's widow left off her supplication and came over to him to see if he needed help. He thanked her politely for her concern and put his head in his hands.

Parkes gave Vela the time he alone needed by inspecting both the HQ and gate sentries. When he returned to Vela, the major was sitting up.

"Parkes, I will testify that you were only obeying my orders throughout. That should take most of the heat off you."

"If there is any heat, sir. The C.O.—"

"Will certainly do his best, I agree. However, eagles can do only so much when stars decide to go nova. If Haskins doesn't produce at least a major flare over this, I'll eat my holster raw."

"Likely enough, sir. But things could be worse. Duchamp could be dead. The Mountaineers could be really involved. We could have got to the shooting point just now, as well as three nights ago. Considering how—"

"Sergeant Major."

"Sir?"

"Have you ever heard of Job's Comforters?"

"Yes, sir."

"Then shut the hell up!"

"Yes, sir."

18

FORBES-BRANDON REMEMBERED being taught that fitness improved the flow of oxygen to the brain. General Haskins seemed to cast a few doubts on this received wisdom.

Although she was fortunate with her metabolism, Forbes-Brandon had still passed up a lot of good meals in the name of fitness. Had she denied herself pleasure to no purpose? She remembered the tag of an old bit of verse:

> For when your life is spent and sun has set
> 'Tis easier to repent than to regret.

She also reminded herself that this grumpiness was her own form of being unsettled by the whole situation. She wished she could be as impassive as Ambassador Xia or Commander Dubignon.

Another silly thought. Xia had nothing to fear from Haskins. Dubignon had very little, as long as she carried out Captain Cooper's orders. Forbes-Brandon didn't know exactly what those orders were; she'd heard rumors that Cooper wanted to stay out from between Haskins and Group Fourteen. Maybe he had good and sufficient reasons; maybe he was just rationalizing his fairly obvious hunger for an admiral's stars.

In any case, orders or no orders, Marie Dubignon wasn't going to be down on the ground with Group Fourteen, calling in supply drops and supporting fires. Her arse wouldn't be on the line either physically or legally. Serenity and detachment came easily under those circumstances.

Forbes-Brandon ignored the sweat trickling down her neck and forced her attention back to Colonel MacLean's narrative.

"... ordered to Camp Kennedy, formerly Advanced Base One. There Major Vela will command our air-assault force against the Survivors' Caves. That force will be essentially our Third Company, reinforced by two platoons of Kabuele company and a Naval Liaison team, moved in two waves. During the movement of each wave, a section of fighters from 31 Squadron will make a sweep of the Cordillera del Sur to detect any enemy radar net or anti-air capabilities. If detected, the rest of the Fighter Flight will be on call for attack."

Haskins frowned. "That involves air operations close to the border of the Republic. My intelligence assessments are that they offer no anti-air threat and would not allow one to be based in their territory."

"Sir, with your permission?" said Forbes-Brandon. MacLean nodded. "I can't offer a formal assessment that contradicts yours." *At least not without getting Lieutenant Tegen in trouble he doesn't deserve.* "But I do want to emphasize something all of us who went to the Republic felt very strongly."

"Yes?" Haskins didn't bother to hide his impatience with even implicit argument from a Navy two-striper.

"The Republic has ties to the terrorists. Or at least some elements in their military do. If they had a chance to damage the Peace Force without any detectable involvement, I believe they would take it."

"Quite possibly," said Haskins. "But is there any covert method of opposing an air assault? One that would justify risking a violation of the Republic's borders? Major Hughes, Captain Dallin. Your assessments, please."

The X.O. of 31 Squadron nodded to Dallin. She frowned. "There are possibilities, using advanced basing of combat vertis and radar stations. Most options that we couldn't detect from *Ark Royal* would give only a marginal capability against an air assault operation."

Hughes nodded. Commander Dubignon looked complacent at the pat on the back to her ship. Forbes-Brandon refrained from looking at either pilot. Nobody who didn't know Dallin well could tell that she'd just told what she believed to be a string of lies. Haskins, please God, didn't know Dallin.

Apparently he didn't. "All right. I'll authorize fighter sweeps over the Survivors' Caves and along the Mountains of Steel. That should turn up anything the Mountaineers may have lurking close enough to do us harm. Fair enough, Colonel MacLean?"

Forbes-Brandon noticed the hesitation in MacLean and the pause before his "Yes, sir." She wasn't surprised, either. Haskins had very neatly put MacLean in a cleft stick. MacLean could cancel the operation because of insufficient air support; Haskins wouldn't order him to push it through regardless.

But if the operation was cancelled, there'd be no further reason for keeping Major Vela out at Camp Kennedy. Sooner rather than later, he'd have to be hauled back to face the music over the confrontation with the Utopian militia. From the few notes Forbes-Brandon had heard, that music sounded rather like the overture to a legal lynching—one that might be pushed through before General Duchamp arrived.

As long as the assault on the Survivors' Caves was on, Vela couldn't be spared. He would also have a chance to distinguish himself so much that this could be waved in the face of the militia. Take that away, and the major would be vulnerable.

Of course, that would also leave Group Fourteen even more underofficered than usual. Then MacLean could always force matters to where Haskins would have to relieve him of command and take over the Group himself. That would wreck the Group, though. Vela would be the first person to refuse to have that price paid for his safety.

Not to mention that Haskins might be shrewd enough to avoid such a confrontation. Taking the Group or putting one of his staff in command would be sticking his neck out far enough for Duchamp to chop it off at will. Haskins had based his career on conscientious attention to detail and minimal risk-taking. He wasn't likely to change now that he was nearly sixty, past hope of further promotion, and hoping only to end his last field assignment without any trouble or black marks.

Haskins turned to the ambassador. "Your Excellency, the political situation is really your province. If your assessment differs from mine . . ."

Xia shook his neat bald head. "No, it does not. At least not in any critical aspects. I have complete confidence in Mediator Goff.

"However, I would also suggest that he is not a complete substitute for an ambassador and staff in the Republica de las Montañas. This is not a situation that we can hope to change soon enough to affect Peace Force operations in support of the railroad. I would like to confer with Mr. Goff as soon as he returns from the Republic. How soon will that be, Colonel?"

"His orders were discretionary, Your Excellency. But I could have him back within three days without affecting his mission or making the Mountaineers suspect anything."

"Very good. In the meantime, I would like a list of his contacts in Barron, Allison, & McNeil. With the general's permission, I would also like the assistance of Colonel Lindholm in following up Mr. Goff's work there."

Now it was Haskins's turn to look discomfited, a sight Forbes-Brandon found distinctly gratifying. He could refuse to allow Lindholm to work with the ambassador, an arrangement that would certainly let the colonel do a good deal of preliminary spadework for General Duchamp. He would also be throwing down the gauntlet to the ambassador, who might then have a plausible case of "noncooperation" to raise against Haskins.

Haskins would then be in almost as much trouble as Major Vela. Not perhaps in the same danger of being arrested and court-martialed, but certainly in grave danger of ending his career under the kind of cloud he feared most.

"You are assigned to the ambassador until further notice," said Haskins. Colonel Lindholm smiled. "Ladies and gentlemen, I think that about finishes our business for this evening. I imagine you would like to get back to your units, so I won't issue dinner invitations. Instead, I'll just say 'Good hunting'."

"Thank you, sir," said MacLean, and turned toward the door. The rest followed him out of the office in silence.

Outside, they gathered around a bench in the park beside the Residency. Commander Dubignon made polite farewells and left. She had an even stronger air than before of wishing to dissociate herself from the proceedings. Colonel Lindholm took Colonel MacLean aside for a few minutes, then joined the ambassador when he came out and left in his car.

With both women gone, Forbes-Brandon found herself breathing more easily. Lindholm's presence was simply a little too overpowering. Her service nickname was "The Valkyrie," and she resembled a Nordic version of Dozer di Leone, only taller, broader, and (in spite of her two doctorates) probably even fitter.

As for Dubignon, the less the commander saw of Forbes-Brandon's loyalty to Group Fourteen, the better. It wouldn't affect whatever decision Cooper had taken about staying out from between Haskins and his Embarked Group. It would only affect Forbes-Brandon's own Efficiency Report.

Somewhat to her surprise, she realized that she wasn't going to lose much sleep over that. Two years ago it would have been different. What had happened in the meantime, other than assignment to Group Fourteen and maybe Hugo Opperman?

She tabled the question as Colonel MacLean returned with the air of a man about to unburden himself.

"Gather 'round, people," he said, putting on his beret. "Now, I won't ask for details, particularly of your methods and who helped. But I do need to know—how successful have you been in arranging for backup air assets?"

He was looking from Dallin to Hughes to Forbes-Brandon, until the two women let Hughes speak. "We can arrange to 'disable' up to three heavy and three light vertis for two days without leaving too many tracks. Beyond two days, somebody's damned well certain to get suspicious, but we're prepared to run the risks—"

MacLean held up a hand. "Thank you. I appreciate the offer, but it may not be necessary. Now that we know how many and for how long, the next question is where?"

It was Forbes-Brandon's turn. "Camp Kennedy is a little public. When the balloon goes up, everybody and their Aunt Eleanor will becoming through. It's been suggested that we set up a staging base on the north slope of the southwestern arm of the Sierra. That would be a good place to put the vertis, and a hard one for anybody to stumble on."

"It would also give us a fueling stop and a second possible approach route to the Survivors' Caves," said MacLean. "Good idea, Lieutenant."

"Thank you, sir, but I can't really take that much credit for it. It was Sergeant Major Parkes who suggested it. He wanted to know if he should arrange for the extra technical people such a base would need." It was nice to be able to pay her debt to Parkes by telling the absolute truth.

MacLean muttered something that sounded like "the next time Parkes makes a suggestion like that, he's bloody well going to take that commission." Then he looked at Dallin and Hughes for confirmation, saw it, and looked back at Forbes-Brandon.

"All right, Lieutenant. I'm sure there's enough credit to go around. But will there be enough support for *Ark* for such a base? Not just fuel drops, but tactical fire support if somebody we can simply shoot stumbles on it?"

Answering that question was a long way down on Forbes-Brandon's list of things she wanted to do. At the moment the list was headed by going to bed with Hugo Opperman. But MacLean would have had to be awesomely stupid not to notice Commander Dubignon's manner.

Forbes-Brandon nodded.

"You're sure, knowing what might be involved?"

"That's why I'm sure, Colonel. Captain Cooper won't do anything like launching an illegal fighter sweep along the border. Just as certainly, he'll launch everything but his spare undershorts if part of the Group is in real trouble. He's only on Haskins's side because Duchamp isn't here, and he's not on the Mountaineers' side at all."

"That confirms my judgment of Captain Cooper. Incidentally, we may have to wait a bit longer than we'd like for General Duchamp. According to Lindholm, P.F. Command didn't realize how fast things might get bad. They held him back to travel with the rest of his staff and a Security Company aboard *Bellerophon*."

"Piss on the Security Company," said Hughes bluntly. "Captain, I think it's time to offer our ace in the hole."

"Right," said Dallin. "Major Hughes and I were both pilots in Project Tollhouse a few years ago."

"The air-combat-capable light vertis?"

"Yes. We both logged about three hundred hours in Tollhouse-fitted lights." Not to mention a respectable number of hours in bed, Forbes-Brandon suspected.

"Right. And 31 Squadron has two complete Tollhouse kits on the strength. Rockets, bombs, guns, racks, sights, software, the works. No armor, but we can fly in battle dress—"

"'We'?"

"Captain Dallin's the only other Tollhouse-qualified pilot who could really be trusted."

"Captain, I must admire your ingenuity," said MacLean. "If you can't get a transfer to fighters, you'll build your own! That's a compliment, incidentally, not a complaint." Dallin's grin implied she wouldn't have cared either way, as long as she had the prospect of an aerial target in her sights.

"Very well. We'll plan on the basis of having both the advanced base and the Tollhouse vertis available. However, I warn all of you. If you've promised what you can't perform, I won't lift a finger to keep off the J.A.G.'s minions. In fact, I'll stand outside the prison every evening and serenade you with my bagpipes. Unless, of course, I'm in there along with you. . . ."

They all looked into the damp Greenhouse night for a moment, wishing they could look into the future as easily. But then, the first soldier to wish that was probably the first caveman to pick up a club.

19

ABOVE SHIPO THE great jutting overhang of black rock blotted out half the sky. Below him the cliff plunged down two hundred *shirhi* to the treetops. From this height the crawling, unclean jungle of Greenhouse looked as kindly as a well-tended lawn.

Shipo turned to Colonel Limón. "I see why you chose this cave. But why the catapult?" He jerked a hand back into the cave, where a human work gang was laying out cutting tools and attachment bolts for the next section. Five sections and the generator were already in place. Two more and the catapult would be able to hurl a combat-loaded light verti out of the cave mouth at flying speed. Or so Limón said.

"Simple enough, when you consider that we're going to have *Ark Royal*'s sensors looking for us sooner rather than later. That means everything that flies around here has to stay low and slow. You saw how the cargo flights came in?"

"Yes." They'd flown up to the cliff just above the treetops, then climbed to the mouth of the cave and hovered. The work gang thrust out a hook attached to a powerful winch, snagged the slung pod, and reeled it in like a giant fish. It showed much skill all around, but to what purpose?

"That overhang blocks out any sort of sensor from directly overhead. So if we get our vertis down to the treetops whenever they're out from under it, *Ark Royal*'s going to have a first-class headache picking us up.

"Where the catapult comes in is getting the combat vertis out and down fast. The cave's too low overhead to let a combat-loaded Model 203 launch in a hurry, at least in V.T.O. mode. It's too short for them to reach flying speed in S.T.O. mode without booster rockets. That would make too many fumes.

"So what we do is let them run up their engines on the cat,

then fire them off. They go over the edge at full power and near flying speed, make a controlled vertical descent to treetop level, and go about their business."

Shipo believed Limón, even though the colonel spoke as smoothly as a *rihin* trying to make a match with a reluctant bond. The machinery of the Hairless Ones always promised marvels and sometimes performed them. If the catapult and the eight vertis it would hurl into the sky performed as Limón promised, they would aid much in the coming victory.

The victory would mean more in all ways if the People could win it themselves, without so much help from the men and machines of the Hairless Ones. Yet it would also be far less likely, and if won at all, won at a price that would leave the Company a hollow shell, sucked dry and ready to throw on the midden heap.

Oh, Limón had helped as much as if he really did want the Company to win its own victory. The vertis had brought in load after load of weapons and ammunition. No three hundred People had ever faced battle so well-armed.

Indeed, the Company was so well-armed that it might be as dangerous to itself as to the Peace Force. The recruits were the soft spot. With Chabon and Koyban both dead, the Company had lost its best trainer and one of its best leaders. There were some natural leaders among the recruits—the Simas twins stood out. But the recruits would either have to be left out of the fight or else furnished with leaders by weakening the experienced platoons.

So be it. "The greater the odds, the more honorable the battle." Both the People and the Hairless Ones had various sayings that all meant essentially this. For once it would be true.

There was more than honor at stake too. A dream as old as the Alliance was pitting People against the Peace Force and beating them. Such a victory would not be forgotten by anyone of either race or any faction. Its consequences might be great or small. Indeed, even preparing to fight it was something of a leap into a swift river.

Yet if the People could stand against the best the Hairless Ones could put into the field—well, from that day forward the Hairless Ones' power would be a little less firm and their sleep a good deal less easy.

Limón was beckoning him away from the mouth of the cave, back toward the rear. As they passed the work gang, the rock cutters started up with a hiss that turned into a rumble, then into a scream. Dust rose; Shipo held his breath and hurried past the gang as the men pulled on their masks and pulled down their earguards.

Limón led Shipo past the "hangar" for the vertis. Several of them had panels open and parts strewn on the floor. The technicians looked like hunters picking over the best parts of slain beasts.

Fifty *shirhi* beyond the hangar Limón turned right, into a cleft so narrow that Shipo had to squeeze through. Inside the cleft was darkness, until Limón turned on his belt light.

Shipo's hands curled into claws. The cave was no more than seven *shirhi* by five, but its floor was as smooth as glass. In the far wall was a neat round doorway with more blackness beyond it. Limón raised the light so that Shipo could see the equally neat round tunnel leading off to . . .

. . . to places he suddenly found he did not want to know, or even imagine. Involuntarily, he shivered.

"Sorry," said Limón. "The temperature shift from outside is a little sharp. But I wanted to show you this before you went back to Company HQ. I thought it might be a shrine built by some of your People. This cave would be perfect for ammunition storage once we blocked up the tunnel, but if that would be desecrating a religious site . . ."

Shipo smiled at the look Limón gave the tunnel. Did that darkness, and thoughts of what it might hide, make even the polished-armor colonel a trifle uneasy? Then he slapped his hips.

"None of the Company have been here long enough to do that much work. Perhaps there have been People here before, although it looks more like Hair—human work. Your technicians haven't been amusing themselves in their free time, have they?"

"What free time?"

"Ah. Then it would seem to be more of the Survivors' work. Perhaps some of those who did not flee downriver to safety, trying to hide from the jungle." He tried not to shiver again. Compared to what his imagination told him might be lurking in the tunnel, the jungle outside seemed almost friendly.

"All right. We'll use it for the ammunition, then, but try to keep it as intact as possible otherwise. After the fighting's over, we may not need this base anymore. Then we can buy some goodwill by letting archeologists amuse themselves here. The Scotians are a lost cause, I fear, but they are not the only archeologists in the Union."

As they made their way back through the cleft, Shipo wondered if Limón would try to tell the same lie to the archeologists.

Or was it a lie? Shipo himself was no pot digger; perhaps the work was human, but of a kind he did not recognize.

And perhaps both his eyes and his instincts were telling him the truth. They said that no human hands had made that smooth floor, that doorway, or that tunnel. They were the work of Those Who Came Before.

If so, were they the only such work around here? Shipo decided to have a discreet search made, beyond the explored limits in the main caves. It could be passed off as a training exercise for the recruits, if they stayed away from any really dangerous areas.

There was no reason that the archeologists, if and when they came, should owe everything to Colonel Limón.

Parkes munched a ration bar and watched the two work gangs finishing their jobs. One was tying down a camouflage net over a heavy-lift verti. No matter how many other kinds of sensors the tech wizards developed, it was still useful to defeat the Mark I Eyeball.

The other party was sliding a large crate labeled UNIVERSITY OF SCOTIA. ARCHEOLOGICAL EXPEDITION. GREENHOUSE from an S.P. pallet on to the ground. It landed with a thump, making a neat row with the other five similarly-labeled crates.

That was one of Jean Grant's contributions to the assault on the caves. The six crates of "archeological gear" contained two complete Tollhouse kits. Three hours' work by a few skilled people, and the two light vertis already tied down under their own nets would be formidable air-combat machines.

Parkes would have been happier if the professor's contribution had stopped there. She would be in trouble with the University authorities if anyone made a fuss, but she wouldn't be putting her life on the line. She'd insisted that someone with archeological knowledge had to go with the first wave, though. Nobody up to and including MacLean had been able to find a polite way of refusing. Everybody up to and including MacLean suspected that if she was refused impolitely, she had a few extra rounds in her magazine. Such as calling up General Haskins or having Tsigo and Kilaa hijack a verti (she had a pilot's license, although she was probably in no shape to fly) . . .

The shortest of the work gang bent over the crate, studied the readouts, and gave a thumbs-up. The other four PFers sat or lounged, while the shorty ran toward Parkes. Even in the twilight, he recognized Warrant Officer Ohara, chief of maintenance for 31 Squadron.

"Hello, Geisha."

"Greetings, Fruit Merchant. Everything's safely delivered. May your ancestors know dishonor if you misuse it."

"Oh, I thought you were out here to keep an eye on your people, so they wouldn't drop anything on their toes . . ."

Ohara mimed a karate chop at Parkes's throat. "On the contrary. I came out here to make sure your people knew enough to stand clear of a takeoff. I hitched a ride with your Captain Dallin. Does she always fly like that?"

"No, usually she's much hotter. I suspect she was catering to your tender stomach. . . ."

This time Ohara mimed a kick to Parkes's groin, then grinned. "Actually, there's nothing left for me to do back in the rear. People I can trust are plugged in just about everwhere they're needed, and I've covered my tracks pretty thoroughly anyway. Somebody I won't name taught me some interesting variations on faking faults in critical components, in return for not being court-martialed for stealing P.F. property. The only way I'll be detected is if Haskins overrides Hughes and the C.O. and brings in somebody from outside who's smarter than I am."

"That won't be too hard to—okay, that'll be a cold day in hell. But . . . Hughes I understand. Your C.O.'s squared too?"

"I found the thief in her flight when I was her crew chief and she was a first lieutenant. She might not have been bounced out on her ear, but I'm damned sure she wouldn't be any kind of colonel now. She owes me more than she's paid so far. By the way, didn't you have a little misappropriation-of-property trouble yourselves, on Bayard?"

Parkes's gut reaction was to stonewall or lie. His higher faculties stamped on that reaction at once. He owed the Geisha a good deal, and the dead Sergeant Major Hatcher nothing at all. Well, maybe not gossiping to everybody and their aunt, but Ohara wasn't everybody, even if she was aunt to twelve and great-aunt to a couple. She worshipped Murphy and Finagle, like any good tech N.C.O. She was also the daughter and granddaughter of PFers who now tended Shinto shrines on Yamato. No Hrothmi ever took bonds or oaths more seriously.

"Tell me why, and oath of silence?"

"You can take the oath for granted. As to why—we're getting three people with some service on Bayard. They're immigrants, and their service was in the Nouvelle Bretagne Light Brigade—"

"You can breathe easy. Hatcher was a mercenary in the Fourth Empire." Parkes told the grim story of how Group First Hatcher

had been blackmailed into acting as a mole for the Group's enemies, leading to the death of Pat Tyndall and eventually to
Hatcher's suicide. By the time he finished, Ohara was looking
both relieved and angry.

"Damn the Fourth Empire. That sewer *has* to be cleaned out
before we can all sleep easily. Suppose the people behind the
terrs here make an alliance with the Emperor?"

"You know that and I know that. But the Union politicos will
lose more sleep over what the job would cost them over what
might happen if they don't do it."

"Oh well, one can always pray. Thanks for the information.
Would you like me to hold the fort here while you fly back to the
rear for the night?"

That was getting his favor repaid faster and better than he'd
have dreamed possible. If he could catch the last verti out of L.Z.
Terwilliger, he could spend a few hours with Jean, instead of just
shaking hands tomorrow morning as she lifted out of Camp Kennedy. That wouldn't be as good as getting his orders recut so he
could go in with the assault, but MacLean and Vela had both dug
in their heels there.

Besides, that would be undercutting Voorhis so that the man
might be damned near useless. Knocking out the Field First on
the eve of an important operation was *not* what they gave you six
stripes and a torch for doing!

It would still touch a raw spot, letting Jean dodge bullets at the
caves while he dodged bugs at Camp Kennedy, but what the hell,
nobody said caring about somebody made things easier, and a
proper good-bye would help....

"Thanks, Geisha. We can figure out who owes whom and how
much after this is over."

"Split a case of Kirin?"

"You think your head's that hard?"

"I don't corrupt my system with all that fruit."

20

THEY LAY ON the spread-out sleeping bags, finding comfort in closeness in spite of the hot night. Forbes-Brandon felt a hand creeping over her thigh to the base of her spine, then massaging gently. She wriggled happily, ready to give herself to the lesser pleasure until they again had the energy for the greater.

After a couple of minutes Opperman's voice sounded in her ear. "Kate, did you ever try it on a camp cot?"

"Once. I confess I was more curious about whether it was possible than I was about my partner. I'd just started enjoying myself when the cot collapsed. Mmmmm, don't stop."

Opperman didn't. When he'd finished with the base of her spine, he gently tipped her over onto her stomach and straddled her. His hands were skilled, but the pleasure they gave couldn't keep a stray thought out of her mind.

Sergeant Major Parkes had learned massage from a Yamato bath girl. What would *his* hands feel like, if they ever had a similar license to roam over her? The thought lasted just long enough for her to note that she'd labeled it as "improbable" rather than impossible.

Meanwhile, Opperman's hands were removing the last of the tension she'd felt ever since she was invited to be a guest of Kabuele Company's mess at dinner tonight. The major clearly intended to give her and Hugo some time together they might not otherwise have. She'd been grateful, but also of two minds about accepting. Kabuele was just as obviously planning to give his officers a chance to look her over, in the tradition of vetting new officers or officers' affiliates.

She'd remained of two minds, until her X.O., Lieutenant Hale, volunteered to set up the entire Naval Liaison mission. She wouldn't have to do anything but initial a printout and climb on the verti, which she could easily do tomorrow morning. After that Major Vela, with suspicious speed, virtually ordered her to accept the invitation.

Another stray thought rambled through Forbes-Brandon's mind. Had a not-so-little little bird put Lieutenant Hale and Major Vela up to their offers—a bird with a long beaklike nose and the six stripes and torch of a Sergeant Major? If so, she owed Parkes all over again. How to pay?

She could always look after Jean Grant. She could do it better than any other officer on the mission too. There were always long periods when apart from self-defense, the Naval Liaison was something of a fifth leg on the sheep.

This was assuming that the little professor couldn't be talked out of going to the Survivors' Caves, to assess them archeologically before they were fought over. Knowing Grant even slightly, Forbes-Brandon wouldn't have bet a single pair of stockings on her being persuadable on that point. She'd have bet her whole wardrobe that Parkes would be making a valiant effort.

About this time thoughts of Parkes wandered back out of her mind, to be replaced by a sensation that almost distracted her from Opperman's soothing hands. She was hungry.

She rolled to grip one of his hands, pulled it under her, hugged it briefly, then sat up. "Hugo, is there anything to eat nearer than the mess?"

Opperman stared, then laughed. "Kate, you should leave your metabolism to science. When I remember what you got through at dinner—"

"The cooks were certainly flattered. And I've been working up an appetite since. With your help, I might add, so don't wash your hands of the matter."

"I won't. There's a refrigerator in the corner, but I don't recall restocking it in the past couple of days. You'll have to take potluck."

Potluck turned out to be a couple of sausages, cold vegetable pie, and two bottles of beer. They demolished everything. The last sausage they finished off holding it between them and nibbling toward each other from opposite ends.

That ended with a long kiss, and the kiss led onward in a way that pleased Forbes-Brandon immensely, but also surprised her. Not Opperman's energy, either, but her own. This was the first time the extra libido supposed to come on the eve of battle had been more than a theoretical concept to her.

It was too hot for the sweat to dry off or even cool down, so they toweled each other afterward, then lay back, touching but hardly caring if touching led anywhere. Forbes-Brandon saw that Opperman was contemplating her left big toe as if it might hold the secrets of the Grand Galactics, or at least the Survivors' Caves.

"Kate, we've had word from Black Star."

" 'We'?"

"Kabuele Company."

"What kind of word?"

"If we finish our commission on Greenhouse with a satisfactory recommendation from BAM, everybody who wants to can come home. In other words, a conditional but full pardon."

"That's wonderful." *Or was it?* "You're not included in the pardon, are you?"

"How could I be? I'm from Nieutrek, not Black Star. The Volksraad probably wouldn't give me a pardon unless I begged for it. I'm damned if I'll do that."

"So where does that leave you? I suspect that you could apply for a Peace Force commission. Even get it if you were willing to drop rank. I'd certainly offer a recommendation—"

"Could you offer one on relevant skills?"

"Captain Opperman, I am a qualified judge of things besides your bedroom performance. Although I would give that a Superior rating if anyone asked. . . ."

"The Peace Force doesn't appeal to me. One reason: I have a nasty feeling that they may be landing on Nieutrek some year in the not-too-distant future. The closed-immigration policy may have been making the best of a bad deal a century ago. How it will look in another generation, I don't know.

"No, I'm going to stick with freelancing. There are others in the Company who feel the same way, enough to form the cadre of a new Company. Trouble is, the Black Star government may be rethinking the policy of sentencing people to a term as a mercenary.

"What they come up with may be no improvement, but it could cut off the flow of recruits. Besides, a white C.O. of a ninety-eight percent *nieblankie* outfit might not look too pretty. It would probably work, but a lot of potential employers might think it wouldn't. That cuts our market way back from the start.

"No, I was thinking of proposing to some other planet or planets that they try the Black Star route. Send me their square pegs instead of trying to hammer them into round holes.

"Once I've got a trained and experienced company, I'd use that as cadre for a battalion. Once the battalion was fully combat ready, I'd hire out the whole outfit on a long-term contract to some planet or country with a long-term need for light infantry—"

"And with plenty of land to award to veterans? You want to found not just a Foreign Legion, but a new colony?"

"Have you ever been tested for ESP?" She shook her head. "I suppose you'd be wasted in Intelligence. In spite of trying to be there two minutes before everybody else, you're a damned good combat officer.

"But—what I want to ask—has it occurred to you that such a battalion would be a lot more capable with a trained Naval Liaison officer? You might spend most of your time plotting regular artillery fire, but there'd be compensations—"

"Enough to be worth exile from the Union? That's what it would amount to, you know."

"Kate, I'm not stupid. Don't start a fight by implying I am. I know what you'd be giving up. But what if by the time you get those two stars, you're so nearly burned out you can't enjoy them? I imagine you've written off marriage and children, but that could be only part of the price."

She hadn't written off children completely; sound ova were on deposit on New Frontier and had been since she was nineteen. As to the rest—this was the first time she'd been offered a partnership that included a military challenge. After eleven years in uniform she knew that was something she couldn't live without.

For better or worse she had a vocation as a military professional, as much as Major Vela or Sergeant Major Parkes. If she was offered a chance to pursue that vocation without giving up a lot of other things—

No *if* about it. Hugo Opperman wouldn't be making an offer like this if he didn't intend to make good on it, or die trying.

And *that* was a bad thought, on the eve of an operation that could easily turn incredibly hairy between one minute and the next. The limited air support and the large element of leap-into-the-unknown would still have worried her if she'd thought worrying would do any good.

What else she would accept from Hugo Opperman in time was in the hands of God, and she would leave it there. Tonight she would accept his company and his desire, tomorrow his leadership in battle.

She rolled over, then bent one leg so that her foot slipped gently down over his flat stomach, into his groin.

"Hugo, are you in shape to finish that massage?"

Jean Grant took a sip of her malt Scotch and rubbed her bare right leg. The dressings were off and the fragment wounds healing nicely. Any plastic surgery would be minor. Parkes was glad. Jeannie had good legs, even if they didn't have the spectacular length and elegance of the Amazon's.

"Are you trying to tell me that the Survivors' Caves *don't* have any archeological significance?"

Parkes took warning from her tone. "I'm not trying to tell you your business, Jean. Don't insult my intelligence. I'm just wondering if you're the best person for the job—and no, I'm not doubting your professional qualifications either. It's just that a couple of other people could do as well. Hell, even Roger Carey would be all right. There won't be any Hrothmi there, at least on our side."

Grant gave a strangled laugh. "I suppose that's one way of getting rid of Carey. Do you think Major Vela could be trusted not to frag him if he had half a chance of getting away with it?"

Common sense and loyalty to Vela wrestled; common sense won. "He'd probably call Carey a sacrifice to the Judgment Lord. Or don't any of your Hrothmi still practice the sacrificial rites?"

"They don't sacrifice sapient beings anymore. I don't ask about anything else. But seriously, John, this protectiveness of yours is getting annoying. Or is there something else?"

This time the wrestling match pitted honesty against pride, and lasted a lot longer. For years Parkes had shied away from using his life story as an explanation for anything, even though he knew his motives for a military career cast a long shadow. It was somewhat like his ancestors' notion that giving others your true name gave them magical power over you.

Well, maybe Jeannie could be trusted with that power. Certainly he hadn't a hope of persuading her without being frank, and little hope of avoiding a messy end to their friendship.

"There's something else. Are you sure you aren't going to the caves because you feel guilty over Alexis Werbel's death?"

Grant looked ready to throw her glass at him. Parkes got ready to duck, then saw her suddenly start shaking. He reached for her; she gently pushed him away and forced a smile.

"Maybe. But what's wrong with that, if I *am* guilty?"

"Guilt's a bad friend to have at your back in battle. It can make you careless or lead you to the wrong decisions. I've been living with guilt for twenty-odd years. There's not much I don't know about it."

Parkes refilled his glass without adding more ice. "My mother died on the operating table when I was twelve. A woman named Red Willow had been angling after my father for years. She reeled him in almost before my mother's ashes were cold.

"As soon as she had a child of her own by my father, she turned against both me and my sister Louise. My father didn't have . . . what it takes to stand up against her, particularly after she gave him another son.

"By then I was sixteen. I could see that Willow was going to be sure neither me nor Louise got anything but scraps from her own kids' table. That meant I'd have to get away from home and make my own way, then help Louise escape too."

The Peace Force offered what looked like the best way. Twenty-two years later, Parkes was quite sure he'd made a good choice, and Louise probably wouldn't have disagreed.

"She's a Navy lieutenant-commander now. Weapons Officer on *Thunderer*, the last time I heard. *Thunderer*'s mostly on training duty these days, but that makes her job all the more important. She's taking wet-behind-the-ears newlies and turning them into Navy people."

Where he and Louise had always disagreed was over his refusal to take a commission. She said he deserved one; he always said he'd think about it. That was the truth: he thought about it a great deal, and always came to the same answer. In saving Louise, he'd abandoned his father to Red Willow. He should have stayed closer to home and fought in his father's defense, instead of fighting the Union's battles fifty light-years away.

A man who could muck things up like that didn't deserve a commission.

"John," said Grant. "I'm glad you've been honest with me. But . . . the way you told me, it sounds as if you know you've made a mistake, not taking a commission."

Parkes looked at the glass he'd just emptied, then at Grant. The empty glass couldn't account for what he thought he'd just heard Jeannie say.

So she'd said it. Had she told the truth?

"Maybe I did make a mistake. But that just makes my point all the more. Besides, I didn't go around thinking I'd got somebody killed. That's a real mess to deal with when you're trying to deal with people shooting at you."

"Are you sure you haven't got anybody killed by refusing that commission?"

Parkes was as surprised as Grant when his glass shattered in his hand. He looked at his bloody hand and the fragments of glass on the sheet, took a deep breath, then let it out without saying anything. He didn't even want to think about what he might have said if he'd spoken.

Grant used the silence. "John, you're a natural leader. The Peace Force needs all it can get, with as much rank as they can handle. Are you sure that nobody's been killed because some platoon went out under a new second lieutenant when it could have been you leading?"

"You can't ever be sure of that, but—"

"Damn it, John, butting is for goats! You can't be sure either way! And there's one thing I'm sure of—you're going to be offered a commission again. The Peace Force is getting ready for a big expansion."

Parkes knew that Group Fourteen's very existence hinted as much, but what evidence did Jean have? "What makes you think that?"

"My brother Duncan works in the Scotia Ministry of Finance. He's seen the projected Peace Force appropriations. They add up to another eighty thousand people over the next five years, and a sixty percent increase in heavy weapons and air support."

"At least that's the interpretation he has from his director. The director's a retired P.F. colonel, so I should think he isn't just talking to improve the air flow in the office."

"I should think not."

Like his own doubts about the wisdom of refusing the commission, Grant's words had a ring of truth in them. His combat infantryman's sixth sense told him so. This was the first time he'd felt it working off the battlefield, but he couldn't mistake it and wouldn't reject it.

"John, the day's coming when it will be your duty to take a commission." Her tone changed as she saw his expression. "I'm sorry. I'm not your military superior, so maybe it's going too far to define 'duty' for you. . . ."

"Maybe. Maybe not." Parkes knew he was dithering, and suddenly felt a wave of gratitude to Jeannie. She wasn't his military superior, but it was a lot safer to dither in front of her than in front of, say, Colonel MacLean or General Duchamp. Just possibly she'd ensured that when one of them leaned on him, he'd answer like a sensible soldier.

He reached for her again, and this time she didn't pull away as his lips met hers and his hands started stroking their way down her back.

21

SHIPO LEANED OVER Gila's shoulder as her decoder spat the message tape into its basket. The decoder belched and fell silent. Gila handed her captain the tape and reached for her bowl of porridge with her free hand. One of Gila's more memorable qualities was her refusal to miss a meal as long as there was food around that nobody else claimed. The Lifegiver only knew how she kept from becoming fat as a *ryqu*.

Shipo scanned the tape. "They're landing at a good place both for them and for us. This will be a splendid fight."

"How many?" said Major Dozo. He did not presume to read the message over Shipo's shoulder. In the two days he'd been with the Company, such little courtesies had won him much honor. His Hrothmi was vile, but the Judgment Lord would forgive that.

"About one company, mixed Peace Force and Kabuele mercenaries. No vehicles, no heavy weapons or equipment. They're taking positions along a line from 467345 to 50010 in Sector Six." The touch of a button lit up the map. Dozo pointed to a position slightly to the southwest of the line.

"If I might speculate—"

"Please do so."

"There will be a second wave, landing there. The perimeter will enclose a secure base for setting up heavy weapons and geoprobes."

"Indeed, that is my thought as well." Would Major Dozo's courtesy extend to letting a Hrothmi launch the air support into action? Shipo chose boldness.

"At your discretion, I suggest that the air support be used to intercept the second wave." He uttered a silent prayer that Dozo's courtesy would extend to letting him know how the P.F. vertis would be tracked for interception. So far Colonel Limón had said not one word on this by no means trivial matter.

"A wise suggestion. With your permission, *Jagrun-te?*"

"Granted."

Dozo shifted frequencies and punched in a series of coded signals. Coded replies came back within a minute. He smiled.

"They'll have three tankers and four interceptors on cockpit alert in twenty minutes. Then all we need is for the PFers to show themselves high enough for the satellites to pick them up."

Shipo pursed his lips in open admiration. "The air-traffic monitor satellites?"

"Of course. Any military radar powerful enough to track the PFers would be hard to emplace and easy to detect. So we tap into the air-traffic control computer in Cervantes. Our people there squirt the data to Limón, and he launches the strike."

"Isn't that rather slow?"

"So are loaded P.F. vertis. Besides, we don't need really precise tracking. We're not trying to hit the vertis from orbit. Just vector our interceptors into their general area. Each flight has one verti with a podded Model 8-U radar instead of missiles. It will home in the others over the last stage."

"Good fortune and good hunting."

"Thank you. We hope for the second, but we'll probably need the first." Dozo's frustration was evident. The wings on his tunic told why; he was a pilot who thought his place should be with the interceptors.

Shipo turned as Piera M'ni Simas entered, loaded with his equipment. He thanked her, took off his cloak, and began shrugging his way into the armored vest. He was calm, as always when he was committed to battle.

Today he was more than calm. He was rejoicing at the chance to honor Chabon's memory by showing how those *she* had trained did against the Peace Force itself.

Katherine Forbes-Brandon leaned back against a rock and adjusted the straps of her pack. The twenty-five-kilo load had been busily undoing all the work of Hugo's hands ever since she boarded the verti. It would also be at least another hour before she could unburden herself.

When the second wave arrived, the ninety soldiers on the ridge above the Caves would become a hundred eighty, with heavy weapons. The crescent would become a circle, enclosing an area large enough for landing supplies dropped from orbit.

With all-round defense and easy resupply, the hundred eighty could hold forever against anything the Caves could produce.

Unless the Grand Galactics were still there? The ridiculous thought still made her uneasy. She forced herself to look at the surrounding terrain, a tangle of man-high flowering bushes exuding a sweetish odor, mixed with trees and outcroppings of rock. She tried to count different shades of green, and gave up at fourteen. It was good territory for ambushes and bad territory for fast maneuvering on foot. This added up to an advantage for the opposition right now, an advantage for the P.F. when the second wave and its vertis arrived.

Fifteen meters away two privates, one from each unit, squatted beside a black cleft in one of the outcroppings. One firmly gripped a yellow rope snaking down into the cleft, while the other watched a pack and a pile of clothes.

Jean Grant was applying her caving skills to the one entrance they'd found so far. She'd also stripped to her underwear to get through the entrance, drawing a round of largely-male applause.

Good luck to you, Professor, she thought. *Although come to think of it, perhaps finding Parkes is pretty good luck already? Let's hope you haven't used up your quota. . . .*

Twenty meters in the opposite direction Major Vela rose from beside the radio and started signaling with his hands. She read the message—the patrol had found another cave entrance, with signs of recent use.

Forbes-Brandon signaled her acknowledgment, unfolded her map, and pulled out her belt calculator. If she was going to be here for a while, she might as well note the coordinates of every piece of ground in sight large enough to land a cargo pod. Which would also keep her from feeling like a 177-centimeter target, as she always did at this stage of an assault. . . .

Squad Leader Nila M'ni Simas open-palmed Shipo. "Report from Major Dozo, Captain. The second Peace Force wave is being tracked. The interceptors are expected to have targets within fifteen minutes."

"Very good." Now, what was the best course of action for the Company? Strike now, or wait until after the interception?

Strike now. The interception would certainly alert the enemy; their nest-looting patrol might do so even sooner. Even if the interception failed, the second wave would hardly come down straight into an unsecured landing zone under heavy fire. The enemy might not be crippled at once, but he would be fighting divided against an opponent united.

Shipo raised his hand to the two launcher crews. The loader of each one picked up one of the rocket-boosted shells and held it over the muzzle. The gunner knelt, one hand adjusting the angle of the tube and the other poised over the firing button.

"Ten rounds, rapid fire!"

Chabon, these are not the people who killed you, but we will take your blood-price from them regardless!

Two charges kicked the first two shells up out of their tubes. Their *craak!* slammed against Shipo's ears like a blow from a cupped hand.

Forbes-Brandon tried to tug her sweat-soaked battle dress away from her skin. It stuck as if it was glued. The yellow rope leading into the caves jerked three times—Grant's signal to be pulled up. The two guards gripped nylon and started pulling. Forbes-Brandon lurched to her feet and moved to where she could guard the privates while they pulled.

The whistle of shells shattered the humid silence. She needed no shout of "Incoming!" to dive for the ground. She hit a grass-shrouded patch of rock, scraping skin from her cheek and picking up bruises. The whistle turned to a scream, then smoke and earth erupted in a line stretching a hundred meters off to the west.

She counted seven bursts, then the eighth shell landed between her and the C.P. The P.F. private dropped the rope with a yell and clapped both hands to the side of her neck, which was dripping blood.

"Keep pulling!" Forbes-Brandon shouted at the Kabuele man. The shelling might collapse the cave on top of Grant. She'd also be helpless if an infantry attack followed the shells and forced her friends back. The soldier nodded and gripped the rope again, while Forbes-Brandon knelt beside the wounded PFer. A field pack on Private McKee's neck stopped the bleeding, but she'd lost quite a bit already.

"Can you walk?"

"I—uck, yes . . . I think so . . ."

More shells bursting, a little farther off. Professor Grant's head emerged from the cleft. She blinked like a mole who's accidentally tunneled into the light.

"Hurry up, Jean! We've got uninvited—"

Whrooom! A different explosion noise. Forbes-Brandon bit

her lip. A shell had touched off somebody's pack of rockets. The pack's wearer had probably gone up with it.

Grant scrambled out onto the grass, wearing even less than she'd gone down in. She brushed herself off and started pulling on her clothes.

Major Vela loomed up through the smoke, standing as blithely as if a meter of steel surrounded him. "We're going to fall back and regroup around Hobson's Pimple. I've already sent the orders. Captain Opperman's patrol will hold here as rearguard, reinforced by one P.F. squad."

Forges-Brandon nodded jerkily. Vela was describing standard P.F. tactics in this kind of situation—the main body breaks contact with the enemy, aided by a rearguard that may not be considered expendable but stands a good chance of being expended, then open the distance to the enemy enough to give your air and orbital fire support a free hand.

Hobson's Pimple was one of the few natural features in the area already named. It offered good fields of fire in all directions. Even the first wave of the assault could hold it against odds. With their fire, they could control an area large enough to allow supply drops. It was too far from the known cave areas to have been the site for the initial landing, but as a fallback position . . .

It would be a fine place to go, call in supporting fires and supply drops, and wonder if Hugo Opperman was dead.

"Sorry, Lieutenant," said Vela. As far as her ringing ears could tell, he really did sound sorry. "But you and the N.L. gang are *not* expendable. So move it!"

Forbes-Brandon allowed herself ten seconds to feel the ancient dilemma—the mission or your buddy/comrade/lover/etc. Another ten seconds told her that the ancient Greeks must have had it easy—both tactics and love told you to stand shields locked with your lover and win or die with him.

The Sacred Band of Thebes had been dead twenty-six hundred years. A modern battlefield had a different set of rules.

Grant was dressed now, shouldering her pack. The Kabuele private was helping McKee to her feet. Forbes-Brandon shouted the rendezvous to the rest of the N.L. team, then faced west, raised her rifle over her head, and pumped it up and down three times.

"Follow me!"

Shipo signaled to the launcher teams, saw them dropping to
the ground, then lay down himself and pulled out his binoculars.
The rugged ground five hundred *shirhi* ahead leaped closer. He
saw a rocket flame from behind a boulder, bursting at the base of
a tree.

No sign of who had launched the rocket. It must have been
one of the veterans. It would have been best to have all the
rockets in the hands of the veterans, but that would have left
some of the recruit-heavy platoons too weak for safety.

Small-arms fire—P.F. explosive bullets—stitched smoke
across a patch of long grass and weeds. A soldier of the People
rolled out of the grass, writhing and clutching a stomach half
blown away. Shipo forced himself not to imagine the screams.
Well, at least he had the next target for the launchers.

He was calculating the most likely place for the enemy rifle-
men when the sound of an approaching verti made him roll over
and look up. He hoped the movement wouldn't attract attention
—then wanted to jump up and shout.

It was one of the vertis from the support flight, banking
steeply over the ridge. Shipo flogged his memory for the vertis'
radio frequency. The fighting had been so fast and furious since
the Company advanced, that he'd almost forgotten there were
such things as vertis!

Memory flowed. He thumbed the radio controls.

"Guardian to Leaf, Guardian to Leaf. Your target will be
found beyond . . ." He hesitated, then gave coordinates marking
off a line that he hoped was beyond any of his own People. He
hoped it wasn't all the way into the rear of the enemy! Improvised air support was better than none at all, but not wholly safe
in a fast-moving ground battle.

The verti's pilot acknowledged, then gave the code word signaling a successful interception and rolled into his strafing run.
Small-arms fire struck sparks from the armor but missed the
shrouded propellors. The belly gun churned up earth where it hit.
The verti banked to circle for a second run. A Company squad
rose from cover and rushed the tree. One fell but the others over-
ran it in a flurry of close-range firing and hand-to-hand combat.
Another of the People didn't rise, but that was one more P.F.
position taken in fair fight.

Two rockets soared up from the enemy's rear. The verti pilot
continued his circle and dropped flares. One rocket turned to

home on the flares. The other was closing on the verti when the sky overhead turned into a sheet of flame. The explosions made Shipo's ears ring. As the ringing faded, the long rumble of the missiles took its place.

Whether the verti was hit by blast, fragments, or the rockets, Shipo never knew. He only saw it flip over on its back and dive straight into the ground. As he pressed himself into the ground, the explosion of its fuel and ammunition felt like a kick in the ribs.

More explosions overhead. The mother *Ark Royal* had come to the rescue of her children, firing salvoes of air-bursting missiles. It would help the P.F. most if the missiles destroyed the Company, but it would help enough if the Company only had to go to ground.

Shipo started calling the squad leaders. He hadn't expected that he'd have radios down to that level. He hoped that they'd all remembered how to use this unexpected gift. Not to mention knowing where their *jagruni* were!

Over and over he gave the same message: take cover until the missiles stop coming, but move at once when they stop. There won't be anything but a rearguard left. Push past them, and we will catch the humans! All worlds will know then that the People can make the Peace Force run, and keep it running!

MacLean had just finished displaying the revised casualty figures from the second wave when Captain Dallin came in. She took one look at the screen and swore.

"*Both* Dog Able Six and Fox Eagle Four?"

"Six may be salvageable," said MacLean. "But Four exploded in the air. No survivors."

The sweat on Parkes's face wasn't entirely due to the demise of the air-conditioning. Lieutenant Simmel and at least twenty-five of Third Company's people were dead, a dozen more missing or dying. The rest of the second wave was marooned on an insect-ridden sandbar a hundred kilometers from anywhere except possibly the enemy air base.

"Is *Ark* scanning for the enemy radar?" asked Dallin. MacLean glared at her. Parkes felt like smiling. The question proved that he wasn't the only one a trifle jangled by the aerial ambush of the second wave.

"She's launched all the fighters. They'll scan with their E.C.M. gear on the way down. Right now *Ark*'s got her hands full trying to keep the enemy's heads down long enough to let our people on the ridge pull back to a defensible position!"

Dallin walked over to the map, so preoccupied that she forgot to light the cigarette dangling from her lips. Parkes knew some of what she must be thinking: that it was a personal insult to her as a pilot that enemy aircraft had been able to do so much damage. He didn't know whether she was madder at the enemy or at General Haskins, who'd bungled them into this situation. He suspected that Dallin would unload on the enemy a lot of what she would have liked to unload on Haskins. He only hoped she wouldn't earn herself a Wooden Cross in the process—although come to think of it, with her it would probably be a Wooden Star of David . . .

Simmel gone. Vela, the Amazon, Jean Grant, and Opperman all marooned on the ridge. It would be an old, cold world if Dallin went too.

For the tenth time Parkes told himself that the first wave was in no more danger of being overrun than he was of slipping in the shower tonight. Although he probably wasn't going to take a shower, or even leave the C.P. . . .

Nothing could alter the fact the P.F. units in similar positions *had* been overrun, or that he couldn't do a damned thing to prevent it. Therefore he told his body to calm down. It might even listen.

Dallin turned away from the map. "As long as we haven't got any intelligence on their base, we're going to have to let them come to us. Colonel, what about flying a bait mission tomorrow morning? One medium verti, loaded with fuel but only two crew. It flies high enough to show up on whatever detectors the opposition has.

"Meanwhile, Steve and I fly the same course, just above the treetops. When our friends come out to play, the ambushers get ambushed."

"That means waiting until morning, I suppose?" said Mac-Lean.

"Unless *Ark* can't drop supplies. Then we could escort a real resupply mission. But I'd rather do the whole thing under V.F.R. conditions, weather permitting. The fewer E.E. we give them to work on, the better."

"Have you discussed this with Major Hughes?"

"His C.O. gave Steve carte blanche, and he passed it on to me." Dallin lit her cigarette and didn't even pretend to notice her slip in first-naming Major Hughes.

"Unless I can think of something better in the next two hours, we'll play it your way," said MacLean. "If those bastards picked up the second wave without any detectable E.E., it may take a while to find their base. That means we either force them to lead with their chin or risk having them pop out and rabbit-punch us any time they damned well please!"

MacLean's clenched fists and figures of speech reminded Parkes that the colonel had been Peace Force middleweight boxing champion as a sergeant. Who would he rather punch now, the enemy pilots or General Haskins?

No way a Sergeant Major could ask that. No way this particular Sergeant Major was going to get much sleep tonight either. Not that he wouldn't be expected to remain on duty, but damn it, he should have a thicker skin by now. Anybody who'd gone through Bifrost—

Anybody who'd gone through Bifrost and all the other battles of Parkes's twenty-two years in uniform could go one of two ways. He could toughen up until nothing bothered him, and by then not be quite human. Or he could slowly lose his ability to see friends die and keep on going. Then the best thing he could do was hang up the uniform before he did something that got more of them killed.

Parkes had the nasty feeling that he'd reached the point where he was balanced between the two choices. And he would have to decide, because he'd seen what happened to people who didn't. It ended either in a funeral or a court-martial, and Parkes was damned if he'd end either way.

MacLean and Dallin had their heads together over the map now. Nobody would miss him. Parkes slipped out into the hall and walked down it to the door. A late afternoon rain was spattering down, already veiling the treetops. It would be wet up on the ridge, and maybe even chilly after sunset. . . .

"Lieutenant."

The soft voice in the rainy twilight was Lieutenant Ngomba's.

"Yes?" said Forbes-Brandon.

"They've brought in Captain Opperman."

Forbes-Brandon leaped to her feet, nearly braining herself on the rock overhang that kept most of the rain off the C.P.

"How . . . ?"

"Rather bad, I'm afraid. You might call it friendly fire that hit him. One of the airbursts knocked loose a boulder, and it rolled over him."

"Oh, hell." Body armor resisted penetration well, crushing not nearly so well. And Hugo had been out there with the bodies of the rearguard for six hours.

"Pete?"

"Yes?" said Lieutenant Hale.

"How long to launch for the next load from *Ark?*"

"Forty-two minutes."

"I'll be back in thirty-five."

She stood up, thanking God for the small favor of not having to hump her pack, and followed Ngomba. They moved downhill slowly and at a crouch. The Hrothmi had fallen back out of small-arms range after their last attempt to storm the Pimple, but they were both determined and well-led. They'd stayed on the heels of their opponents all the way to the Pimple, in spite of missiles from orbit, only withdrawing after two determined attacks. People like that could easily think of infiltrating snipers after dark.

Ngomba was just turning right around a clump of bushes when the twilight lit up with tracer and grenades. All of it was well downhill.

"Sounds . . . like they're locking . . . the barn door after the horse is stolen," came a voice from the other side of the bushes. Forbes-Brandon started, not only at the pain in the voice, but at even hearing it.

"Kate?"

"Yes, it's me."

"Come on . . . around where I can see you."

She stumbled around the bush, to kneel beside a man lying on one groundsheet and covered with another. Nothing showed except a face darkened with bruises and one hand wrapped in a field dressing.

She laid her own hand lightly on Hugo's, afraid her voice would break if she spoke. After a moment his fingers curled around hers. The movement made him gasp.

"Hugo, have the medics—"

"The bastards wanted to slow me down. Heart, everything. That way I might . . . might not bleed out before medevac comes."

"We're supposed to get a medevac flight, as soon as the second load from orbit arrives. It's got heavy weapons, so we can keep our friends' furry heads down—"

"And . . . how long?"

"Another three hours, maximum."

"You mean, minimum."

"Maybe, but—"

"Kate, I know you'll do your best and so . . . will *Ark*. But . . . this is the end of my road. I want . . . to walk the rest of the way . . . with my eyes open. Look at you, mostly. Too bad . . . you have to keep your clothes on."

"Flattery will—oh, damn," she said, dabbing at her eyes.

"Don't . . . worry, Kate. It hurt a lot more . . . to lie down on an anthill, the first . . . first time I ever had a girl."

"Was it ants for you? My first time outdoors, it was a bull in the next pasture. We thought the fence would hold, but it was a big bull." Her eyes needed more than dabbing now, but she ignored them.

"Kate, promise me one thing. Those Hrothmi . . . People down there. Damned good soldiers. Don't . . . let them be killed—"

"We aren't going to turn them over to those bloody bedamned militia! They'll probably be shipped home—"

"Home. And when they get there, governments who want to suck up to us will kill them, for being soldiers good enough to give the Peace Force a standup fight! Don't let it happen, Kate. Please."

"I'll do everything I can." Which might not be very much, considering that most generals didn't take lieutenants' suggestions all that seriously.

But one of the generals who did was supposed to be on the way to Greenhouse. If he arrived in time to influence matters . . .

"Please, Kate."

"Will you let the medics slow you down if I promise?"

"Only after you go back on duty."

That was now about thirty minutes. Would it make a difference? Did she have any choice, confronted with Hugo's stubbornness?

"I'll lay the matter before everyone I can reach. Word of honor." She bent over to kiss him, and didn't straighten up for nearly a minute.

22

It was a rarely bright morning for Greenhouse. Silver patches of sunlight raced across the river as Dallin and Hughes flew along it. The tops of the trees on the banks were twenty meters above them.

Five hundred meters higher and four kilometers ahead, the two medium vertis acting as bait were cruising steadily toward the Pimple. Neither carried more than its normal flight crew of two. Both carried useful cargoes. Goose Zebra One carried a resupply of ammunition for the Pimple's defenders. Eagle Peter Three carried a filled collapsible fuel tank and an aerial refueling kit.

Both additions to the plan were the idea of 31 Squadron's C.O. As she put it, "I'm an optimist. I assume that the bait will get through without being eaten by the fish. I also might as well be hung for a sheep as for a lamb."

Both Dallin and Hughes had protested, pointing out that the loads would reduce the bait vertis' maneuverability. The C.O. pointed out that even empty medium vertis were as maneuverable as drunken seahoppers. Then she threatened to pull rank. Dallin and Hughes yielded with as much grace as they could muster at three o'clock in the morning, and went off to get a little sleep.

The message portion of Dallin's heads-up display read: "Course change to 323 true. Mark—five, four, three, two—"

On "one," Dallin's hands danced over control plates. As if they'd been tied together, the two vertis climbed. They skimmed meters above the treetops as they settled into their new course. The two bait vertis came into sight five kilometers ahead. If visibility held, the two flights would be in visual contact from now on, able to communicate securely by tight-focused laser beam.

Dallin said a mental prayer for security of communications and everything else. The Hrothmi *jagruni* around the Pimple—

nobody called them terrorists anymore—couldn't win outright. The P.F./Kabuele defenders had too much firepower and the high ground as well.

With air support to disrupt or delay their opponents' reinforcements, the Hrothmi could hold on for quite a while. When they had to withdraw, they could make a fighting retreat to the caves, from which they'd have to be winkled out like meat from a snail.

The whole process would be a bloody mess, from start to finish.

Without air support for the Hrothmi, the buildup on the Pimple could go faster. When the defenders went over to the offensive, they might impress even these tough *jagruni* with the wisdom of surrendering. At worst, they could get between the Hrothmi and the caves and destroy them in the open.

That would also be a bloody mess, but most of the blood shed would be Hrothmi. Dallin realized that thought didn't make her feel much better. Maybe she'd been studying Hrothmi and listening to Major Vela too much.

The message indicator flashed: "Sabra One has possible radar-scan indication. Heads up, Sonny!" It was the tanker verti.

She tapped back an acknowledgment.

The two interceptor vertis separated until they were a kilometer apart. Dallin checked the fuel. They were going to need a drink if the fighting went on for more than a few minutes. Fortunately the Pimple had a fuel blivet they could tap, even if the enemy got lucky with the tanker.

Radar, weapons sensors, and I.F.F. all screamed a warning at once. A moment later Dallin caught sight of five dots climbing steeply from behind a ridge. The two bait vertis separated, heading for the treetops, their work done. Now all they had to do was stay in the air and preferably out of their friends' way.

Dallin opened her throttles and swung into a turn. Hughes was climbing rapidly, to engage the two enemies who were also continuing to climb. The enemy's tactics looked like sending three after the bait while two stayed high to provide cover.

Smoke a good long way behind Sabra Two now—a decoy, or maybe a missile spooked into detonating prematurely. Each bait verti carried E.C.M. gear, chaff, and a couple of close-range missiles for self-defense. Enough to delay the enemy, not enough to fight off a salvo of missiles or the close-range gunnery used yesterday.

Dallin pulled g's as she turned. For a moment she lost sight of both Hughes and the enemy. When she saw clearly again, Hughes had fired a missile. It raced toward the enemy top cover, and enemy jamming screamed in her ear. Then there was only flame and smoke and tumbling pieces where one of the enemy vertis had been.

The three of the low section were hot on the trail of the bait. The remaining enemy from the high section was turning into Hughes, apparently intending a head-on pass with both guns and missiles.

Hughes must have hit him as he straightened out, because he came straight at his opponent. Between one heartbeat and the next, Dallin knew what was going to happen.

"Break, Steve!"

Her mouth was still open from the shout when the two vertis collided head on. Dallin forced herself to see the much larger cloud of smoke, flame, and falling wreckage—closing your eyes in combat was suicidally stupid. Then she swallowed hard, looked again, made sure there were no parachutes, and went into a full-throttle dive.

The enemy low section had lost sight of her in their eagerness to close with what they must have thought were helpless targets. Dallin was able to dive down and get on their tails before the two bait vertis separated. A missile took out one enemy just as he noticed he was being followed.

One survivor went into an Immelman turn to face Dallin. He'd forgotten that this slowed him down, and he never knew that he was facing a prize winner in air-to-air gunnery. He might have guessed it in the seconds it took Dallin to saw one wing off with her belly gun. If so, it was knowledge acquired too late to be useful.

By the time the fourth enemy hit the jungle, the bait flight was nearly out of Dallin's sight. Visibility was deteriorating; she saw the last enemy trying to sneak away, ducking from one patch of mist to the next. He was moving slowly, as if damaged or wounded.

Closing, Dallin saw that he was running on one engine. Circling around him, she indicated with emphatic hand signals that he should land by the river and surrender. It took her ten minutes to herd him to the river and watch him land on a sandbank. She took another minute to make one firing pass, putting a burst into his tail that made sure he wouldn't repair the damage and lift out.

It was only after this that she realized everyone had been trying to reach her. She called Sabra One, arranged for an aerial refueling, and poured on the power. She wanted to catch up with the bait section. Though she and Steve had accounted for all the enemies they'd seen, that didn't mean there couldn't be more.

As the jungle below blurred into a featureless green rug, she wiped the sweat off her face and looked at the clock display. It had been eighteen minutes from the time they'd sighted the five enemies, give or take a few seconds. Plenty of time for a good man—no, five good people, even if Steve Hughes had been the best—plenty of time for them to die.

She slapped her radio to RECEIVE and started answering the urgent questions that poured in. By the time she'd caught up with the tanker and was maneuvering to plug into its hose, she knew what came next.

She was glad that her next mission would be based out of the Pimple. The Amazon deserved to hear the word about Hugo Opperman from a friend.

Forbes-Brandon saw Captain Dallin walking up the hill, past the line of stretcher bearers carrying the wounded down to Goose Zebra One. She unfolded cramped legs, stood up, and went down to greet the pilot.

"I heard about Major Hughes. I'm sorry."

Dallin shrugged. Either she'd finished her crying or else wasn't ready to start yet. Probably the second; the fighting was a long way from over. The Hrothmi weren't taking a shot at the tempting target of the three grounded vertis. That only proved that they didn't want to draw a retaliatory bombardment.

Jagruni who'd tried a platoon-sized infiltration at night against the Peace Force's night sensors and Kabuele Company's night-fighting skills weren't going to give up easily. There were going to be lots more bodies of both species when the reinforced defenders of the Pimple moved out after lunch. Field First Voorhis was leading a platoon, and half the squads were led by corporals or privates.

Reflexively, Forbes-Brandon looked at the line of shrouded bodies to her left, human and Hrothmi mingled. Then she saw that Captain Dallin seemed to be waiting to say something more. Certainty of what it was flowed through her like an icy underground stream.

"Hugo Opperman's dead, isn't he?"

Dallin nodded. "The word came just before I took off." She pulled the taller woman's head down and kissed her. "Being sorry won't bring him back, either, but I am."

"They say Bifrost was worse," said Forbes-Brandon, knowing

her voice would shake if she let it. "Maybe I'll ask the Fruit Merchant sometime."

"You do that. And if you want a shoulder to cry on, you could do worse than his."

"Thanks."

Small-arms fire sputtered downhill. A moment later two launchers *whoomped* from the top of the hill. Smoke mushroomed beyond the perimeter. The small-arms fire continued.

"Hard to discourage, aren't they?" said Dallin. She threw down her cigarette and stamped it into the mud. "Time for me to go and do my Forward Air Controller act for the alpha strike they're laying on."

"They have a fix on the enemy airbase?"

"Within a few square kilometers, yes. The opposition had two tankers following the interceptors. A battle station blew one from orbit with a fragment bus. The other ran for it, got lost, and shouted for help. We had enough people listening to get a fix on where the reply came from."

Go on talking technicalities, and maybe it won't hurt so much. "You have orbital backup?"

Dallin noded. "*Ark*'s maneuvering to be in optimum position when we arrive. She's ready to launch anything short of nukes. Her fighters will be refueling and be the second strike if one's needed."

"Perfect." Except that a world without Hugo Opperman was a long way from perfect. One she could live in, undoubtedly, but perfect? Hardly.

They shook hands. Dallin turned and ran downhill toward her verti. Forbes-Brandon watched her vault into the cockpit and slide her canopy shut, as the ground crew unhooked the fueling hose. They stepped back and waved as the engines started, then waved again as the verti broke free of the mud and drifted away at low altitude. Dallin was too experienced to climb too soon and be an easy target for an enemy who might not have expended their missiles and certainly hadn't expended their aggressiveness.

Forbes-Brandon realized she should be thankful for the persistence of the Hrothmi. As long as the fight lasted, she would have something to keep her mind occupied. She could face the loneliness of the battlefield, or even its dangers. It was what might come afterward that made her uneasy.

As she started uphill again, it began to rain.

• • •

Colonel Limón stood at the foot of the shaft leading to the surface. He counted off his men as they started climbing the fiber rungs bonded to the rock. With only one flyable verti left, the underground base no longer had any purpose.

In a conventional war they would have shut down only temporarily, until the Republic's air force had regained air superiority. In this war they had done as much as they could by making the battle of the Peace Force against the Hrothmi more expensive.

Would it be enough to weaken the PFers' willingness to defend the Hrothmi homesteaders of Utopia against the Utopians? Certainly it would be a good start. Limón had a number of ideas for continuing the process. When he returned to Cervantes, he would start work on some of them.

He hoped he would have Major Dozo's help, but the major's chances of getting away from the Battle of the Pimple looked dim. A good man, and a loss to be regretted. The crew of the airbase would have less trouble. Up the shaft to the surface, then a quick dash into the cover of the forest. This high, the forest was passable for fit men loaded with immunization shots and carrying plenty of water.

Two days' travel should be more than enough to bring them to a safe L.Z., pickup, and a comfortable flight home. Long before they reached the pickup, the time fuses would detonate the demolition charges in the caves, leaving no clear traces—

The cave quivered like a drum struck with a giant padded club. From high up the shaft, someone shouted in wordless fear or surprise.

More impacts, more shouts. On the fifth impact a bolt holding the catapult to the rock floor sheered. It banged off the wall, spraying bits of rock over Limón, hard enough to draw blood.

He was wiping his cheek when the worst shock of all came. The shaft filled with dust and screams, cut off suddenly as it collapsed. The last man on the ladder came hurtling back down, to land at Limón's feet. After him came a huge slab of stone, landing squarely on top of him. He not only died, he spattered.

Limón controlled his stomach with a desperate effort as he fumbled his respirator out of its pouch. The last verti had toppled over from the last shock, and was leaking fuel. As Limón watched, the fuel crept across the floor to the arcing power line to the catapult.

The cave roared into flames. Limón ran toward the cave mouth. If he could hide there until the fuel burned out, he might escape death by burning or suffocation. Then he could go out the secret rear entrance, if the earthquake hadn't collapsed it too.

He reached the comparatively fresh air at the mouth of the cave, to see a Peace Force verti cruising by, almost at a level with him. It was then that he knew the shocks had not been earthquakes, but burrowing warheads hurled from orbit.

He thought of simply stepping off the edge, but a soldier's curiousity made him sit down and wait the ten minutes it took for Captain Dallin to call up the alpha strike. He was still sitting when the missiles homed in on the heat pulse from the dying fire. They collapsed the cave and blew the overhang completely free of the cliff. A million tons of rock and what was left of Colonel Limón plunged into the jungle below.

About half an hour after the radio at the airbase went silent, Shipo heard a single pistol shot. It seemed to come from Major Dozo's position.

Cautiously Shipo raised his head. When this drew no fire, he even more cautiously crawled out of his hole and walked, crouching, to Dozo's position. He made the whole twenty-*shirhi* trip without a shot being fired at him, but didn't find this encouraging. The PFers and Kabuele people must be resting, gathering their strength and orienting their reinforcements before counterattacking.

Major Dozo's position held no surprise. The major's right hand held his pistol, and the ruin of his head showed where the shot had gone. His two guards were running their hands nervously over their rifles.

"Did he leave any messages for me?" said Shipo.

The older guard nodded. "He . . . he said it had been an honor to serve with you and your People. He also said that he could not afford to be a prisoner."

So Dozo's knowledge of Limón's plans and perhaps those of others had been his death sentence. Shipo was not surprised at this either. He mourned, because a good soldier had died from something other than the chance of battle. Still, that left him free to do what he thought best.

By the time he'd walked back to his own position, standing upright and still drawing no fire, he knew what to do.

"Gila?"

"Yes, Captain?"

"Signal to all units. Kuurim Two."

"Two?"

"Yes."

Gila began tapping out the signal on her radio. Shipo sat down and started looking for his pipe. He had one filling of good *kasir* left, and couldn't think of a better occasion for smoking. The Peace Forcers might not take his pipe, but it could be a while before they let him have anything to put in it.

He'd made a cloud of yellow smoke around his head by the time Gila finished her signaling. Then she drew her pistol.

"Kuurim Two, Gila. Not One."

Kuurim One was the order he'd have given if through some foul chance they'd been defeated by Utopian militia. It would give every one of the company permission to end their own lives. Kuurim Two only called for destroying weapons and equipment.

"I know, Captain." She pointed the pistol at the radio and fired twice. Bits of plastic and copper sprayed the position. Like an echo, Shipo heard other shots from the positions around him, along with breaking or tearing noises, curses, and the occasional sob.

Parkes peeled another banana and stuck out a hand. Corporal Dietsch put a beer into it without being asked. Parkes drained the beer without taking it from his lips, then addressed himself to the banana.

This was his third beer, and he decided against having a fourth. He'd started on the first already half drunk with sheer relief. No doubt a fight against Hrothmi resisting to the last round would have been an interesting exercise in minor tactics, to say nothing of adding chapters to the Peace Force texts on fighting underground. Parkes was perfectly happy not to see those chapters, and also to not see another forty-odd names written up on a casualty list already much too long.

Forty-seven dead, forty-one wounded was the total from Group Fourteen, Kabuele Company, and 31 Squadron. Not much compared to Group Nine's toll on Bifrost, when both dead and wounded ran into three figures. But enough to make Parkes realize he could no longer shrug off casualties with the notion, "Well, Bifrost was worse."

It had been, but big battle or little, every soldier's death was of the same importance to him personally. And the death of anyone in Group Fourteen—his warbond-kin, as the Hrothmi would put it—chipped away a little of him. How much more did he have to give before he had nothing left—for his sister, for a civilian career, for a woman—if he was unreasonably lucky—for himself?

Parkes changed his mind about that fourth beer and stuck out his hand. After a moment he realized Dietsch hadn't put anything in it.

"Dietsch, what the hell—"

"We're out of bananas, and I don't think more beer's too good an idea."

"Look, Dietsch, if you're bucking for a transfer to Medical Company, I'm sure Laughton can be made warm for your form. In the meantime—"

"With all due respect, First, I just saw Colonel MacLean roll up. The Valkyrie's with him, and she's talking about what she just heard from General Duchamp."

"Duchamp? He's in-system?"

"Sounds a lot like it. Pity he didn't come about ten days sooner."

That was as much as Dietsch would risk saying out loud in Parkes's presence, but his face filled in the details. If Duchamp had come sooner, a lot of dead and wounded might be alive and whole.

Agreement on that point reconciled Parkes to not having another beer. He stood up and managed to be fully squared-away when MacLean and Lindholm came in.

23

"So, Captain Dallin," said General Duchamp. "You do not wish a transfer to a fighter squadron?"

Dallin shook her head. Katherine Forbes-Brandon controlled an impulse to gape. Dallin turning down her long-standing dream? Was the heat giving hallucinations?

Then Dallin smiled. The smile took years off her age, making her look much as she might have when she and Stephen Hughes were lovers and test pilots on Project Tollhouse.

"Sir, under other circumstances I wouldn't even ask what squadron. But I don't feel this is the right time for me to leave Group Fourteen. I can't help thinking that we have a few more battles to fight together. A decoration I'll be happy to accept, if there's going to be one for Major Hughes as well."

"Are you bargaining with General Duchamp?" said General Haskins. It was his fourth attempt to contribute something to the discussion, and no more successful than the first three.

Duchamp looked at Haskins until the junior man seemed to have shrunk the necessary meter or so, then said mildly: "If I wish to let her do so, that is my decision."

Since Haskins was not yet overtly suicidal, all he said was, "Yes, sir."

Duchamp stood up. "As for decorations for Major Hughes or anyone else—I am sure I bring no news when I say that the bureaucracy of doing justice to good soldiering has grown no thinner since Bifrost. Without anyone else's permission, however, I can repeat what I said at first. Well done, Group Fourteen. You resolved a very ugly situation in the highest traditions of the Peace Force."

He did not add, "Although it should not have been allowed to become that ugly in the first place." He did not need to.

"Thank you all," Duchamp went on. "I am sure we shall find

occasions to meet less formally before *Ark Royal* heads home. Meanwhile, I should like to speak with Lieutenant Forbes-Brandon privately."

Even Haskins didn't try to linger after such a dismissal, although MacLean, Vela, and Dallin were all trying not to look curiously at Forbes-Brandon as they left. Duchamp closed the door personally, then returned to his desk, sat down, and began to play with a paperweight carved of rock from the Pimple.

Forbes-Brandon was as curious as the others about the purpose of this meeting. A year ago she knew she would also have been nervous, even irritable, ready to defend herself on any and all counts, starting with her relationship with Hugo Opperman. Now . . . well, she remembered what Hugo had said once:

"Don't assume you'll get an E.R. downcheck if you aren't as alert as an M.D.S. Let the other party take the offensive, then counterattack after they've committed themselves. It worked well enough for your compatriot the Duke of Wellington, so why not try it yourself?"

Hugo, you put more into me (and the image made her smile) *than you took out. I won't stop either missing or thanking you for a long time.*

She put Opperman into the back of her mind and concentrated on looking over the general in front of her. She'd seen Duchamp only twice, once when he gave a series of lectures on leadership at the Naval Academy, and once briefly at a reception after Bifrost. His black hair was much grayer and a trifle thinner, but his two-meter frame was still lean and hard, and the mild, almost scholarly look in the wide gray eyes was probably still as deceptive.

"Lieutenant," said Duchamp.

"Sir?"

"I'm not going to pry into your relationship with Captain Opperman. It involved no neglect of duty of any sort, let alone of a kind I would feel called on to notice officially. I shall impress that opinion on anyone who might think otherwise."

He did not even hint at who the "anyone" might be, and maybe it was doing Captain Cooper an injustice to think of him. Still, it was nice to have Duchamp on her side. When he impressed an opinion on a junior officer, that officer did well to walk out of the interview on his feet.

"I do wish to draw on your personal association with Captain Opperman for one piece of advice. What is the best tribute the

Peace Force can pay him? He deserves something, I think you will agree."

For a moment Forbes-Brandon knew exactly what it felt like to be taken up to a high place and offered all the kingdoms of the earth. Then the euphoria faded, and she found herself explaining concisely and clearly Opperman's proposal for a Hrothmi Foreign Legion.

Duchamp was smiling by the time she finished. When she had, he laughed out loud, then opened his desk drawer and fished out a flask of brandy and two glasses.

"This is not a question that deserves an answer, but I will ask it anyway. Did Captain Opperman know how powerfully the image of *La Légion* works on me and many other senior officers?"

"I don't know, sir. *I* knew that, which is another reason I put it before you."

"Not a bad reason, either, although no civilian will find that easy to understand. Something they will find easy to understand, though, is something they will not like. Such a legion could teach Hrothmi not only that the Hairless Ones can be beaten but how to do it."

His tone said that an answer to that question was not optional. She shrugged. "They'll learn it sooner rather than later, with such a legion or without it. All the *jagruni* who fought on the Pimple have seen the Peace Force retreating in front of them. A Hrothmi Foreign Legion may turn those memories to good use, and it will certainly be less barbarous."

"Yes. We must avoid a descent into barbarism at any cost. The Peace Force has stood against that for a century, and will go on standing against it no matter who—" He broke off with more haste than grace, covering himself by pouring out two glasses of brandy.

"A toast, then. To the memory of Captain Opperman, and the future of the Hrothmi Foreign Legion!"

The "brandy" was actually *eau-de-vie* and tasted like distilled crankcase drippings, but she was too happy to care. Not that she was going to wait around for the machinery to grind out a Hrothmi Foreign Legion to pay her own tribute to Hugo.

Weather forecasts had predicted a sickeningly hot day for Hugo Opperman's memorial service, so it was held at 0800. In spite of this, everyone who was invited showed up half an hour early. A few Utopian militiamen showed up uninvited but stayed well back.

MacLean, Vela, and Parkes put their heads together about letting them stay. "I'll be happy to play bouncer," said Parkes. "But you can find decent soldiers in the worst outfits. Besides, a brawl now would be a rotten tribute to Captain Opperman. The Am— Lieutenant Forbes-Brandon—she's not feeling too good as it is. Why not let 'em stay?"

"Why not indeed?" said Major Vela, although his sideways look at Parkes said a good deal more. Parkes ignored it and saluted. MacLean and Vela returned the salute, and all three returned to their places as Major Kabuele stepped forward.

No, Lieutenant-Colonel Kabuele now. His shoulders carried black and white shields instead of silver palm leaves. The Black Star government was clearly not sitting on its hands where Kabuele Company was concerned; he wasn't the sort of mercenary officer who promoted himself.

Better find out a little more about what was in the works. If Voorhis really was resigning to stay here on Greenhouse as security chief for the railroad when it was finished, he might get a flying start if he had a few K.D. people joining his cadre. Voorhis had done a damned good job on the Pimple, even if he hadn't been able to cope with the job of Field First; he deserved a little help as he parachuted out of the P.F.

"Ladies and gentlemen," said Kabuele, saluting. "We meet here to say farewell to the body of Captain Hugo Opperman. This is not such a sad occasion as it might be, because his spirit lives on. It will always be with us." Parkes sneaked a glance at Forbes-Brandon, and wasn't wholly surprised to see her nodding.

"Captain Opperman hated long speeches and long ceremonies in bad weather. Since I do not wish him to haunt me, I will avoid both.

"I will say this. He saw himself as an exile from Nieutrek. If he was, it was because he saw how some of his home world's policies might end with injustice. Rather than become part of that injustice, he became a freelance soldier. He did not seek to become a white leader among black freelances, but that was his fate.

"Among us, he was not white, we were not black. We were all soldiers together, and Kabuele Company was home to all of us. Now his ashes will lie among ours, and with them, join the soil of Greenhouse, to bring forth new life.

"Farewell, Hugo Opperman."

Parkes expected the Company bugler to blow Taps then. Instead the Amazon stepped forward.

"I won't claim to have known Hugo as long or as well as anyone in Kabuele Company. So it is with great respect and reluctance that I venture to disagree with Colonel Kabuele. Captain Opperman didn't want to go back to Nieutrek, that is certain.

"I'm also certain he had a home that wasn't Kabuele Company somewhere in his heart. He dreamed of it, and in his dreams saw it clearly enough to offer to share it with me. Instead he died here on the hills of Greenhouse before he saw it with his eyes."

Forbes-Brandon swallowed, took a deep breath, then opened her mouth and began to sing.

> "There was a soldier, a Scottish soldier,
> Who wandered far away, who soldiered far away.
> There was none bolder, with good broad shoulders.
> He fought in many a fray and fought and won."

This was the first time Parkes had heard her sing sober. Her contralto *was* good.

But she shouldn't have to sing all alone. He knew the song too. His voice was nothing to boast about, but somehow he had to join her before anyone else did. As easily as if he were stepping into a hot shower after a long field exercise, Parkes broke out of ranks and strode toward Forbes-Brandon. His voice joined hers a second before MacLean's, ten seconds before Jean Grant's.

> "Because these green hills are not Highland hills
> Or the island hills, they're not my land's hills.
> And fair as these green foreign hills may be,
> They are not the hills of home."

Halfway through the second stanza there were twenty people singing. By the time the third began, it was fifty and Kilaa beating out the rythmn on a Hrothmi drum.

They finished the song with a whole reservoir of feeling yet undrained, so there was nothing to do but go through it again. And again, and again. Parkes stopped counting after the eighth repetition, when he suspected that everyone who wasn't tone-deaf had joined in.

Somewhere along the line singers started dropping out as

spontaneously as they'd joined in. The effect was a slow, fading fall, until at last Katherine Forbes-Brandon was singing alone on the last repetition of the last stanza.

> "And now this soldier, this Scottish soldier,
> Will wander far no more and soldier far no more.
> And on a hillside, a Scottish hillside,
> You'll see a piper play his soldier home.
> He's seen the glory, he's told the story,
> Of battles glorious, of deeds victorious.
> The bugles cease now, he is at peace now,
> Far from those green hills of Tyrol.
> Because these green hills are not Highland hills
> Or the island hills, they're not my land's hills.
> And fair as these green foreign hills may be,
> They are not the hills of home."

A silence purged of grief and every other emotion. Parkes had room for only one question.

Wouldn't it have been better if there were a piper?

Then the bugler broke the silence with Taps, and Parkes knew there should have been a piper. He didn't like the bagpipes, so the thought should have surprised him. Instead it came easily and stayed.

Fourteen wasn't shipping out for another ten days at least, but Parkes had heard that Jean Grant was moving out to the Survivors' Caves tomorrow. The evening rain was starting as the guard from the Security Company passed him through. it was pouring down by the time Grant let him into her tent.

She looked good even in field clothes, and she felt so good when they kissed that Parkes almost regretted the finality of the farewell coming up. At least neither of them would have anything on their consciences; affairs that had begun better had ended worse.

At last she broke away and began rummaging for the malt Scotch. Over her shoulder she said, "Your Sergeant Voorhis was around today."

Parkes grinned. "Jean, I know it's traditional among camp followers to transfer affections every time the higher-ups transfer the unit, but—" She made a small noise that might have been a laugh but might not have been. On the chance that he'd hit a nerve, Parkes hastily added, "That was a joke, Jean."

"I know. Besides, I'm not a camp follower. Ever since I got tenure, the camps follow me." She turned around with two glasses in her hands. "Sorry there's no ice, but we're winding things down here. I may come cadging a meal at the mess tonight, if they'll have me."

"Be my guest?"

"Why not?"

"Then it's a date. Seriously, be nice to Chuck Voorhis. He's pulling the plug and signing on as a security officer with BAM, then with the railroad when it's finished. He'll probably be helping with security at the Caves too."

"Forgive me if this is asking something out of line, but how good is he?"

"Meaning why is he resigning? He found that overcoming the network between me and Dozer and Vela was more than he could manage. Small-group politics wasn't one of his talents. He's a good field man, though, and if the K.C. cadre throws up somebody to do his paperwork and diplomacy . . . well, you could do a lot worse."

"Good. I suspect we are going to need on-site security, and a lot of it. Never mind any leftover terrorists either. When those pictures of Grand Galactic traces Shipo provided start circulating, it will be a circus on the ridge. Every university with a faculty member who ever read a book on archeology will send somebody. We'll need security people for traffic control, if nothing worse!"

"That's about all you'll need, plus protecting any relics that turn up. The terrs have had their day."

"How's that, with the Game Master in the field and Mountaineer backing?"

"The Game Master never made enough contact with Limón and his friends to matter. We have Alexis Werbel to thank for that. She made a difference, killing her father. How big a difference, we'll never know, but I'm damned sure she didn't throw her life away."

Which is not a lie as far as I know, and even if it turns out to be one, the Wise One will forgive bigger lies than this in a good cause.

"That's good to know," said Jean in a small voice, turning away for a moment and taking a big drink of her whiskey. "But what about the Mountaineer government?"

"Limón and his friends weren't the government. They were a faction in Military Intelligence and Procurement who were being winked at by the politicians who wanted to sabotage the railroad. Their reasons were obvious—the railroad would help the Utopians acquire an industrial base.

"Limón, Dozo, and company were playing for higher stakes. Not without the knowledge of the politicians, I suspect, but without any active support that couldn't be repudiated if it hit the fan."

"Cynical bastards."

"Very. But what Limón wanted was to play progressive immiseration games. Provoke the Utopians into really tightening the screws on the Hrothmi homesteaders, until they rebelled. Then the Mountaineers could intervene to save them. In the process they'd come to rule the whole continent with the hearty approval of everybody up to the Union Senate.

"Needless to say, the politicians are now washing their hands in public, in the best Pontius Pilate tradition. They certainly won't try anything else until after Arthur Goff leaves. By the time he ships out, the Union should finally have an ambassador in Cervantes. With a good military attaché, he should give you plenty of warning of any more trouble. The diplomats do have their uses sometimes."

"You sound bitter, John."

"Chalk it up to fifty-five dead. No, fifty-six. Hagood died this morning. They couldn't keep his liver and kidneys going, no matter what they hooked him up to."

"I'm sorry. Did he have any family?"

"A father, I think. His parents split up right after he was born." Parkes sipped his whiskey. "I know that it was Haskins's screwing up that killed a lot of them, but right now I just don't like anybody who hasn't been shot at as much as I should. You excepted—and come to think of it, you've joined the Benevolent and Protective Association of Them What Has Been Shot At. We'll have to welcome you properly tonight." He toasted her.

"Maybe, but I'm still a civilian."

"So?"

"So that means we . . . we really don't have much of a future together."

"Damn."

"John, I'm sorry, but—"

"No, wait, Jean." He smiled. "You've just put me in a nasty dilemma. If I sound terribly disappointed, I'll be lying. But if I sound relieved, I'll be insulting you. Which would you rather have, the lie or the insult?"

"Neither, if that's available. I appreciate your making it easy for me. Would you like a little explanation?"

"Is that intended as a reward or a punishment?"

"Well . . . the worst it will do is tell you something you already know. I don't think any woman who hasn't worn a uniform in combat has much of a chance with you. And I don't think any other woman should try for you seriously as long as Katherine Forbes-Brandon is alive."

Parkes stared at Jean Grant and decided she wasn't joking. He stared into his glass and saw only amber whiskey. He looked up at the roof of the tent, quivering under the assault of the rain. His mind seemed to be full of half-formed thoughts twitching with a semblance of life, but none of them coming clear.

After a while he gave up hoping that any of them would, drained his glass, and rose. "Let's get squared away for dinner. If you're lucky, General Duchamp will show up and sing 'Le Boudin' halfway through the drinks."

"The what?"

"'Le Boudin'. It means 'blood pudding.' There's an old French Foreign Legion marching song about it. In fact, I think it *was* the Legion's marching song, and that's where the Tenth Brigade on Clovis picked it up. They grew out of the Legion regiment there at the time of the Collapse War. Better ask the Amazon. She's more of an expert on old songs than I am."

"A marching song about blood pudding?"

"Would I lie to you?"

"No, or at least not about anything important. But blood pudding? I tell you, soldiers *are* different."

"Yes, but wouldn't it be a dull Universe if we were all the same?"

MORE SCIENCE FICTION ADVENTURE!

BESTSELLING
Science Fiction
and
Fantasy

ACE
SCIENCE FICTION
SPECIALS

Under the brilliant editorship of Terry Carr, the award-winning <u>Ace Science Fiction Specials</u> were <u>the</u> imprint for literate, quality sf.

Now, once again under the leadership of Terry Carr, <u>The New Ace SF Specials</u> have been created to seek out the talents and titles that will lead science fiction into the 21st Century.